# THE CITADEL

*Of*

# STAIRS

## The Armory, Book One

D1414475

*By*

## PORTER ALBAN

*To you...*

# TABLE OF CONTENTS

# — CHAPTER 1 —

## One Piece at a Time

The comet trailed flames across the black, star-pocked heavens. Nobody saw it. Nobody made a wish. It headed toward a blue, green and brown ball that hung in the black expanse and shattered into five pieces when it hit the atmosphere.

If one had been close by, if one's skin was tough enough to withstand the heat or had ears sharp enough to hear over the thunder of the comet's sundering, one might have heard five voices coming from each of the five pieces as they scattered and trailed flames toward the planet.

One growled a prayer to a dead god.

The other four screamed: "Fuuuuuuuuuuck!

# THE FIRST PIECE

## It's a bird, it's a plane, it's a monk (he's a dick).

I t was just before dawn in the village, and the fisher folk were sleepily untangling their nets when the ocean between their boats exploded. Three of their vessels were swamped by waves, and they all clutched hard to the rigging to avoid being thrown over. Everybody got wet. The water was warm as tears and salty steam made brief fog as the ocean sizzled and a glowing mass sank to the bottom, cooling as it went. A minute later, one of the fisherwomen shouted for help as her anchor chain tugged and the boat dipped.

Something had them.

Her son put his mother behind him and grabbed a gutting knife. He'd always feared its keen edge, but as the chain rattled and the boat bucked, he knew it wasn't enough knife for whatever had them hooked. A hand burst out of the water and grabbed the gunwale. They stared as a hooded figure flopped over the side to lay gasping and choking in the gut-strewn scuppers. He struggled weakly in his ocean-soaked cloak. Beneath he wore battered leathers. He was not very tall, but massively built and he hacked water and phlegm through a tangled gray beard. He reached out a hand toward the mother and son.

"Wat— plea—" the man croaked.

The fisherman's son cautiously handed him a jug and the stranger drank greedily. A small boy who had been watching from the docks ran to get the sheriff.

"Thank you," the stranger whispered. "May the—" He coughed, gagged and spat over the side, then continued. "May the Vigil guide your steps," he said, his head sinking back. "May he watch your path through the world."

"Who?" The young man said.

"Did you find anybody else?" The stranger asked.

"Did you fall out of the sky?"

The robed man closed his eyes. He seemed to be listening. Or feeling. Then he nodded solemnly. "No. They are not here." He kicked his legs free of his wet cloak and knelt. He adjusted his soaked hood and clasped his hands under his chin, muttering under his breath. His hands were large and gnarled, the knuckles thick and scarred, misshapen into nearly one bony mass. The fisherwoman and her son looked at each other. Then the robed man stood.

"Your kindness will not be forgotten," he said, dove over the side and swam toward the shore.

"If that's a mermaid you can keep 'em," the young man muttered.

The fallen stranger dragged himself up the gravely beach and walked into the village, trailing ocean as he went. Dawn was breaking over the slumped buildings, and from the far end of the street hurried a man in a dented steel cuirass. He was still buckling it as he fumbled with an old pistol and a chipped, rusty sword.

"You there! Stranger!" the man called, "I'm the sheriff."

The stranger stopped in the center of the road and said nothing as the sheriff approached.

"They told me... are you the one who fell out of the sky?" The sheriff asked.

"Do you protect this place?"

"I'm the sheriff," the man repeated. He was past middle age, but still held his sword and pistol in unsure hands.

"I need your steel," the stranger said.

"My what?"

"Your sword, your armor and your pistol."

"Maybe you should sit down for a second, stranger."

The stranger tilted his head. "You seem like a kind man. I will make this easy as I am able. By way of apology."

"For what?"

The man in the robe walked closer.

"Stay back," the sheriff said and lifted his pistol. But he'd waited too long and had forgotten to load it.

To his credit, he at least managed to pull the trigger.

The gun clicked dry, and the cloaked man punched him in the chin. The sheriff fell sputtering to the ground, and the stranger considered him a moment, then knelt and hit the sheriff a second time, knocking him out. He stripped the sheriff's steel cuirass and chainmail collar, ripping the leather straps like they were paper. The stranger took his sword and broke his pistol, discarding the useless wood and

5

putting the steel pieces in the pocket of his robe. He stood up and looked at the shocked villagers.

"He will recover," the stranger called to them. "Is there a metalworker here?"

The villagers didn't answer. Only then did the stranger notice the spired stone building. The other homes seemed to grow away from it like it was the centerpiece of an arch or a crescent. At its spire was a crude wooden carving of a harpoon crossed with an oar.

"Is this your place of worship?" The robed man called. Then he looked down at the still-unconscious constable at his feet. "Is it?"

"That's the Giving Place," a small voice said with brave and nasal defiance. The robed man looked up to see the boy who had run for the sheriff. In his little hand was a wooden sword.

"And what do you give there?" The stranger asked the boy.

"We give to the sea, the sea gives to us," the little boy said.

"What if I am a gift of the sea?"

"Sometimes the sea brings death," the little boy said, and tightened his grip on his toy sword. "It took my brother."

The robed stranger almost smiled. "You are brave, little one, but you cannot fight this war.

Not yet. My faith, and my fists, are bigger." The little boy backed up a single step, but his eyes were still afire. The man crouched down so that he was on eye level with him.

"But it will not always be so," he rumbled. "Find me then, and if you choose, I will answer for what happens next."

"What's going to happen?" The little boy asked. His voice shook.

The robed man walked past the little boy to the doors of the Giving Place. Fearful villagers peeked from alleys and doorways. Some even held tools turned weapons in half-hearted fingers. The robed man shouted to them.

"What I do, I do in the Vigil's name," he bellowed, "That you may know it lives! That you believe! That you never forget!"

"You're doing this for a virgin?" One of the villagers called back.

The robed man growled an inaudible prayer and kicked through the doors of their temple. There was a shriek from inside and an elderly man dressed in vestments made from fishing net flew out of the broken doorway and landed in the mud with a grunt. The villagers helped their sea priest to his feet and listened in fear as the robed stranger had what sounded like a temper tantrum in their holy place. Amid the sounds of breaking glass and splintering wood, the villagers began to close in with their marlinspikes, gutting knives and mooring pins held like clubs. There was a crash from inside the temple and then a triumphant groan before the robed stranger emerged with two blazing torches in his bleeding hands.

"Mark me," he called to them, "you have raised your uncaring sea into a false god. You have mistaken luck for favor and silence for wisdom."

The villagers stepped forward with their weapons. The tallest of their number, a rangy woman with a face harder than the crags of the surrounding cliffs, was whirling a length of rusty boat chain with a towing hook at the end.

"If I return and find this monument to apostasy rebuilt," the stranger called, "I will pull it down again."

Then he tossed the two torches behind him into the building. The woman with the chain lunged forward and swung overhand. The boat chain whistled through the air toward the stranger's head, but just before it struck him, he stepped to one side and caught the chain by its hook and ripped it from her grasp.

"Good," the stranger said and coiled the chain and hook around his waist, "more steel."

The other villagers scattered to fetch buckets and water. Leaving the hardened woman to face the stranger alone. She shifted her feet uncertainly, but her face was still a stone. "If I see you again," she said, her fists balled at her sides. "I'll kill you. I don't care if you were sent by the sea."

"The sea did not send me. It is not listening to you," the robed stranger said. "I must leave, but mark what I said."

"Get out," the woman said and moved to join in as the villagers formed a bucket line.

The man in the robe walked past her and out of town — the sheriff's armor and sword dangling from his left hand and the boat chain around his waist. He walked through sunrise and sunset without stopping, eventually he reached another town, one that had a blacksmith. He dumped the sheriff's armor, sword and gun metal on the table and piled the rusty chain beside them. He told the blacksmith what he wanted. The steel was melted and reshaped into dozens of overlapping, studded steel plates the size of knuckles, and slightly curved bands affixed to leather straps.

When the blacksmith finished, the stranger from the sky pushed him protesting from his own smithy and barred the door. While the man kicked at the heavy wood and yelled to be let back in and paid, the man in the robe took a small chisel and hammer and knelt, praying as he inscribed symbol after symbol into the newly forged steel. Then he slid his hands into the contraptions and tightened the straps. He inspected his gleaming hands and forearms that were both his armor and his weapons. He grunted with satisfaction.

"I am whole," he said.

His work concluded, the stranger opened the door and pushed past the protesting smith and walked out of the town, ignoring the shouts and threats behind him. The blacksmith dashed into his smithy, grabbed his heaviest hammer and chased after the stranger. When he caught up, the smith swung his hammer at the back of the stranger's head, but the man was already moving to one side. He wrapped one arm around the hammer and knocked the smith's hands off the handle with the other. He stepped back from the gasping smith and considered the tool.

"No," the stranger said quietly and tossed it into the gutter, "I have enough steel."

The stranger walked away from the smith and followed the road until it forked.

He held his face up as if sniffing the air.

He could feel them. They were not close.

He took the right-hand fork.

His name was Vice.

# THE SECOND PIECE

## Wanna buy some magic meth?

The Festival of the Five ran for fifteen days, five times three praises for the pillars that held the heavens high, the ground low, and prevented both from crashing into one another and ending the world. For three hundred years the festival had run. All work in the capital stopped, the gutters ran with wine and the revels rang among the rooftops like flocks of bright, circling birds. It was the third night, and fireworks painted the sky in a staccato drowning of light and sound.

Nobody saw the comet fragment rush out of the sky as if one of the Five had failed to hold up their end, if for only a moment.

The burning chunk of skyrock struck a six-story apartment building. Only those who lived nearby, and few enough of those, rushed to search for survivors.

There was only one, but he was not found.

The sole survivor dragged himself, coughing and covered in dust, away from the rubble and cleaned his face at a communal pump. He walked the narrow streets between the celebrating citizens, jostled this way and that by their joy, until he found an apothecary's shop. He entered through a back window that he broke with a paving stone he'd pried out of the street, and roamed the shelves and cupboards, ticking his fingers across the labeled jars by the light of a small lamp. He filled the pouches and pockets in his leather coat and apron. He mixed other components and poured the blends into glass vials, some of which he sealed with wax, others with corks. These he slid the vials into a bandolier around his waist. He made painkillers and sedatives, corrosives, flammables and medicines from the book in his memory, far beyond anything this apothecary had ever heard of or seen, and he grumbled under his breath at the paucity of the shop's stock.

"They might as well pray for all the good this shit will do them."

He left the looted apothecary and visited tavern after tavern, sipping warm beer he didn't want and wine so foul he wondered if the vintner had drowned his family in the vat.

And he watched.

In the seventh tavern he saw four people follow a fifth out the back door. The four returned, animated and jerky, their movements snapping like flickering candlelight. He went through the back door and into the alley behind the tavern. A tall, thin man was counting coins under a street lantern.

"I'll have what they did," the alchemist said to him.

The man stopped counting and gave him a hard look. "No idea what you're talking about."

"What was it? Lizard Crystal? Dark Sip?"

The thin man shook his head. "Never heard of that. Go back inside before you piss me off."

"Kyne's Pitch? An amalgam of dern root sap and dried barkleaf?" He held up a stack of silver coins. "I'm a customer, not the law."

The dealer cocked his head to one side. "You sound like a scholar. You from the university?"

"Just visiting. I want to try whatever you sold those four. They looked like they were trying to dance a jig on hot, broken glass."

"This ain't brandy, mate."

"I certainly hope not."

The dealer shrugged and held out a folded packet of paper and took the silver coins. The alchemist took the packet, knowing he'd likely paid four times what it was worth, and stuck his finger inside. He rubbed the powder between his fingertips, studying the grit, and then touched his tongue.

"Hey, idiot, you're supposed to snort it," the dealer said.

The alchemist ignored him. He smacked his lips and rolled his tongue around his mouth. Then he did take a pinch of the powder and snort it. He cocked his head as a faint rush danced across his skull from his septum to the middle of his spine. The feeling was over in moments. It was a sludgy sort of thing that jangled his nerves like cans on a string.

He took a vial from his pocket and sipped. The sedative washed away the cheap narcotics. Amateurs, he thought.

"Good, right?" The dealer asked with a grin.

"Not really. It's insipid. You're using too much dern root sap. And you didn't let it age. It needs a full week at least, not," he paused and tasted from the packet again, "two days. "

"Mate, that right there's the best Dance in three towns."

"Dance, you call it? Interesting. But I doubt it. Take me to your boss."

"Far as you're concerned, I am the boss. Now, fuck off. I'm busy."

"Too busy to make this Dance of yours twice as addictive and potent with half the ingredients?"

"Is that right, schoolboy?"

The alchemist tossed the dealer a vial. "Sell that to your next customer. I'll be inside."

"What is it?"

"Not Dance."

"How do I know it's safe?"

The alchemist shook his head and went back inside. He was sipping a brandy when the dealer sat down across from him.

"What was that shit?" the dealer asked. "They already want more."

The alchemist smiled. "Take me to your boss. I'll make all he can sell and teach him the recipe. For the right price."

"She. You better hope you can deliver like you say. If you bought that around here, she's gonna want to know everything. And believe me, you'll tell her. But if you waste her time..."

The alchemist looked bored. "Consider me sufficiently threatened."

"C'mon," the dealer said. "Let's go see the Spider."

The alchemist rolled his eyes. Just once he wanted to meet a crime boss named Sally, or maybe William.

✳✳✳

The Spider was a stout woman with short arms and a knife scar that bisected her face and a ruined left eye that she left uncovered.

While the festival raged, the alchemist mixed Dance as pure and fast as a never-ending fall into a bottomless pit, and just as implacable. His blend did not need to age. Within a day it flooded the festival. As the Spider counted the earnings, the glint from the coins matched the one in her good eye. That sparkle that told the alchemist she'd wasn't ever going to let this golden goose fly free.

But he'd suspected as much.

The next day, when most of the Spider's crew came to resupply, the alchemist added a few of the compounds he made in the apothecary's shop to his cauldron. He immediately dosed himself with a powerful tincture that smothered emotion and added more coals to the fire. As the heat rose, the chemicals bubbled and blended,

17

and a thick smoke boiled out of the cauldron and filled the room.

The gangsters sniffed the air and wrinkled their noses.

One sneezed.

And then, the first one screamed.

Through a clinical detachment, the alchemist saw the same visions they did: Monsters dredged from a hundred nights of forgotten nightmares. While the gangsters went mad, gibbering and striking at the invisible threats that surrounded them, the alchemist waved away the imaginary horrors and helped himself to their stores of coin and chemicals. He stole vial after vial and filled them with what he needed, using their facilities to do his blending while the hardened men and women of Spider's underworld fief softened and went insane.

"I hope they have an asylum," he mused as he walked between the flailing dealers, strong-arms and sneak thieves while they begged for mercy from gods only they could see.

Across the room lay the Spider, contorted on the floor amid the gold she'd just finished counting. She stared with unseeing eye, trapped in her body as the evils of her mind capered before her. Drool ran from the corner of her mouth, and she was making a faint grinding noise in the back of her throat. The alchemist knelt by her side and checked her pulse. It was faint.

"Interesting," he muttered. "Spider, I'm afraid you've had a stroke. It seems you have weak veins." The alchemist pried open her clenched fingers and put the gold coin she'd been clutching in his pocket.

He spent the night in an expensive hotel until the tincture wore off and he could once again feel the pull that told him where to go. He bought passage with a caravan and rode out of the city.

His name was Pitch.

# THE THIRD PIECE

## I can shoot the hair off a gnat's ass at fifty paces.

S he lay at the bottom of the crater with her hands behind her head and stared up at the sky. Compared to the return, the crater was very peaceful. It was so quiet. Almost as quiet as that place inside her mind that was hers all alone, a space so hushed it was almost violent. The moon was so bright and big that if she stared long enough, she almost felt like she was rushing toward it.

She sighed as the sun rose, stood up and went to find a war. She needed to resupply.

But as she walked over hill and dale, all she found were farms and fields. So much was green and lush, the vistas so bucolic, that she wondered if her comet hadn't taken a wrong turn and dumped her straight into some other god's heaven. Farmers paused in their work to wave as she passed. One shepherd offered to share his lunch, and the invitation didn't come with a suggestive, lecherous glint.

"This place is absurd," she muttered as she walked. She wasn't going to find a battle here unless she started it, and even then it might not evolve past a strongly worded argument. She walked until she came to a good-sized town, and sitting in a tavern with a cup of ale that tasted like sunshine, she heard some men by the counter talking. She left her cup on her table.

"Sorry, couldn't help but overhear," she said. "What's this about a shooting competition?"

The men turned, startled. "Lord Dunne always wins. He's the best shot in the canton."

"Who's Lord Dunne?"

"Where are you from that you don't know Lord Dunne?"

"Not here."

"Where's your gun?"

"Also not here. Lost over the side," she said, already bored with the conversation.

"Of what? You sailed here?"

"Sort of."

"But the ocean's miles away!"

"It was a river boat."

"River?" The man chuckled good naturedly, as if she'd made a joke. "The Wynde's too shallow."

"It was a chariot of fire in the sky. Never mind," she said with an aggravated noise. Both men flinched as if she'd slapped them. "Where do I find this Lord Dunne?"

"His factor's office is near the town hall," one of the men said in a small voice. "But he always wins."

"Great. Thanks. Ah, sorry for snapping at you."

The men instantly brightened and one chirped: "Oh, that's okay!"

I have got to get out of here before I lose my mind, she thought.

The factor was a pretty, young man with long fingers and a pair of glasses that glinted in the lamplight that spilled across his ledger. His pen made precise trips back and forth across the page, leaving elegant black scrawls in their wake. There was an antique wheel-lock rifle hanging on the wall above him.

"Yes?" he asked without looking up.

"I hear there's a shooting competition," she said.

His eyes stayed on the ledger, his pen poised above the page. "His grace is holding it in four days, as you well know."

"Actually, I don't."

The young man looked up. "Ah, I apologize. You are visiting then?"

"Just arrived."

"Well, his grace typically offers a modest prize for first place, but since you are new here, I feel I should warn you: His grace always wins. He's the best shot in the five cantons."

"So I hear. Good for him. I don't have time to enter anyway."

"Then what can I do for you? I don't mean to be rude, but I am very busy."

"How much will his grace pay me not to enter."

The young man looked startled. "I beg your pardon?"

"You manage the man's business, yes? Does that mean you have access to discretionary funds?"

"His grace trusts me to run the day to day, yes."

The woman nodded to the rifle. "Does that work?"

The young man glanced at the antique. "I would assume so, though it's very old. His grace is quite fastidious about his firearms."

"Perfect. What would you say to a wager?"

The factor smiled. "With me? Madam, I am not a gifted shot."

"Anybody knows good shooting when they see it. Come with me and I'll show you shooting nobody in this little paradise has even dreamed of."

"Please, madam," the young man said and gestured plaintively at his ledger, "this has been quite diverting, but I am far too busy."

"C'mon," she said with a rakish wink, "aren't you just the least bit curious?"

The young man hesitated, and she smiled at him. "It's a lovely day. And I'm not going to leave you alone until you say yes."

"I... very well."

They left the building and walked through the main street of the town. She stopped by a group of children playing marbles in the dirt.

"Just a moment," she said to the factor, and then approached the children. She spoke to them for several moments, gesturing to the marbles and then took a silver chain from around her neck. It was hung with an old silver coin, the center of which had been punched with a ragged hole. She traded it, chain and all, for one of the brighter glass orbs.

She and the factor climbed the top of a hill just outside town with a crabapple tree on top. She took what looked like a thick string from her pocket and made one end a kind of knotted basket around the marble. The other end she tied to a low branch, so the marble hung glinting in the air.

"It's a small target," the factor said, "but I have seen his grace perform similar tricks."

She looked back at him and, with a wink, tapped the marble to send it swinging back and forth. She walked a few dozen feet from and checked the old rifle's pan, pulled back the dog and inspected the flint. The factor had been right. It was fresh. She loaded and charged the weapon, and then poured powder into the pan.

"It's a very old gun," the factor called, almost like an apology.

"That doesn't matter," she called back with a smile. "You were right, his grace is careful with his weapons."

She lifted the weapon to her shoulder, sighted down the barrel at the swinging marble, and pulled the trigger. It shattered in a shower of sunlight.

The factor's mouth fell open. Finally, he clapped his hands. "That was very impressive," he said.

She reloaded and fired four more times, picking four crabapples from the branches by shooting through their stems. She collected two of them and offered one to the factor, who was cleaning his glasses as if a smudge on the lens might explain what he just saw.

"So, what's the grand prize for this contest?" She asked.

"Five hundred silver," he said.

"How many years has he held it?"

"Fifteen."

"And he's never lost?"

The factor mutely shook his head.

She smiled sweetly and handed back the rifle. "His grace doesn't want me entering this contest."

"I am sure I cannot speak to his grace's mind," the factor demurred.

"Three hundred silver and I leave town without firing another shot."

"You don't have a gun."

The woman waved away the point. "I'm sure one of the neighboring lords would lend me one. They might even pay me for my trouble on top of the prize. I bet at least one of them would love to see the 'best shot in the five cantons' get embarrassed by a stranger."

The factor thought for several moments.

"Two hundred and fifty silver."

"Deal," she said and bit into the apple. She spat the piece into the dirt. It was bitter.

She collected her silver and returned to the children, who were still shooting marbles in the dirt. She traded five silver coins for the return of her pendant, then hitched a ride with a merchant who was heading in the direction of the pull in her chest. In a coastal city that she didn't bother to learn the name of, she boarded a ship. At the next port of call, she found a gunsmith and bought two long rifles, a pair of sawed down shotguns, two pistols and three derringers. She bought lead, a slug mold, cartridges and several pouches of black powder. She bought pig-iron bombshells and fuses, both slow and fast.

Her name was Powder.

# THE FOURTH PIECE

## I can show you that thing your wife likes.

T he highwaymen were having a very good month after the snowmelt.

The crocuses had sprouted, and winter's meager sun had given way to joyous, chill dawns that promised warm afternoons. Best of all the carriage wheels were turning again. Wagoneers, shipping caravans and wealthy visitors — with nothing better to do than call upon each other — were all on the road once more, and the highwaymen were there to shear their flock.

They were celebrating around the fire in their forest hideout, a collection of canopy dwellings connected by rope-bridges, rough plank walkways and pulley systems. Darn's wife had just given birth and Gow, their chief, raised his glass in a toast, vowing they would all make sure this new, young life wanted for nothing. Darn and his wife named her Gowa after their leader, and if there was a sentimental tear in the old bandit leader's eye over the gesture, nobody mentioned it.

Then there was a sound like thunder a hundred times over and half their hideout was on fire.

A dozen of the highwaymen were killed in the impact. Their celebratory circle was now a smoking crater crosshatched by fallen, scorched trees. Men and women ran around coughing and screaming. Some were burning. Most were dead.

A stranger with broad shoulders that tapered to a dancer's waist crawled out of the rubble and bodies. He hacked, spat in the ashes and looked around at the blazing chaos.

"Well. That's fucked up," he muttered.

"You! Who are you?!"

It was Darn. Tears streamed down his face, and he looked around at the ruins of the only place he'd ever called home.

"That's really your first question?" the stranger asked.

"Was this your doing!?" Darn screamed, drawing his sword.

"I really don't think you're focusing on the right things," the stranger said and gestured as a woman ran past, screaming and very much on fire. "That for example."

"I'm going to kill you."

"This shit isn't my fault! I wasn't steering it!"

"Who then? The king? His majesty would burn women and children?"

"He's a king," the stranger said and shrugged. "Definitely. But this isn't his doing either. Look, I'm really sorry, but... Wait, which king are you talking about?"

Darn lunged at the stranger with his blade. But the stranger vanished. Darn glanced around and realized he'd lost his sword. A familiar point and edge were sticking out of his chest. He coughed. His sternum felt cold.

"Sorcerer," he gasped.

"Hardly," the stranger said from behind him, "but since you're dying, I'm not gonna argue."

Darn fell. The stranger sighed and looked around.

"Really sorry about this. But I do have to go. Uh... good luck to..." He looked around, but there was nobody left. Those able had fled for their lives from the wildfire devouring the trees. "Well, to somebody. I guess."

The stranger looted Darn's pockets, found a few gold coins, and then considered the sword he'd shoved through the bandit's breadbasket. It was dull and the edge was chipped. "You know what? Why don't you just hang onto that?"

The stranger walked out of the camp and picked his way through the forest until he found a road. He followed that until the walls of a city loomed on the horizon. He passed through the gates without an issue, as he had neither cargo nor weapon. He ate in a market and drank a cup of wine. At a notice board he saw a leaflet warning about bandits on the road.

"Don't think you'll have to worry about that anymore," he muttered.

Then he noticed another leaflet, this one decorated with a pair of stylized, crossed swords.

"Oh, hello," he whispered and ripped it from the board.

The stranger asked for directions until he stood before a building on a quiet, clean street. From inside came the clashing of swords, a kind of music he could always dance to. The hall was vast and open, the floor was decorated with footwork diagrams, and pillars padded with old straw mattresses held up the ceiling. Several pairs of men and women were fencing with a variety of weapons of either dull metal or wood.

At the far end a handsome, middle-aged man looked on and called corrections. The stranger licked his lips as he looked at the wall behind the instructor. On it hung blades of every sort imaginable. There were slender rapiers and stout cleavers, a falchion with its big-bellied blade, a claymore. There were axes and knives for dueling and for throwing. The instructor noticed the visitor and crossed the floor, stepping elegantly between the clusters of sparring students, their blades sometimes passing no more than a half-inch from his skin. The stranger shivered. There was a tingle in his belly.

"Good morning, sir," the fencing master said. "Are you interested in the art of self-defense?"

The stranger smiled. "No, thanks. I'm quite set there."

"Oh? Has a master walked into my academy?"

The stranger laughed with delight. "I've had many teachers who would disagree."

The fencing master's arrogance was as graceful as his movements and rugged as his jaw line. "Then why are you here?"

"I crave a contest."

"I will summon one of my students. I believe that Delan would be happy to oblige you. He's one of my best."

"Care to lay a wager on it?" The stranger said, holding out a stack of gold coins he'd stolen from Darn's pocket.

The fencing master's lip curled. "I know your sort. Killing drunk fools behind taverns for copper. Here we don't profit from blood."

"Everybody profits from blood. I'm just a working man."

"I'll not have my students injured by some street fighter's back-alley tricks."

"What you call tricks, I call a living. But no dirty fighting. I promise. Skill against skill alone."

"You don't even have a weapon."

"Pawned it for a pretty smile," the stranger said with an abashed grin that had brought him luck so many times in the past. "You'll lend me one, won't you?"

The fencing master chuckled. "A charming rogue, aren't you?"

"Do you really think so?" The stranger winked.

"I admire your dash, sir. You level a challenge in another man's house and ask to borrow a sword in the same breath. I admit, I stand intrigued."

"And to put money in your pocket. Let's make it friendly. First blood?"

"Very well. But you won't be fencing with one of my students."

"I was hoping not."

The fencing master cocked his head to one side and pursed his lips. The stranger couldn't take his eyes off the salt and pepper in the master's beard, or a muscle in his neck that stood out like taut rigging. At a gesture, his students cleared a space at the center of the hall and the fencing master beckoned the stranger forward. "Do you have a preference in sword?"

The stranger shrugged. "Whatever's handy."

The fencing master snorted. "Rego," he called and one of his students stepped forward. "Fetch a pair of sabers."

"How fitting," the stranger said with a smile.

"Why do you say that?"

"I'll tell you later."

Rego brought over two sabers. They were metal, but their edges were dull.

"No," the fencing master said, "fetch the sharp ones."

Rego looked startled, but took a pair of plain but well-formed blades down from the wall. Each had a simple knuckle bow guard.

"On your guard, sir," the fencing master said once Rego had handed over the weapon to the stranger, who spun the sword around his wrist and then dropped it.

"Sorry. Bit out of practice, I guess."

The fencing master scowled as he waited for the stranger to pick up the blade.

"I seem to have nicked the edge a bit," the stranger said with a sheepish grin.

"I am waiting, sir."

"Well, we can't have that," the stranger said and lunged forward with a sweeping overhead cut that the fencing master caught on the roof of his own sword and stepped around.

They circled each other, flickering and testing, the weapons made blurring shapes in the air. The stranger parried a hard downward cut and then spun away to create some distance. The watching students clicked their tongues in disapproval. Spins were needless, dangerous flash. They were for festival exhibitions and the theater, not battle.

The fencing master's style was blunt and formal. He was a cliff to the stranger's wind. He moved as little as possible, his style that of a fighter who hadn't stepped outside his own academy in many years. His students had affected him as much as he taught them, but the stranger was a repository of tricks, most of which had outlived their trades and the fighters who practiced them. He turned aside an oncoming thrust with the knuckle bow of his sword — a nearly impossible gambit that no sensible swordsman would even consider — and then snapped down the flat of his blade on the master's sword, and then flicked out his saber again, nicking the outside of the older swordsman's arm. It was barely more than a paper cut.

The stranger darted back out of range and pointed with the tip of his weapon.

"Red there," he said. He was barely breathing hard. The fencing master, his lungs moving like bellows, squinted at his sleeve.

"Right you are, sir. Well fought."

"To you as well."

"I'll fetch your gold."

"I'd rather you fetch some wine."

The fencing master grinned and several of the students laughed. The master's students departed shortly after, leaving just he and the stranger sitting at a table near the back of the academy sharing the last of a bottle of red.

"I must say, your style is unlike any I've encountered," the fencing master said, pouring out the last of the full-bodied vintage. "Who taught you?"

The stranger shrugged modestly. "Be faster to mention who didn't. But no names you would recognize, many of them are dead, sad to say. On one battlefield or another."

"Are you a soldier? In whose army?"

"Whoever's paying."

"You're a mercenary?"

"I'm a lover of life, sir. A poet. An adventurer and admirer of the world's delights," he said with wink. "But a man has to eat. I hope I haven't cost you any esteem among your students."

The fencing master shook his head with a wry grin. "I would have preferred to be the victor of our little contest, but it provides a good lesson to them. To be cautious. That there is always somebody better. And that," he said with a sigh, "age catches up with us all."

"You're not so old," the stranger said and leaned forward placing his hand on the fencing master's knee.

The man looked down. "What are you doing?"

"Isn't it obvious?" the stranger said, sliding his chair closer until their knees were nearly touching. His grin was playful. "I'm sure there's still much I could stand to learn. I could use an experienced teacher."

The fencing master stood up faster than any movement he'd made during their match. "What you're suggesting is disgusting."

"Oh, come now. I've no problem being the lock to your key if that's the issue."

"Moreover, it is illegal. I could have you hanged!"

"Hanged? What kind of backwards shithole is this?"

"I'll have satisfaction from you, sir."

"Now we're talking! You had me there for a minute."

"At dawn," the fencing master said, looking down his nose at the stranger.

"Oh, you're fucking kidding!" the stranger said. "Calm down. A simple 'no' is just fine. It happens... though I admit, not often."

"At dawn, sir. The field outside town. You would have passed it on your way to the north gate."

"Look, can we not just forget about this?"

"We will not. Now get out."

The stranger rolled his eyes and stood up. "I'm keeping the sword, since you're going to act like a virgin whose ass I just pinched."

"You won't be so flip when we're crossing blades for true."

"I can promise you I will be. Drove my instructors crazy."

"On a real field, your back alley-tricks won't save you."

The stranger thought about all the back alleys he'd fought in, all the years and battlefields with their reddened mud, all the gutters and shadowed rooftops. He looked at the handsome fencing master, who was little more than a schoolboy by comparison if he believed dirty tricks would be less help in a real duel.

"At dawn then," the stranger said, ice in his voice.

\*\*\*

The fencing master slept poorly that night. He'd stayed in his study on the ground floor of his home to avoid disturbing or worrying his wife. It had been many years since his last duel. The house was quiet and he filled a metal basin with water from the pump out back. He had just carried it back into the kitchen when he heard feet coming down the stairs.

"Is that you, my love?" he called. "I am sorry if I woke you."

The stranger walked through the doorway of the kitchen, still buckling his trousers with his borrowed sword under one arm.

"Good morning," the stranger said.

"What are you doing in my house?" the fencing master said, fear frosting his ribcage.

"You really should fuck your wife before a duel. I mean, what if it's the last time?"

"My wife?"

"But don't worry. I took care of that for you. Is there coffee?"

The fencing master dropped the basin with a clang. Water spread across the floor until it was nearly touching the stranger's boots.

"Shhh! You're going to wake her. She's sleeping so peacefully. You should see her. She has the most adorable little smi-"

"You..." the master's face was pale as he spoke very quietly. "You violated my wife?"

"Violated?" the stranger scoffed. "What do you take me for? I'll have you know I never have to force anybody. Ever. She's a lovely woman. We met while she was tending the roses outside your door."

"The field. Now," the fencing master grated and grabbed his sword and belt from the kitchen table.

The stranger ignored him. "Going forward I might suggest spending just a little less time with your students polishing their swordplay and a little more at home, polishing yours, if you know what I mean. All I had to do was compliment those roses and-"

"The. Fucking. Field!" The master said from between clenched teeth.

"Do you want to walk together?"

The fencing master stared for several seconds. "What?"

"Might be a little awkward, but on the way, I can tell you about this thing your wife likes. I would have taught it to you, if you weren't such a prude."

"I am going to kill you."

"So, that's a 'no' to coffee?"

The fencing master drew his blade and lunged across the room with a howl, swinging for the stranger's neck. But the stranger vanished. The fencing master felt a hand on the back of his head and then saw the heavy kitchen table rushing at his face. His world went black.

The stranger looked down at the unconscious man and sighed. "Really would be too much to kill you on top of everything else. Plus, I think it would make your wife sad. Despite her recent indiscretion, and who can blame her after all, she really does seem to love you."

He trussed the fencing master's arms and legs, and dragged him into his study, where he laid him out along the couch on which he'd spent the night.

"You never know," the stranger said. "Your wife might like finding you this way, since you're so tightly wrapped already. Maybe I've just expanded your marriage."

The stranger went through the fencing master's pockets and took out the key to his academy. He left the house, stopped to pluck a single rose to tuck into the collar of his coat, and then he traced his steps back to the academy to properly arm himself.

His name was Saber.

# THE FIFTH PIECE

## Overqualified for the job.

The steer chewed a mouthful of grass and stared off into space, thinking long thoughts. He was sort of a loner, and the ranchers always had a hard time getting him back into the paddock. Every time he was let out to graze, he wandered further. His returns were more like quests for the ranchers, and the trip home was often punctuated with many variations of "c'mon, stupid, let's go." But he wasn't stupid. He was probably the smartest of all the cattle. It was why he ranged so far, and also why he was the sole casualty when a comet fell out of the sky and turned the deepest thought of his life into a crater.

The woman who stood up out of the smoking dent in the earth — wondering why the air smelled so strongly of roast beef — was nearly seven feet tall and thickly built. She squinted in the bright sunlight. Then she looked down and saw a leg with a hoof.

"Oh," she said. "Cow."

There was an uneasy tugging in her chest. She climbed out of the crater and walked until four men on horseback rode into her path.

"You see it?" The lead horseman asked.

"See what?" she asked. She was nearly on eye level with the man on horseback, and the four looked at her nervously, though she carried no weapon.

"The comet!" the rancher said. "Did you see that comet fall out of the sky?"

"I heard something," she lied, "but I didn't see a comet."

"Wim," the lead horseman said, "go check it out."

The large woman started walking away.

"Wait," he said.

"Nope."

"Where's your horse?"

"Lost."

"You can't just leave."

"And yet," she said as she passed.

"No, I mean, there's nothing for miles. It'll take you an age to walk to the nearest town."

"Oh. That sort of can't."

"Ride with us. We'll take you back to the ranch. The boss'll know what to do."

Wim, the one who'd gone to look for the comet, returned. "Bad news."

"What? You find it?" The lead horseman said.

"Yeah," Wim said. "There's a big crater out near the edge of the graze lands. George is dead."

"The comet hit George?"

"Looks like it. Only a leg left. It's got our brand."

"Aw, hell."

There was a moment of silence for George.

"Well," the lead horseman said, "guess we won't be having to chase him back into the pen at the end of the day anymore. Wim, let this lady get up behind you. We're gonna take her to see the boss."

Wim's horse eyed the large woman with what might have been apprehension. It sighed heavily as she climbed up and settled herself behind the saddle. She towered over Wim.

"Is the ranch far?" she asked.

"Just a few minutes ride," Wim said. When he nudged the horse into a walk, it whinnied plaintively as if to say it would feel like days.

The rolling hills passed in gentle green curves, and a breeze gave some relief from the heat. The house they reached was a sprawling, single story building of wood and stone. It was surrounded by miles of fencing, and several dogs frisked and barked around the horses' hooves as they rode through the main gate and dismounted by front steps that led to a wraparound porch.

"Vert!" One of the ranchers called as they walked up the steps and into the shade of the eaves.

A short, slender man wearing a pair of thin eyeglasses walked out onto the porch and gave the tall woman standing over his men a startled look.

"You find where it fell?" he asked.

"Found a big crater," Wim said. "George is at the bottom of it. What's left of him, anyway."

Vert sighed and rubbed the back of his neck. "Well, we're taking them in tomorrow anyway. Saves him wandering during the run."

"Lost money though."

"Wolf was gonna get him one day anyway, way he ranged. Ma'am, what can I do for you?"

"We found her out near the crater," Wim said. "Just walking."

"Lady can probably speak for herself," Vert said. Wim shut his mouth with a click. "Ma'am?"

"How close is the nearest town?" she asked.

"Three days if you're riding. You planning to walk? Long and hot, and you don't seem to have any supplies."

"Wolves," she lied, "I was thrown clear of my horse, but they chased her off. My gear's with her."

"You're lucky to be alive," Vert said.

The woman shrugged.

"Well," Vert said, "we're driving the herd into town tomorrow. Guess we can see clear to giving you a ride."

"I don't have any money."

Vert waved his hand away. "Won't hear of it. You'll eat with us and bunk with the men tonight. Ordinarily I'd have you stay in the house, you being a lady and the men being the rowdy sort and all, but somehow I don't think you'll have a problem."

The woman looked around at the ranchers who'd found her. "No. And thank you."

Dinner was a chorus of wet chewing until the men had finished eating and then the gentle rumble of sated conversation. The woman was silent throughout, as if she were the only one in the room. Later, she drifted off to sleep on her own bunk surrounded by ranch hands, largely ignored save for the occasional nervous glance. She ignored the tugging feeling. She'd follow it when she could.

In the morning as they prepared to leave, she assumed she'd have to ride double again but Vert told her he needed every spare hand to keep the cattle together. Instead, he told her to ride next to him on the bench of a wagon. After she'd sat down, he handed across a shotgun.

"I'll drive, but hand that to me quick if we run into rustlers."

She broke open the barrel to check the load, closed it again, and laid it across her lap.

"You drive, I'll shoot," she said.

"Should have guessed. Soldier?

"Once."

"Not much of a talker, are you?"

"When I have to."

"We're gonna get along just fine."

49

They rode in silence over the rolling terrain until they reached a dirt road. They followed it for three days and slept under the wagons at night. The road grew busier closer to the town, but the herd was given primacy in the traffic, other people shuffling to the sides to let it pass. The ranchers knew their business and not one steer strayed from formation as they drove them into an enclosure just outside the cluster of low buildings that made up the town. She stepped down with Vert when he stopped the carriage.

"We'll go into town in a bit," Vert said, "but for now I have to see to my herd."

"I understand."

"It's time for slaughter. We'll finish that up in a few days. Don't know your plans, but maybe you can grab a ride with one of the wagons that'll take the meat and the skins on from here."

She nodded.

Vert walked into the main building of the holding area. His ranchers milled around outside, filling their pipes to smoke and talking in low voices about not much of anything. Vert came out of the house a moment later and walked up to her.

"So, I think I might have gotten you a lift," he said.

"My thanks."

"But the slaughter crew is down a couple of men, so I'm gonna send mine to help. Wagoneers're gonna chip in too. They hate the work, bless 'em, it's a dirty job. They tell me it'll be a few days before they can set out."

"Two days?"

"More like three. At least. Sorry, but there's no avoiding it. Unless you want to walk."

She frowned and stared at the road.

"Or..." Vert said.

"Or what?" she asked.

"Don't suppose you know how to swing a bolt?"

"A bolt?"

"Like a big hammer."

She raised an eyebrow. "You don't say?"

Vert led the woman into the enclosure. On the far side was another gate. She could smell old blood and fresh shit. Past the gate their boots sank into a muddy slurry. There was a steer chained up, its eyes rolling nervously at the humans. To one side was a large hammer with a steel head. She walked over to the massive tool and lifted it easily. The steer watched her approach with one large, rolling eye as she, without breaking stride, swung the hammer overhand and brained the animal. After it dropped a ranch hand ran over and checked it.

"It's dead," he said with awe, "killed it in one blow."

Vert walked over to her. "Usually, that's just the stun before we bleed them out."

She shrugged. "That bad?"

"Not remotely," Vert said, "can you do that consistently?"

"Not a problem."

"They're gonna love you," Vert said with a nod and went to speak with the manager.

She worked in the slaughter yard that day and the next, standing alongside the other workers and braining steer from dawn to dusk. The smell of blood drove the animals into nervous frenzy. She retired exhausted at the end of the first day. At the end of the second, the abattoir manager came out and shook her hand. It vanished inside hers.

"Be happy to get you a ride into the next town," he said, "you can get on with your journey from there."

"How far to the coast?" she asked.

The manager squinted as he thought. "About fifty miles to the next town. It's near the river. You can get a ride on a barge from there to the coast."

"Thanks."

"I should be thanking you. This job normally takes another full day, even two." He handed her a clinking pouch. "Normally, the wagoneers sell their passenger spots, but you ride for free."

"Thank you."

He nodded. "They leave at dawn."

She walked into town. At the general store she bought one of the bolts she'd been swinging for the last two days and asked the proprietor if there was a blacksmith.

"We've got one. Mostly he works with tack and horseshoes. What do you need fixed?"

She hefted the maul she'd just purchased.

"But that's brand new!"

"Where's the smith?"

She walked until she heard the telltale din of steel on steel. The smith nodded as she spoke, only a little startled at what she was asking for.

"Not gonna work for cattle," he muttered, "too messy."

"It's not for cows."

He looked her up and down. "No. I guess not."

When she walked out to the wagon the next day, the striking surfaces of her new hammer had jagged surfaces. The haft had been covered in leather and the handle capped with a nasty spike. The wagon driver gave the brutal weapon only a single glance as she climbed up onto the seat.

"Hope that's not for cows."

"It's not."

"Make an awful mess."

She turned to look at him. "Yup."

The man nodded and snapped the reins. The woman leaned back and sighed, her hands gently resting on the haft of the hammer. Within a few moments the rocking of the wagon had put her to sleep.

Her name was Dagger.

# TOGETHER

## Took you long enough.

E ach of the five followed that pulling feeling, getting ever closer to each other.

At a crossroads of four shipping routes, near the coast of a kingdom none of them bothered to learn the name of, the five came together at the tavern in the center of town and stood for several moments, basking in their proximity.

"Good to see you," Dagger said, and held up a scrap she'd torn from a clumsily printed newspaper in a nearby town. It was an advertisement.

"Found us a job," she said. "Should keep the Vigil's coffers full. And ours."

"Our retirement fund?" Saber asked with a smirk.

"Can't do this forever, Saber," Dagger said.

"All evidence to the contrary," Pitch said.

Vice clasped his hands. "The road is as long as it must be. Let the quality of each step decide its value. Distance and time are unworthy measurements."

Saber took the piece of paper from Dagger. "Yeah, thanks for that, Vice." He read with a raised eyebrow. "We're going to some place called Doll's Fart?"

They were The Armory.

# — CHAPTER 2 —

## A strike in Dahlsvaart.

The Armory paused on a ridge of red rock that loomed high over Dahlsvaart. It was less a town than a collection of factories that a town had formed between like lichen in sun-starved cracks. The smoke-stacked buildings reached for the sky like fingers on malformed hands, and though the factories were quiet, the reek of scorched iron and oil still whispered on a faint wind. A well-maintained road led to a gate in the high walls.

"Looks like they didn't lie about the strike," Saber said. "Industry town like this? The sky should be full of smoke."

"Why would they lie?" Powder asked, resettling the rifles strapped over her shoulder.

"Could have been a trap," Saber shrugged.

"Trap seems doubtful," Pitch said.

"Why? Plenty of people want to kill us," Saber said.

"Sure, but we've never been here before," the alchemist answered.

"You sure?"

The alchemist frowned. "Actually, no."

"Let's move," Dagger said. "Somebody's war is running out of bullets."

The guards at the gate gave the band of mercenaries a nervous look and stepped into their path.

"What's your business here?" one of them asked. His uniform was cleaner than the others and pressed. "You can't enter Dahlsvaart with those weapons."

Past him, The Armory could see slogans painted on the buildings in shaky letters. Discarded leaflets dusted the street. One of them blew through the gate on a fateful wind and fetched up between Dagger's boots. She bent to pick up the tattered scrap. Most of it was too weathered and dirty to read, but block letters shouted "Wurkers' Ryts." Pitch peered at it over Dagger's shoulder.

"They got the punctuation right," he said with a chuckle.

Dagger handed over the advertisement she'd found. "We're here at your mayor's invitation."

"I wasn't informed about that," the guard said.

"Does your boss tell you everything?"

"I work for the city."

"This isn't a city. It's a business."

The guard shifted his feet. "You still can't bring those weapons inside."

Vice walked up beside Dagger. "This town has forgotten its purpose. People must serve a town if it is to survive, but a town should remember that without people it is just a shell for hermit ghosts."

"What?" The guard said with an uneasy look at the monk, whose words issued from the shadow of his hood. The guard stared at the Vice's armored hands.

Dagger gave Vice a sidelong glance. "These aren't weapons, constable, they're tools. We're here to repair the most important part of your machinery. Which way to the mayor's office?"

***

"Ah, more mercenaries. Excellent," Mayor Roth said.

He was a tall, slender man who might have towered over Dagger if he'd been able to stand up straight. He looked like a dandelion struggling with a broken stem.

"Now, you're the third band of mercenaries I've hired to do this job. What makes you think you'll be successful?" Roth said as he stared at Dagger over grasping fingers formed in a steeple. Dagger wondered what the pose was supposed to signify. Maybe it just made him feel better. If her fingers were that long and strange, she'd try to keep the mutinous things occupied too.

"We cost more," Dagger said.

Roth grunted. "I could see to raising the amount, but I only pay once the job's done. And there are conditions."

"That's your right," Dagger said. "But too many rules and this problem won't get solved."

Roth pointed a finger that looked like a spear with gout. "No damage to my factories or the town. My workers have created enough havoc with their petty sabotage."

Dagger waited. When the mayor said nothing more, she spoke.

"Anything else?"

"That is all of it."

"Loss of life?"

Roth waved the question away. "I have men and women waiting in nearby towns that don't have our opportunities. They're eager to work, but there's no point in bringing them in now." The mayor reached into a safe behind his desk and took out a stack of thin gold bars. He put them on the table. "If you're successful, this is yours."

Dagger barely glanced at the stack of metal. "No."

Roth raised an eyebrow. "This is a king's fortune. Any moneychanger in town can convert this to coin without blinking. "

Dagger looked at Pitch and then nodded toward the gold on the table. Pitch picked up one of the bars. "It could be purer," he said.

"The amount is fine," Dagger said, "but the money changers in town work for you, Mayor Roth. We have a deal, but that had better be coin by the time we're finished. We're here to get paid, not pay you."

Pitch set the gold back on the desk. "And we know what this is worth," he said. "Short us and we'll sell our services to the workers. Cheap."

Mayor Roth nodded. "Deal. But cross me and you won't leave this town alive."

"As if that matters," Dagger said.

The mayor looked at her strangely but let the comment pass.

The Armory went to an inn to prepare. It must have been empty for weeks because of the workers' boycotts, but the landlord was still sour over his new 'guests.' They weren't paying either. The landlord sent food and drink up to their room carried by a sullen employee who looked like he could have been the landlord's son. The Armory took the food and shooed him out.

"Who wants what?" Dagger said as she picked at the lukewarm stew with a scowl. She was not talking about the food.

"I'll take the leaders when they're in the open, Captain," Powder said. "Shouldn't be too much trouble. Several of the tallest buildings are near the plazas where they protest. Good sight lines. And when we know where they cached their weapons and supplies, I'll destroy them."

Saber nodded at Powder. "I'll take the ones that go to ground and hide."

"I'll handle the strikes themselves," Pitch said. "The pot's already close to boiling. We just need to turn up the heat. If somebody can get hold of one of their leaders, they'll talk to me. I'll get Saber and Powder the names and locations they need."

"I will get you your leader to speak with, Pitch," Vice rumbled. "The workers are men of faith. I will shatter their symbols and cast down their false deities."

"This isn't a holy war, Vice," Dagger said.

"All we do, we do in the Vigil's name. What is that if not a holy war?"

Saber grinned. "I always wanted to be a holy warrior."

"Saber," Vice said, "you could never be holy, not even if I boiled you for a year in blessed waters."

"Vice, was that a joke? Did Vice just make a joke?" Saber said.

"When that's all done," Dagger said, "I'll break whatever force assembles in response."

"So, the easy job then?" Saber said with a smirk.

"Know your role, Saber." Dagger said. "You want me to do the creeping and cutting, you'll have to wait until somebody hires us to kill a giant."

Saber laughed. "You'd just get Pitch to poison it."

"I wonder how much poison I'd need to kill a giant," Pitch mused with a faraway expression.

"Remember that one army?" Powder asked. "The one that worshipped a rabid sheep? It took a whole barrel."

"It's not the same ratio at all, Powder," Pitch said. "That was a lot of small doses in their cook pots. But a giant would need..." He went quiet, doing calculations in his head.

"Figure it out later, Pitch," Dagger said. "Let's get some sleep. Busy days ahead."

# PITCH

## Trouble in a bottle.

Pitch sat up on the lumpy mattress and groaned into his hands.

Mornings were loathsome and he preferred to pretend they didn't exist. With mumbling fingers, he dropped several leaves and a crystal into a steel bowl and ground them with a pestle until they were dust. He carefully dumped the powder onto a reasonably clean book and snorted most of it, the rest he rubbed into his eyes. In moments, the room's colors took on a much more pleasant hue and he could have counted every crack in the old floorboards after a single glance. He gathered his equipment and stepped out the door with the dash of a bantam rooster.

The first of the protests was assembled outside a dry goods shop that the workers patronized, paying with the scrip that made for over half their wage and was useless outside the town.

Pitch hovered around the edge of the crowd and looked for late arrivals and stragglers. Most of the demonstrators seemed genuinely impassioned and far too alert. He wanted one who was just there for the show, but not the big ones, the angry ones, or the ones moving with the nervous, excited energy of the fire starter.

There.

Watching from a corner on the edge of the action, shaking her fist and howling with a dull-eyed enthusiasm was a stout, drink-aged woman. She was about his size and dressed like the other workers. Pitch made his way over to her, shouting inarticulately as he went. When he moved beside her, she grinned at him as if they were watching some sporting contest and swayed unsteadily. Pitch showed her a little stoppered vial in the palm of his hand. Her eyes widened. She looked around and back at him. Pitch nodded encouragingly and she snatched the vial and ducked into a nearby alley to open her present.

Pitch counted to fifty and then followed. He found her slumped and snoozing happily with a smile worthy of a saint's portrait.

"I envy you the dreams you are having," he said. "My gift to you. Now, for your gift to me." He took off his coat and hid it behind an empty refuse can, then removed her jacket and cap and put them on. He could have bought clothes, but then they'd have looked new. With his disguise in place, he slithered into the very center of the protest, listening for the cadence of their shouts and matching them until he'd gotten the words right.

"Copper's for kettles! Paper is for books! Pay in silver!"

"No more sweat and callous for their scrip and malice!"

"Scrip won't grip! Fuck the company coin!"

Pitch wondered what failed poet had written that last chant.

Overlooking the protest on a hastily erected stage of wooden planks and sawhorses was one of the leaders. He called the chants like conducting an orchestra, screaming through the mouthpiece of a tin speaking horn. The crowd seemed to move in slow motion around Pitch as he rode the wave of his own chemicals. This particular blend created a hyper focus that turned the grains of sand in time's hourglass into molasses, but this morning he'd also cut a sedative into it which was about to be vital.

He took a cloth bundle from his pocket and unwrapped six four-inch vials of paper-thin glass sealed with red wax. As he shouldered his way through the thick of the crowd, he dropped the first vial. It landed in the dirty street where the stomping, shuffling heels of crowd would find it. It broke. Chemicals hit air. They blended and smoked. The fumes traveled up past the workers' boots to their dirty trousers, climbed past their belts and used the buttons of their shirts like stairs until they entered screaming mouths and flaring nostrils. Excited pulses and hot blood would carry them the rest of the way.

The fumes hit Pitch too but were smothered by the sedative.

He dropped another vial. Then another.

There is no ardor like the chemical, Pitch thought. Take one crowd, add passion. Sprinkle with years of frustration, sore backs and hungry bellies. Dash with righteous fury and deglaze with herd mentality.

Pitch's blends would put beneath that protest stew a blaze worthy of a dragon's throat. He felt the crowd's vibration change when he was halfway through it. He dropped another vial and then another. Better hurry, he thought, and dropped the last of his payload and popped out the far end of the mob.

He returned to the snoozing woman and laid her coat and hat beside her, then collected his own from their hiding spot and went to lean against a building across the street to watch.

The mob's shouts fell out of sync and became angrier. They shoved and pushed each other. They looked away from the stage and glared at the guardsmen lingering at the edge of the plaza. Arguments and scuffles broke out. He saw a hand flash a knife. A large worker knelt to pry loose a paving stone.

Only one ingredient left, Pitch thought.

Pitch approached the guardsmen who'd been sent to monitor the demonstration. What did any brewing conflicted need to boil over?

"Constable," Pitch said to one of them.

"What do you want?" the uniformed guard said, his eyes focused on the mob. That clears up another question, Pitch thought. They don't all know who I am. He wondered why Roth hadn't told all his hardcases that there were mercenaries here to quell the strike.

"I'm not from here," the alchemist said, "just came to do some business. I thought you should know I saw weapons in that crowd."

"They're armed?" One of the other guards asked.

"I saw at least two pistols," Pitch lied. "And knives. It's not the whole crowd. But there's a group in the middle. I think they're planning something."

The guards looked at each other and fingered the truncheons hanging from their belts. Pitch could almost hear their brains doing the math of conflict. There were few less-appealing equations than a club divided by a bullet.

"Get moving, merchant," one of the guards said. "Can't vouch for your safety anymore."

"Understood, constable. Thank you for your service."

Pitch walked away from the protest. He heard a gun go off. Screams spiked.

The final ingredient was beyond even his ability to replicate.

Authority.

He hurried down a side street. He had four more protests to visit.

## VICE

**Gimme that old time religion.**

Vice rose with the dawn and drank half a flagon of water. He ate a plain, dry barley cake and a cold chunk of mutton left over from last night. He knelt to speak with the Vigil. As usual, his god didn't answer, even in his imagination. Such was the nature of a dead god. He left his room to begin the day's work and passed Saber's. The duelist was sharpening the tools of his trade. He looked up as the monk loomed in his doorway.

"Morning, Vice," Saber said. "I'll be ready when you are."

Vice nodded. He commandeered a cart that the innkeeper used to shop for supplies at the market and pushed it through the streets. He considered the task ahead of him.

The town's god was a worker's nondescript deity: Fairness. The laborers had prayed it into existence when they'd left their shops and assembly lines.

Its principles were all borrowed things — scraps of a hundred other faiths, picked up over the years like coins found in the street — and their leaders would be weak priests all, regurgitating these tenets as if they were their own, from hazy memory and half-remembered euphorias. They didn't even have an afterlife. They were too concerned with the small, dirty machinations of this one. Their churches were union meeting places in the back rooms of silenced factories and the corners of empty warehouses. Sermons were desperate and fragmented, each a feeble grasping at an imagined freedom, a deliverance spoken of in an aspirational manner. But if they succeeded here, if The Armory failed, it was possible theirs might become a true, new faith with an infant god, still slimy from the womb. Vice idly wondered which scrap of the heavens that god would have claimed for itself, but the issue was irrelevant.

The Armory had arrived.

He had arrived.

Vice pushed the cart to a coffee house where the mayor's bullymen waited for him. He walked to the table of uniforms and stood over them until they stopped talking and looked up.

"Yeah?" One of them said.

Vice scowled. "Would you make us both look foolish by demanding that I ask?" He reached out one armored hand and snapped his fingers with a dull clang. One of the guards took out a piece of paper. On it were four addresses.

"Just four?" Vice said.

"That we know of," the guard said.

"What a timid faith," Vice said. "Nascent. Unborn. What could it change and become if allowed to grow? If I was not here to abort it, to strangle it with its birth cord?"

One of the guards winced. Vice pinned him with a hard stare. Did he sympathize with the workers and their faith? Or was he just a father?

"The loss of a child is a terrible tragedy," Vice said to him. "Know that yours slumbers in the arms of a god of the true faith."

"What the fuck are you talking about?" The guard asked.

Vice nodded knowingly. "To the ignorant all truth sounds strange. If you do not understand, do not be concerned. That truth was not for you."

The guard who might be a father blinked. "What?"

Vice left the guards to their coffee. What small lives to have, so unexamined, he thought, for only through aggressive study could a small life attain meaning and become vast.

He followed the note in his pocket to the first address, pushing the cart among the pedestrians with his hood up, feeling as he always did when he walked among people — as one forever apart.

Not even my footsteps sound the same as the unguided, he thought.

The first church was a low building and Vice paused to watch the faithful file in. He left the cart near the door and walked to an open window to listen as the workers took their seats. A portly man huffed his way to a podium.

"The sermon begins," Vice muttered.

"As many of you know," the portly man said in hard voice, "we lost Lucius, Kenell and Darvish in the riots yesterday."

Vice sniffed. Ah, Pitch you did your work well, didn't you? With chemicals you earn your place in one faith's hell and another's heaven.

What a winding path to walk, paved with the fallen.

"I know many of you are worried," the union official continued. "Some of you are afraid. But you must stand strong. Roth's shown us he's growing desperate, ordering his enforcers to use violence like that. It means the strike is working, but as I've told you so many times, this fight can't be stopped. But we'll win. As long as you all stand strong and stand together. It's fine to grieve, but if you really want to honor them, keep going. You must have the strength to walk on, even when the distance is unknown!"

Vice examined his armored fists and made sure the cords were taut. He clasped his hands below his chin and bent his head.

"Watcher in the Darkness," he whispered, "I know you are looking on from somewhere, no matter how far. Only a weak man demands his god's protection. I am not weak. For by leaving my steps unguided, you have made me strong. Know that all I do, I do in your name. As I speak it through my actions, so do you live on."

Vice lifted his head and walked into the building.

The portly leader glanced at Vice sharply but did not pause his sermon. Instead, he spoke even louder and with greater passion. He shook his little fist and sent ripples through the crowd.

Ah, Vice thought, as it is with every dissipated priest. They show their worshippers with every gesture that they are different, that they are better. But who could trust such a man, such a faith? So unsharpened by life, unsullied by action? Did he mean to present his visage as the dream, the goal? As the embodiment of successful deeds done, when those deeds would always be done by others?

"Are you the keeper of this faith?" Vice called to man behind the podium.

The workers turned in their chairs to glare at Vice, their sunken cheeks and hollow eyes told of fear, fatigue and deprivation. And still they listened to this feeble visage of plenty with his straining belt and groomed mustache, Vice thought.

The monk addressed the workers next. "Is he your paragon? Your guide?"

"Faith?" The leader said, "Nothing like that here. This isn't a church, it's a private meeting for workers. What's your business here?"

"No faith?" Vice said with a sweeping gesture for the room. "No faith?! You open your mouth and lies pour forth like a poisoned waterfall. No faith. Bah! You drip with faith. This temple overflows with it. Look at you all in your neat little rows, eagerly supping from the spiritual feast this man has laid out for you!"

The man behind the podium rubbed the bridge of his nose. "Look, I don't know who you are, but this is a private meeting for the mistreated workers of Dahlsvaart. You're obviously not a laborer so—"

"How do you know?" Vice asked as he walked up the central path between the rows of chairs. "How do you know that I do not labor? Can you guess my trade, priest?"

"I'm not a priest!"

"Of course you are. You stand before a congregation. You talk of salvation, deliverance. Of long roads walked blindly. What is that if not a priest?"

"This has nothing to do with the gods. We are—"

"You are here," Vice interrupted him, "to make these men believe that they can change their fates. That at the far side of this long trial there is a better life waiting. What is that if not a religion? What is such an idea if not godly?"

"Okay, I'm done," the union official said. "Fitz, Jons, get this nutcase out of here. We've got shit to do."

Two big, broad-shouldered men got up and approached Vice. Chairs squeaked as the workers made space around the monk and soon there was a circle a few feet from the podium.

"C'mon. Time to go," one of the big men said.

Vice spread his arms wide. Each of the men glanced at his armored hands and paused. "Is it time?" the monk asked. "Truly? Are we called to the beyond this day? Because I tell you, I have been there and returned again and again. There is nothing at the end for me. What waits for you? Do you know? Has your overfed priest told you yet?"

"Boys, just get this crazy prick outta here!" the man at the podium yelled.

"He calls you boys," Vice said. "Are you his sons to be so spoken to?"

The monk threw back his hood and fixed his piercing, mad eyes upon them. "I tell you now, your faith is weak. You follow men incapable of taking up the banner they so casually ask you to suffer under. But that is the way of most priests," Vice said and paused to give each man a significant look. "Most, but not all."

"You're a priest?" One of them asked with a quick glance at the fat man behind the podium, who made a helpless gesture in reply.

"I am a man of faith bereft," Vice said. "But though my god is dead, its power is greater than your own because my faith has never died. Yours toddles from its cradle on unsteady feet, a feckless, celestial child ready to knock down the world without a care for you. When you need this infant god most, it will abandon you."

The union leader slammed his hand down on the podium. "Why are you two still talking? Get him the fuck out of here!"

The men took Vice by the arms and walked him toward the door. Vice whispered to them. "Faith must be strongest in the dark. The unshakable pillar beneath the world when all is chaos, when all is devoid of light, of meaning. It must be the golden rope that lets one climb from the depths of life's dry well. Is yours such a faith?"

One of the big men shrugged. "I don't know, buddy. Sorry about this. You know, if you are a priest."

"No," Vice said to him with a beatific smile, "it is I who am sorry. I have come to test your faith. Always an ugly task. But fear not, I bring deliverance. I bring truth. I bring a breaking, after which there will be nothing but light."

"Whatever you say," the other large man said as they neared the door. But then Vice stopped and though they tugged, they could not move him. The men grunted and yanked, but Vice stood firm.

"C'mon, old man. Don't make us get rough."

"Why?" Vice asked. "Why not? I have come to be exactly that! I am the anvil against which your faith might become steel... or scrap metal."

Vice spun and ripped his arms free of their grip. He darted left and low, and his shoulder took one man beneath the arm and cracked his ribs. He fell gasping and Vice turned to the other, casually catching his punch against his armored forearm. The fist shattered against the steel, and before the man could even moan, Vice destroyed his collarbone and shoulder with a falling, overhand strike worthy of a rockslide.

"Rejoice!" Vice boomed as the two big men fell and the chairs squeaked as the rest of the workers in the room leapt to their feet and into the brawl. "I have come to shatter the lie of your faith with the golden truth! Rejoice, for this day you are cupped in the memory of a true god!"

The fat man behind the podium screamed. "For the last time, asshole, this isn't a church!"

Vice bulled through the workers and rushed the stage. He kicked aside the podium and took the fat man by the head and turned his face to the workers. They stopped and watched as Vice whispered to his hostage. "Look at them! Look at your flock, priest. See them come together with the light of the true faith in their eyes! What is this, if not a place of worship?"

"You're out of your fucking mind," the fat man said, struggling to free his head from Vice's plated grip.

"No. I am quite sane. Now watch as I tear down your temple, stone by stone."

Vice released the union leader's head and shoved him aside. He turned to the mob before the podium and smiled.

"Come then," he called, "show me the truth of your faith!"

The workers rushed the monk of a dead god. They tried to grab and overwhelm him with numbers, but he had spoken true. He was the anvil. They were barely pig iron. When each had fallen, broken or cowering on the floor in search of their fighting spirit, Vice returned to the leader quivering behind what was left of his podium. He might as well have tried to hide behind a single blade of grass.

"Your altar will not save you," Vice said softly. The man only stared up at this walking, sermonizing cataclysm. "Walk or be carried?"

"What?"

"Carried then," Vice said. He trussed the union leader's arms and legs, gagged him and threw him over his shoulder. He carried him outside and dumped the man into the cart, covered him with a horse blanket and wheeled the cart through the streets toward the tavern, where Pitch was waiting in the basement.

# SABER

## Doing it in the dark.

Saber looked down at his bed and smirked. This was by far the prettiest company he'd ever had across a set of rented sheets, and it broke his heart a little to have to leave any of them, especially when the candles had lit them with such a golden glow. He took a deep breath and sighed. Time to make some hard choices.

"I'm sorry, my dears," he whispered.

On the bed were several swords, a dozen knives of different lengths and types, curved, straight, hooked and jagged. A long sword lay suggestively between a curved saber with a half-basket hilt and a broad-bladed, single edged short sword with a simple brass d-guard. That one would be short enough to bring. He also chose a pair of heavy blades, more like cleavers, and then stripped the scabbards he wouldn't need from his leathers while he sipped strong coffee. Dagger filled the doorway with her shoulders.

"Sun's down," she said. "You ready?"

Saber nodded. "Nearly. It's just such a delicate choice, you know?"

"You're a romantic, Saber," Dagger chuckled.

Saber winked at her. "There's a certain poetry in a good departure. How can we appreciate a memory if we try and live it forever?"

"We do live forever."

"No, Dagger. We die forever."

Dagger only grunted. "No poetry in tonight's work."

"Alas, but one can't live on wine alone! There must also be bread," Saber said and drained his coffee. "Did Vice and Pitch come through?"

In answer, Dagger dropped a stack of pages torn from a notebook on the table by Saber's bed. "The man was quite the talker once Pitch got hold of him. You've got a long, bloody night ahead."

Saber shuffled the pages. Names. Addresses. Maps. Directions. Even guard rotations. The workers had themselves a very organized strike. "Has Powder left already?"

Dagger nodded.

Saber sheathed the d-guard short sword at his hip and several knives under his arms, against his thighs and across his chest. He slid the cleavers home in overlapping scabbards on the small of his back, and tightened every buckle and smeared the metal with lampblack to hide the glint. He swept a long coat over all of it, clapped a hat on his head and slipped out the window that led to the alley behind the tavern.

At night, Dahlsvaart was hushed. The leaders of the strike had struck a deal with Roth and his guards, a kind of good faith detente, to keep the streets relatively quiet after the sun went down.

Saber knew that bargain — all bargains in fact — would be off the table by sunrise.

Ordinary factory workers wouldn't have been much of a problem, dark alleys or not. But the factories of Dahlsvaart did not make engine parts or nails — they made guns, cannons and swords. Roth had reported a lot of missing inventory, some of which was certain to be stored beneath the floorboards of the workers' homes.

Saber kept to the alleys. The town had some indoor plumbing, but in the poorer warrens of the workers' quarter, public troughs were more common. Saber covered his mouth with a cloth and waved away the hungry flies. Music wafted from the windows. Evening meals and entertainments were being taken with tired, tense families eager for the strike to end. He tucked himself into a corner below a glowing window and held Pitch's map up to the dim light.

The first address was just ahead.

The building was seven stories tall, and Pitch's notes indicated the hall past the front door would be lined with guards, even at night. The roof on the other hand...

Saber slipped behind the building, tested a drainpipe for strength and climbed, the treads of his soft boots tacking against the building's rough stucco. He dragged himself up onto the roof and froze.

A wooden hut with a door had been built over the hatch that led down into the building. Next to the door was a man in a chair. Saber waited. He looked from hand to hand for a weapon, but the man only had a bottle loosely gripped in his fingers. Saber edged closer. The man was snoring and there was rifle across his lap. The barrel had been sawed down to the stock.

Powder would disapprove, Saber thought. You lose a lot of range with a short barrel.

Saber grinned and shook his head. This sleeping guard had probably just learned to pull a trigger yesterday, after just enough instruction to learn which end made all the noise before some idiot leader put the weapon in his hands. The guard twitched in some dream, and his hand opened. The bottle fell and shattered. The guard snorted awake, and Saber spun around to the deep shadows on the far side of the hut.

"Who's there?" The guard called. Saber drew one of his knives and held it against his leg.

"I can see you," the guard said in a loud, theatrical tone.

Saber frowned. Whatever he's looking at, it's not me.

"That's right, you better run!"

The door of the hut banged open, and a short woman rushed out, gun up and ready.

"Shilba? What is it?" She asked.

"Somebody was trying to get up onto the roof."

"Where did they go?"

"I chased them off. They ran."

"Where? Right off the edge?" the woman asked, her tone dubious. Saber took out another knife and prepared to throw it.

"What's this?" she asked.

Saber ducked further back into the shadows. He heard the sound of glass grating.

"Just some broken glass," Shilba said.

The woman sniffed the air. "Were you drinking up here?"

"No!"

"Again? After Roderick told you what would happen?"

"I wasn't!"

"Shilba, do you want another beating!? He might kill you next time."

"I wasn't drinking," Shilba whined.

Saber peered around the edge of the hut and watched as the woman gathered up what was left of Shilba's bottle and tossed it over the edge.

"You're lucky it was me," she said. "Somebody else would tell."

"I wasn't drinking," Shilba muttered.

The woman went back into the hut and slammed the door, leaving Shilba alone with his sullen protests. Saber heard another slam from inside the hut as she went through the hatch that led down into the building. He crept slowly around the hut and marked Shilba's position by his faint, indignant muttering, by the creak of the chair as Shilba sat back down and finally by the click of wood as Shilba set his rifle on the ground.

Saber rushed around the hut, grabbed Shilba by the chin and drove a knife through his voice box. As Shilba gurgled and tried to swallow steel, Saber yanked the blade free and slammed it into his chest over and over, digging a well in his lungs. Saber propped the dead man up and unloaded the rifle before laying it back across his lap.

"Sorry, Shilba," he whispered. "You were right. Somebody was trying to get onto the roof."

Saber slipped through the door of the hut, opened the hatch that led into the building and ghosted his way down the shadowed stairwell.

Good that it's dark, he thought. This was such an ugly way to practice his craft, on catlike feet against untested opponents disarmed by sleep and lack of proper training.

He wouldn't want to watch it either.

# POWDER

## Whatever you do,
## don't look up.

It had taken a bit of an argument with the innkeeper to get a spare table moved into her room. He huffed like an ox stuck in a mud hole when the gunner asked for a tablecloth too, and whined that she'd better not be expecting him to throw a banquet.

"Nobody's going to want to eat what I'm serving," Powder murmured. The innkeeper's eyes dropped to the pistols holstered under her arms. She patted his shoulder. "Just get me the table. Then go away."

She laid the table with the tools of her trade. Two rifles, one longer than the other by several inches, a pair of short-barreled shotguns, four revolvers and three derringers, two over-under varieties and one with four barrels bound together. She put aside the shotguns and two of the revolvers. She'd be working at a distance tonight. Then she stripped two pistols, cleaned and oiled them, and loaded them along with two derringers, because she knew you can't always pick your distance. Then she set the first rifle, the longer of the two, in the center of the table and gave it the same treatment as the pistols.

"Nearly ready?" Dagger asked, coming into the room and leaning her hammer against the wall. She sat on the bed, which creaked under her bulk.

"Just about, Captain," Powder said. She kept her eyes on Dagger while her hands stripped and oiled the second rifle, even though it was brand new.

"How's that look?" Dagger nodded to the weapon. It had been supplied by Roth's factor and had come off an assembly line right there in town.

"Dahlsvaart's finest?" Powder snorted. "Good enough. I'll be happy to leave it where I shoot it."

"Job should be relaxing," Dagger said, "You won't have to shoot around us."

"That's true. Just a pleasant little night on the town," Powder said.

"Just don't go dancing on the rooftops and getting seen."

"More Saber's thing than mine, Captain," Powder said. "Speaking of which, did Pitch finish?"

Dagger put a sheaf of tattered papers on the table by Powder's weapons.

"Saber goes low, you go high," Dagger said.

"As ever."

Powder set aside the weapon and wiped her oily hands on a rag. She looked over the names adorning a series of hand-drawn maps. "Pitch still squeezing the guy?"

"If you call frolicking in a field of daises getting squeezed. Pitch thinks he's almost empty. The daisies are about to go away."

Powder hmmed as she stopped at the second piece of paper.

"What?" Dagger asked.

"A friendly target?"

"We don't have friends here," Dagger said. "Roth wanted an excuse to use force. We're going to give it to him. Don't kill them, just make a point."

"I could remove the buttons on their shirts one by one if you like."

"A slightly stronger point than that."

Powder chuckled.

"And Powder? It's overcast."

Powder gave a theatrical little shiver. "You know just what to say to a girl, Captain."

"Save it for harassing Saber. He's the only one still has those appetites."

"I think he's just going through the motions."

"Sometimes that's all you have."

***

Powder crept to the edge of the roof overlooking the small square and looked down on the shouting protesters. Roth had ordered extra street lamps and the square was bathed in amber.

She took a small telescope from her bag and trained it on the crowd. After Pitch's chemically orchestrated riot, they'd been smarter this evening. More union officials were in the throng, marked by finer clothes and cleaner faces. They kept a stronger handle on their powder keg of foot soldiers: A patted shoulder here, a restrained touch there, leaning in to talk directly into an ear. Not one of the workers was carrying anything that looked like a weapon, but Powder knew the odds. You couldn't count on every one of your soldiers to obey orders, and among all that swarming, ragged cloth there would be knives, clubs and even a pistol or two.

She trained the telescope on the town guards ringing the plaza. They were another story. Their faces were tense. They all carried pistols.

But for the moment, the protest was careful and calm.

That wouldn't do at all.

Powder opened her leather case and took out her rifles. She wanted one target wounded and angry, and the other messy and dead. Tonight she had switched own rifle's barrel for a narrower bore. It was loaded with a small bullet under a quarter-load of powder, it would only kill with perfect shot placement, but the Dahlsvaart rifle held a much larger, crosshatched round under a full load. A scalpel and a bludgeon. She unfolded a black canvas shroud and lay down on the roof, pulling the shroud over her body as she rested the barrel on the edge. She set the second rifle by her side and took aim at one of the guards.

"Right or left, my son?" She noted the holstered pistol was on his left side. "Ah, you're a lefty. I'll be nice. Leave you the arm you jerk off with."

She aimed for the edge of his right shoulder. The gun barked. The guard screamed and fell.

The other guards crouched and pulled their weapons. If they'd been trained soldiers, Powder might have been worried about them guessing her position, but instead they pointed their pistols at the protesters. Some of the shouting workers had heard the shot, and they turned to look at the guards instead of looking up. She saw them draw knives and truncheons from their clothes as their panicked leaders tried to keep them calm.

"Oh, no you don't," Powder muttered.

She grabbed the Dahlsvaart rifle and sighted at the protesters as ripples of conflict worked their way through the crowd.

"C'mon," Powder whispered. "Not just any leader. I need the big dog. Where are you?"

One by one, the workers and even the union officials turned this way and that, looking for orders. Soon there was one figure among that sea of faces to which all others seemed to look: a woman wearing a metal worker's leather apron who raised her hands and yelled for order. The apron was spotless. Her laborer's clothes were brand new. She raised her hands and turned rapidly, desperately giving orders to preserve the protest and prevent a mob.

"There you are," Powdered whispered. The guards moved in and tense standoffs sparked along the edges of the throng.

Powder squeezed the trigger.

The bullet turned the leader's sternum into a broken bowl and ripped out of her back in spurt of bone-flecked gore. The protest shrank in on itself like one organism, held for a moment, and burst outward. Guns fired, guards fell, truncheons swung. Powder pulled back from the roof and packed up most of her weapons.

She left Dahlsvaart rifle where Mayor Roth's agents would find it.

Her night wasn't finished yet.

*** 

Powder descended the iron stairs down the side of the building and collected the satchel she'd stashed under a pile of refuse. She brushed off the wetter bits of the camouflage, and gently slung the bag over her shoulder.

What was inside could not be jostled.

She went first to two apartment buildings that Pitch indicated on his map with hash marks and numbers. Around the back, she found the brittle shack of a public toilet and covered her face with a scarf. She expected the usual human stench but there was nothing but a faint wisp. The outhouses hadn't been used in months.

She flipped back the lid of one of the toilets to reveal a hidden ladder and climbed down into a hollowed-out basement. She lit a small lantern and by its slender light saw stacks of crates. Inside one were rifles, in another were short, single edged swords — the kind an artillery soldier might rely on once the quarters were close and the guns were quiet. In one corner were several sealed barrels of black powder.

"Shit," she muttered, "that's double what Pitch said was here."

She set the lantern on a crate of guns and knelt with her satchel. Packed inside, among scrap leather and raw wool still greasy with lanolin, were two iron boxes and two hourglasses filled with viscous liquid that had been carefully packed, liquid side down. She and Pitch had created the boxes together after making two prototypes barely bigger than matchboxes, the first of which they used to blow a hole in the paved yard behind the inn. The second, Pitch had kept with a grin, saying "you never know."

Powder took out the first. Made of a thin cast iron, a blow with a hammer would shatter it, while a larger force would turn it into a burst of slag shrapnel. She took out one of the hourglasses. The empty end was flat and sealed with a wax of Pitch's invention. Holding it carefully, liquid side down, Powder took a deep breath. Once installed, she'd have an hour to get clear. She set the iron box on top of one of the barrels of gunpowder, and then carefully set the hourglass, wax side down, into a hole in the top of the box. The liquid dripped. The wax smoked. It started to dissolve.

Powder slung her bag and quickly climbed back to the street. She had to get to the other cache before the first blew and the workers went to check on their stolen weapons.

Pitch's intel was off. If the other cache was the same size, it suggested the workers had more weapons than Roth's men had thought, and far more gunpowder. It also meant the devices would do far more damage.

Oh well, Powder thought, no plan survives reality.

She hurried. Behind her, acid chewed wax.

Powder found the second cache in an abandoned building with a ragged hole in the side. She planted the last device, ran to a nearby factory and climbed the external stairs to the roof. She's just settled when the first device went off. The ground rumbled and a gout of fire shot up into the night sky.

She aimed at the hole in the building and waited. Only minutes later, a half dozen workers rushed up the street and inside to check their cache. Powder swore. The bomb had been designed to make it look like the arms hadn't been stored properly and gone up on their own. It would take a bomber of Powder's skill, or Pitch's education, to look at the scorch patterns and find evidence of a hidden hand. She was sure there was nobody like that here, not even on the mayor's staff. If there had been, The Armory might never have been hired.

But if even one of the workers survived the blast, they'd all know it hadn't been an accident.

"Fuck," she muttered.

She heard a single, panicked shout of alarm from inside the building and then a figure sprinted out. Powder's rifle snapped. The worker dropped face down, curled up and writhing, just before a blast of sound and roaring white light stole Powder's night vision.

When the sunspots cleared, the building was a pile of rubble. Powder grinned. They'd been stupid enough to fiddle with the device. Power rubbed her eyes and looked through her scope for the man she'd shot, but the fallen building had buried him.

"Time for bed," Powder muttered. She climbed down and threaded her way through side streets to the inn.

# — CHAPTER 3 —

## An ugly problem with a stupid solution.

The shouting that woke Dagger seemed at first like some vestige of a dream. There was a battlefield. There was always a battlefield. She sat up in bed, groggily rubbing her eyes as the sound worked its way through the fog of last night's drink. She wasn't quite sure what she was hearing, but it didn't sound good.

Her bedroom door opened and Powder stuck her head in.

"Better get up, Captain. We're mildly fucked."

"Is there coffee?"

"Downstairs."

"That's something."

"Hence mildly," Powder said and left.

Dagger put on her leathers and picked up her hammer. She recognized what she was hearing.

A mob.

In the common room of the inn the rest of The Armory stood tensely armed and peeking through the windows at the crowd. Dagger looked out herself and saw an assembly of city guards and workers. She smirked.

"Mercenaries!" a leader of the guard shouted through a speaking horn. Dagger recognized it as the same kind used by the strike leaders. "You've brought chaos and destruction! Come out quietly. You have my word you'll receive a fair trial."

"Roth," Dagger muttered. "That rat fuck."

"I guess he sold us out," Powder said as she loaded her guns between sips of hot coffee.

"I want you all to leave," the innkeeper said, his voice quivering, even as he served coffee and laid out a tray with bread and cheese.

"Is there a back door?" Dagger asked him.

"Yes," the innkeeper said, "you have to—"

Saber interrupted him. "There's a bunch of armed morons out there too."

"There's your answer," she told the innkeeper as Saber handed her a cup of coffee.

"Mercenaries!" The shrill voice came again.

"A couple of these idiots actually have pitchforks," Pitch said from a window.

"Pretty standard mob fare, Pitch," Saber said, with a theatrical leer at the service girl as he bit into a piece of bread. She skittered away.

"Saber," Pitch said, "this is a factory town. They're not farmers. Why would they even have pitchforks?"

"There is a stable."

"Oh."

Saber grinned. "Aren't you the smart one?"

"Some problems are beneath me."

"It's okay, Pitch. I won't tell everybody."

"Powder," Dagger said, "I'm going out to talk to the mayor."

"I'm on it, Captain," Powder said, picked up her rifle and dashed up the stairs to the roof.

"Sure that's a good idea, boss?" Saber asked.

"Where's Vice?" Dagger asked.

"Where do you think?" Pitch said and pointed at the ceiling. "Upstairs praying."

Dagger swung her hammer up onto her shoulder. "Tell him to find out how many we need for an exit. We might be coming in hot."

Then she walked out to face the mob.

"Fuck," Saber muttered and went upstairs. He found Vice on his knees, shirtless except for his scars.

103

"Vice?" Saber asked. "Don't suppose you can hear me in there?"

"Do not be an idiot, Saber."

"You might want to get ready. It's about to get hairy."

"To what end should I be ready? I scorn the physical. It is transient."

Saber rolled his eyes.

"Temporary," Vice said.

"I know what transient means, Vice. It's about to get more temporary-er."

"That is not a word."

"Dagger says find out how many."

"It is certain, then?"

"How long have you been up here with your head in the clouds?"

"My faith is—"

"Your faith can't be louder than half the town and all the guards screaming for our fucking heads, Vice. Get your shit together."

"I will ask," Vice said.

***

Dagger walked out into the square, the far side and most of the nearby alleys were packed with

104

screaming figures riding the rush of righteousness and numbers.

"Roth! Let's talk!" she called and stopped in the center of the street. She rested her hammer head-down between her boots and folded her arms. The mayor stepped out from between the ranks of his guards, gesturing that a few should follow him. Five men walked to meet her.

"What is this, Roth?" Dagger asked, with a nod to the mob surrounding them.

"You went too far, mercenary."

"Call me Dagger."

The mayor and the guards looked at the hammer between her feet.

"It's ironic," Dagger said.

"You don't seem to understand," the mayor said. "At a wave of my hand these people will tear you apart."

Dagger shrugged. "Pay us. We'll leave."

"Pay you? For bombing buildings, murdering innocent community leaders and shooting my guards?"

"Workers shot your guard and we didn't bomb anything," Dagger lied, knowing the quality of Powder and Pitch's work meant he had no proof. "Your workers stole gunpowder from your factories and stored it like dickheads. Take it up with them."

"You were hired to put down the strike, not destroy half the town! You made our divisions greater than ever."

Dagger looked around at the crowd. "Looks like you've got unity now."

Roth smiled smugly. "When I explained that outside consultants created this issue, the union leaders expressed a willingness to bargain."

Dagger rolled her eyes. "Just pay us. Trust me, it'll be cheaper."

"Look around," Roth countered. "I could let you walk free and that would be payment enough."

"The Armory always gets paid, Roth. Gold or souls."

"I don't know what that means."

"Pay us and you never will."

Roth crossed his arms. "Throw down your weapons and surrender. I'll have my men escort you to the city gates."

"Oh, I'm sure."

"You have my word."

"Uh huh. Roth, we were working in the shadows before. You don't want us working in the light. Trust me, you can't afford it."

Roth pursed his lips and peered at her like a vulture looking at a rat with three broken legs. "I could see to giving you... one quarter of what you were promised."

Dagger sighed and pretended to think it over. "Your terms are acceptable."

"Very wise. I am glad we could come to an agreement."

Dagger smiled thinly and leaned over in a deep, ironic bow.

Roth's head disappeared in a burst of red. The sound of a gunshot came a fraction of a second later.

Dagger stood to her full height and picked up her hammer. To the music of the crowd's enraged, confused screaming, she shattered the little cluster of Roth's guards still fumbling to raise their weapons. The man who caught the brunt of her blow flew several feet, cartwheeling bonelessly with a square dent in his ribcage. Dagger stepped in and swung again, smashing a knee to pulp, then around in an arc to crush a man's head. She thrust with the head of her weapon and a guard stumbled back spitting teeth.

The last guard backed away and the crowd rushed forward.

Dagger turned and sprinted for the tavern while Powder covered her, dropping citizen and guard alike from the roof. The mob's few, untrained guns sent up little puffs of dust around Dagger as she neared the door.

Pitch and Saber threw it open.

As the first of the mob closed the distance, Dagger dove through as Pitch heaved a thin glass jar over her. It shattered against the paving stones. The liquid inside sizzled when it hit the air and became a sickly yellow-and-pale-blue fog.

The mob ran into the mist heedlessly as Pitch and Saber slammed and locked the door behind Dagger. A moment later the screams of rage and the meaty slam of fists hitting the door and walls of the tavern turned to howls of terror and demands to be let in and away from the terrifying visions that walked among them.

The Armory barricaded the door with a banquet table.

"I hate running," Dagger said, catching her breath. "What's our status?"

"Vice says twenty," Saber said.

"Twenty!?"

"He might have told them we were in a hurry."

Dagger snarled. "Somebody needs to teach our holy man how to bargain."

"Do you get to do that with god?" Saber asked.

"If the god's dead and you're dealing with his fucking butler?" Dagger asked, rubbing the bridge of her nose. "Okay. Twenty. Anybody keeping count? Roth's down. I dropped two for sure. Another's on the way but gangrene will take too long. Powder!"

The sharpshooter was coming down the stairs. "I got five I'm sure of," she said, "and if anybody tries to come in through the hatch on the roof, we'll get another two. Three if we're lucky."

"You left a bomb up there?" Saber asked.

"Of course. Why? Did you want to guard the hatch?"

Dagger looked at Pitch. "That stuff you threw lethal?"

Pitch shrugged. "One or two might die of a heart attack."

"Next time throw poison."

"Sure, boss," Pitch said dryly. "Next time I'll throw poison gas while you're still outside. Everybody get in close. Somebody get the monk."

"I'll get him," Saber said, pausing only long enough to stop by one of the street level windows and thrust his sword through the bars and into a workman fumbling at them with a pry bar. "Six!" he called and dashed upstairs.

"Fourteen left," Dagger muttered.

"What about them?" Pitch asked, pointing at the innkeeper and his staff, who were clumped in a corner with eyes like dinner plates. It was hard to know who they were more worried about: the mob outside mindlessly battering at the walls of the inn, or the killers inside talking about a death toll like it was a grocery list. Dagger looked at them.

"It would be an easy four more," she mused.

"You sure, Captain?" Powder said, even as she raised one of her scatterguns. The innkeeper and his staff shrunk closer together.

"We're in a bit of a bind, Powder. Case you didn't notice."

"It's a battlefield, Captain. Not a butcher shop."

Dagger swore. "Lock them in the basement."

"Let's go," Powder said and herded the inn's staff and owner ahead of her gun barrels to the basement steps. "You'll be safer down there."

"This is my inn, you can't just— we have—" the innkeeper said, but his feet knew their business even if his mouth was propping up his dignity.

"We can. We are," Powder said, as she shoved them ahead of her. "Blah, blah. Protest, whine, snivel. Menacing threat. Move the asses I just saved!"

Vice clumped down the stairs. He'd shed his hooded coat, and his white beard seemed to blaze in the dim light. Dagger met him at the bottom.

"Twenty, Vice? Really?"

Vice nodded. "The machinery of the heavens winds down, grows less efficient in its disrepair. We ask much and deliver little. Such is the way of mortals when they provide sustenance to the gods. What can such short lives know of hunger that spans eons?"

"Vice..." Dagger said, rubbing her face in frustration.

"Enough," Pitch called. "Everybody gather close. We can debate theological economics when we're dead."

The Armory stood in a tight circle and leaned in as Pitch took a vial from his rig, shook it thoroughly and pulled out the cork. Blue-tinted vapor wafted out and one by one they inhaled deep from the vial. The lights of the inn brightened, their heartbeats slowed, the air caught fire. They could smell the sweat, fear and rusty steel of the slavering mob that battered the walls. Dagger leaned back, pinched the bridge of her nose and snorted hard into the back of her throat. Tension swept away on a chill, dispassionate calm. She looked at the others as their eyes and hands steadied.

"That burns," Dagger said. She smacked her lips. "Peach? Where did you find peaches?"

"Peach brandy," Pitch said with a grin. "It needed some flavor."

"Nice touch," Dagger said. "Pitch, lace the windows with evil shit. Powder, load up for close range. Saber, put your dancing shoes on and ready your short blades. Vice, don't get killed first."

Vice spread his arms. "That is in the hands of —"

Dagger cut him off with an impatient wave. "Just fucking don't, alright?"

"Yes, Dagger."

The door shuddered.

"They found a battering ram," Saber noted. "I wonder what they're using."

"Maybe Mayor Whatshisdick's corpse," Powder said.

"Too light," Dagger said. "Especially without his head."

Pitch went to the door and rigged a sealed jar of paper-thin glass above the jam, then spread a thick gel on the inside of the window frames. Powder checked and loaded four short-barreled pistols and holstered them around her body. She tucked her derringers into her belt and boot tops. Dagger wrapped both hands around the haft of her hammer and stood a few feet from the door, waiting for the inevitable breach.

Steel whined on stone as the workers pried away the bars over the windows. Overhead there was an explosion.

"They're inside," Saber said and dashed up the stairs to hold the top, a short sword in one hand and a knife in the other, the knuckle guards of both studded with sharp spikes to rake and puncture. At the top, a town guard and a worker stepped over the rubble and bodies. Saber ducked a club and slashed the inside of the man's arm, severing the arteries at the bend of his elbow. The worker staggered, fell and bled out as Saber raked his knife guard across the face of the other man and ran him through.

Downstairs, the front door screamed off its hinges and five workers jammed themselves in the doorway in a knot. The jar above the door fell and the thin glass shattered over their heads. Acid sizzled, eating through clothes and skin. They howled and rolled in a futile effort to put out invisible, hungry heat.

The next workers and guards that came through, Dagger scattered with her hammer, shoving them back with a thrust of the massive steel head. Powder spun around Dagger's shoulder with a pistol in each hand and burned the invaders down, firing as they fell. Townsfolk that climbed in the windows touched Pitch's gel and began to choke and froth at the mouth a second later. Two fell dead, and two others were so distracted from drowning inside their own lungs that they fell easily to Vice's armored fists. Pitch tossed a clay sphere through the open window and a wall of white-hot fire rose up, burning unnaturally on the paving stones.

Dagger gave up counting in the chaos.

"Kitchen!" Dagger shouted and brained a worker with her hammer, then reversed it to stab another with the sharp spike on the haft. At the top of the stairs Saber ran through a worker, kneed another in the balls and carved his dagger in a tight circle around the man's neck. Blood sprayed the duelist's boots and trousers. Saber leapt over the high railing and landed lightly but slipped in the blood on the floor and fell on his ass. Dagger dragged him to his feet by his collar.

"That was graceful," she said.

"I am a jungle cat."

The Armory backed into the kitchen through its big double doors as the townsfolk boiled into the common room and absorbed the ground The Armory could not hope to hold. The kitchen was a dead end, but with only one way in or out, they had a chance to bottleneck the assault and ruin its power of numbers.

"Pitch, burn the—" Dagger was calling as a clay jar sailed over her head and hit the top of the doorway, breaking and scattering flames across the wood.

"—door," Dagger finished with a satisfied nod. "Well done. Where are we?"

"Eight that I am sure of," Vice said.

"Two from the stairs," Saber said, "four likely, but two already there."

"You felt them go?" Dagger asked Vice. "They're not just outside raving or waiting to die?"

"I believe Saber is right. But it is hard to be sure."

"That leaves four more," Dagger said.

"Easy enough," Powder muttered as she fed bullets into her hungry guns.

"I've never killed a whole town before," Pitch muttered.

"What about that time with the reservoir?" Saber asked.

"I told you about that?"

"You were very stoned," Saber said, apologetically.

Pitch sighed. "That makes sense."

"We don't have to kill the whole town," Dagger said.

"Four more," Powder intoned and nodded when her guns were ready.

A shot rang from outside and half of Dagger's head vanished.

"Fuck," Saber muttered.

"Oh, now I'm pissed," Powder muttered.

"You can feel anger?" Pitch asked her.

"More the memory of the anger I know I should be feeling."

"Interesting," said and scratched his chin. "Remind me to take some detailed notes later."

"Science can wait," Saber said as he and Vice grabbed Dagger's body by the shoulders. The Armory moved as one and flipped over the heavy prep table and took cover behind it. Made of heavy wood and steel, it would provide cover from gunfire. Powder snapped off a shot from over the top and dropped a figure coming in through the door.

"Three," she called. "Do your thing, Vice!"

Vice knelt across Dagger's dead body and clasped his hands, muttering in a guttural language. Saber met the next cluster of townsfolk through the door and gutted the first under his clumsy swing. Pitch stood, put a slender tube to his mouth and puffed hard. A dart lodged in a man's cheek and he fell thrashing, his face as purple and swollen as a late-summer plum. Powder opened up with her scatterguns and two more attackers vanished from the waist up. The walls were spattered with red. Vice's prayers rose into a shout.

"One more," Saber whispered as townsfolk swarmed the room as Pitch's flame barrier finally burned itself out. A bottle that trailed a flaming rag flew through the door and shattered against Pitch's head. He went up like a torch and Powder kicked him back from Vice. Pitch fell smoking, clawing and beating at himself weakly until the fire took his life. The townsfolk rushed them and smothered Powder under a pile of bodies, pummeling and kicking and swinging truncheons that crushed her skull even as they also hit each other. One man fell screaming around a shattered kneecap. Saber met their crush, tackled them away from Vice and fell back with two guards on top of him. He sank his knife into a man's gut and dug upwards, wriggling his hand like he was stirring a butter churn.

"You're the last one," Saber grated as the man sputtered and coughed warm red across his face. Saber tasted salt and grinned as the second guard put a pistol under his chin and pulled the trigger, blowing out the top of the duelist's skull.

"Vigil, we are coming," Vice said with satisfaction as the townsfolk grabbed him, swarmed him under and beat him to death.

The last living member of The Armory died with an ecstatic, broken smile.

# — CHAPTER 4 —

## The toll.

D agger gasped, sat up and gently touched her head. It was very much intact.

She was on a dusty stone floor, cracked and aged as if a hundred armies had marched across it. The space she sat in had borders of shadow that gave one the sense of a hidden, limitless distance. The pale light overhead had no apparent source, but she knew from experience that walking in any direction would carry one no further from it. Dagger scanned the expanse until she saw four other shadows.

"We all here?" Dagger called softly.

"Yeah," Saber answered as he gingerly touched beneath his chin and the top of his head. He sighed with relief.

"Sound off," Dagger said.

"Arms, legs and idiots accounted for," Powder said and gently shook Pitch. The alchemist coughed, clutched around his body and laid back down with a groaned swear. Vice was already on his knees, praying gratitude for their deliverance. Dagger did not disturb him. She could see his armored hands were clean again, not so much as a bloody scrap of hair or skin decorating the rivets that studded the banded steel.

"Everybody got all their shit?" she asked and patted her hammer. The rest nodded or grunted in answer.

"You have arrived safe," a dry voice whispered.

The figure was a few respectful feet away, shrouded in flowing cloth. Its hands were clasped at what could have been its waist. Its face, if it had one, was hidden by the deep shadow of its hood. For all The Armory knew, the servants of the Vigil may as well have been stone obelisks in monks' robes. Their garments had no color, no weave of fiber, no pattern. Even the wrinkles seemed painted on. Its whisper came from the space around each of their ears, not the figure itself.

"Thank you for the exit," Dagger said.

"You paid the toll for the return, and several others besides. How is our little brother? The one who actually believes," the figure said wryly.

Dagger turned to look at Vice, who was still on his knees, his face contorting with the force of his prayer.

"Ecstatic," Dagger muttered.

"He's a good servant," the robed figure said. "As for the rest of you, we're grateful. Even the Watcher in the Darkness, though his eyes have closed, is grateful."

"How do you know?" Dagger asked. She would have preferred that Vice make this kind of small talk with his god's servants, but at least they spoke to her in an ordinary manner, instead of like some religious text.

"Faith, I suppose," the figure replied. "Come. Your return is nearly ready."

"Already?"

"We need you down there, not up here. Don't forget that."

"Be hard to forget."

"Yes. Forgive me," its tone held genuine compassion, "You all serve the Vigil, and it's appreciated. But the machinery must be tended. Our stores are running dry. We are on edge."

Dagger nodded. "We'll go. Better not to rock the boat."

"Or the afterlife in this case," the robed figure said with a dusty chuckle, "such as it is. This is not a place for the living. Come. We must hurry. The cargo you brought us must be processed before their gods notice the theft."

"Do they even have a god?" Dagger asked, recalling that she'd seen no churches in the industry town.

"Where there is value, there is always a claim, however faint."

Dagger gestured and the rest of The Armory followed. Powder was about to rouse Vice from his prayers, but Dagger stopped her.

"Leave him. He'll follow when he's ready."

The four mercenaries followed the Vigil's servant into the shadows. The pale light paced them and seemed to shine a path on the floor ahead. It led them to a much larger, weakly lit space in the shadows like an anemic dome.

More robed figures milled around the edges of the dark boundary, tending to clumps of gray-scale people who seemed to buzz and flicker. Dagger was sure if she stared hard enough, she might have been able to see through them. Their shoulders were, one and

122

all, slumped and defeated. Every now and then, one would look up and glance around this limbo they waited in, fruitlessly and forever, and then return their eyes to the space between their feet as if words of consolation were written on the stones.

What was not empty, or filled with milling, disconsolate souls, was wound back and across with old machinery that stuttered and rumbled. Pipes coiled like serpents, leading to and from a network of boilers, funnels and large tanks. The robed figure led The Armory to a cage suspended a dozen feet above the ground. Inside were the people they'd killed just before the end in Dahlsvaart. They shouted and rattled the cage bars. Unlike the others in this place, they were full color and tangible. Some still held the weapons they'd died with and were fruitlessly trying to break free. This was not the beyond their faiths had promised. Many of them had probably given up on gods in this age of industry and had expected a velvety blackness when their eyes closed for the last time.

"Twenty is steep for a return," Dagger said. "Where's the rest of them?" She asked. There looked to be less than twenty souls in the cage, not nearly as many as The Armory had killed before Roth turned on them. She looked for the former mayor and found him in the middle of the throng. His eyes were staring at nothing. His lanky arms were wrapped around his knees. Two of his citizens were standing on him in an attempt to reach the top of the cage.

"Twenty was just for your exit and return," the Vigil's servant said. "The others you... collected—"

"You mean killed."

"Yes, I suppose. Those went to repairs the moment they arrived. The machines have grown far less efficient," the robed figure said.

They passed a trio of the robed figures around a large vat beneath which burned gray fire. Pipes connected to the vat's belly extended away into the darkness. Robed servants of the Vigil grabbed a soul from Dahlsvaart and pushed him protesting into the vat and he screamed once before he was melted down to nothing, and the pipes glowed dully as his soul was piped away. Tools and machinery clanked somewhere in the darkness.

"Less efficient..." the Vigil's servant continued. "Let us be honest. It is falling apart. We fix it as best we can but..."

"But you didn't build it."

"No," the robed figure said sadly. "And every year, the prayers from below grow fainter and fewer. More of our believers come here to wait forever. So, we must continue to steal."

Dagger nodded. Nothing lasted forever. Not even heaven. "Works out in our favor."

"Yes, it does."

"Let us the fuck out of here!" One of the workers screamed from the cage.

"Shortly," the robed figured said. Vice pushed his way through the rest of The Armory to kneel before the robed figure.

"Rise, little brother," the robed figure said in a more formal tone. "The one you are kneeling to can no longer see it, and I am not fit to stand in the Watcher's place."

"It's all breaking down isn't it?" Vice said.

"It is," the robed figure said. "There are so few out in the world keeping us sustained. You must soon return to offer protection. To affirm their faith."

"We are ready. Where?"

"Speak for yourself," Saber said, "I could use a break."

"A town," the Vigil's servant said. "Their lives have been... interrupted. There is a mortal threat. We think. Perhaps a few hundred souls."

"You think?" Dagger asked.

"We only just became aware of them. They are not praying to us."

"What do you mean?" Dagger asked. "How could you hear them? Are you listening to the other gods' prayers?"

"No, though we are trying to," the servant said. "We stumbled across them. Their prayers are not directed to any god. It's as if they've never had gods at all, but still they cast their eyes skyward and beg deliverance. If we were to answer them, then we would become the place they turned to for help. They would be new faithful. That is enormous power."

"How long have they been praying?"

"We don't know. It is odd. As if something suddenly allowed the prayers to come through. They are indistinct, as if partially hidden. They sound tired and I fear they are close to giving up."

"So, they could have been praying for years," Dagger said. "Decades even."

"That is possible."

"That's a long time."

"No, it is not."

"They could already be dead."

"No. We hear them still, and the signal has even grown clearer."

Some of the stolen souls in the cage still screamed to be freed. Others sat, dejected and confused. Some shouted to friends they recognized outside the cage, the others The Armory had killed in Dahlsvaart, as the servants of the Vigil prodded and forced these extra souls, one by one, into the rendering cauldron. The servants of the Vigil collected the glowing material in buckets and used it like hot metal to patch and repair their various contraptions.

"These souls are fine for now," the Vigil's servant said and gestured to the cage. "They'll power the machines a bit longer. But they're nothing compared to the sustained prayers of the living. Render what aid you can. Save them. Tell them of us. Win new converts."

"Maybe we leave out that god is dead?" Dagger suggested.

"That would be wise," the Vigil's servant said.

Dagger nodded. "Prep the return. We're ready."

The servant threw a lever. Mechanisms coughed and heaved to life and the cage holding the souls of Dahlsvaart moved until it was above a funnel. A different servant threw another lever and the funnel rattled and shook with a sharp whine of steel-on-steel. The souls in the cage stopped protesting to look down. Then they started screaming again. Several tried to climb the bars and each other in a raw panic, stomping and trampling and kicking. Dagger didn't know what they saw exactly, and didn't ever want to, but she imagined a lot of really fast teeth.

The cage bottom split and dumped its cargo into the funnel. A few of the workers managed to catch the edge of the funnel or hang onto the bars of the cage, but the rest fell slid in with a wet, chewing sound. The Vigil's servants went around the cage with long poles and casually prodded the clinging souls until they fell.

"Into the Soul Hole you go," Saber muttered.

"The what?" Powder asked.

"That's what I call the big meat grinder," Saber said. "Soul Hole."

"That isn't meat it's grinding," Pitch said.

Lights blazed on all the machines in the room as they coughed into dusty half-life. The light overhead brightened and the shimmering clusters of the Vigil's faithful sighed and raised their hoods to their heaven's sun.

Dagger gestured and The Armory followed the Vigil's servant to a platform bathed in light.

"Your chariot," it said.

"Will it hold this time?" Dagger asked, "Or will we and our weapons get scattered to the four winds again?"

"That was a fresh malfunction. We have adjusted."

The Armory stood upon the platform. "Go ahead," Dagger said.

Somewhere, yet another switch was thrown. The Vigil's heaven blurred and faded to black as star stone formed from the very air and encased The Armory.

Then they were hurtling through the heavens in an igneous ball, as fast as if they'd been fired from the bore of Powder's gun.

# — CHAPTER 5 —

## Well, this is just needlessly fucked up.

This time, the comet held.

It made a new clearing in the forest. The air was hot, wet and thick enough to chew. The Armory climbed out of the earth's new, smoking dent and looked around as they brushed stardust and charred forest from their clothes.

"Now what?" Powder asked.

Dagger sniffed the air. Then she sniffed again. "Smell that?"

"Smells like rot and death," Pitch said.

"Smells like work," Dagger countered.

"If that's a job," Pitch said, "somebody did it already. A week ago, at least."

The work wasn't hard to find. They just followed their noses.

The mining yard reeked of salty copper, machine oil and rust. It had rained recently, and the earthen, muddy pit of the yard sat at the center of the forest idyll like an abscess, filled with stagnant pools and swarming insects. The Armory walked past dormant, rusting machines and snapped tow chains that the mud was trying to swallow. Even the sagging buildings that still stood listed and rebelled against their foundations.

"Nature is trying to reclaim the futile works of man," Vice said.

"Would we know nature if not for the contrast provided by the futile works of man?" Pitch asked him.

Vice opened his mouth to say something. Then closed it. He looked confused.

"What?" Pitch asked him, "you're the only one that gets to say weird shit in a big, official voice?"

At the center of the yard, wood posts were driven into the mud in a spiral pattern. They were carved with symbols and adorned with feathers, beaded leather thongs and bits of polished metal and bone. Beyond them were three gaping adits that led down into the mine.

"The hell is this?" Saber asked, cautiously prodding at the dangling fetishes with the point of a knife.

Vice spat in the dirt. "Heathen iconography. They think something evil is the mines."

"And this is supposed to ward it off?" Saber asked.

"Perhaps," Vice said. "Or to keep it confined to the tunnels."

"Any idea what it is?" Dagger asked Vice. "Could this be why the Vigil's servants heard the prayers?"

"Not from this blasphemy," Vice answered. "The Vigil does not believe in the existence of evil as humans think of it."

"Finally," Pitch said, "something we agree on."

"Humans," Vice continued, "think of evil as the opposite of whatever a majority believes correct. But the Vigil would define evil as chaos, an environment antithetical to progress and growth. Humans are not chaotic by nature. They always seek order, no matter how ugly or brutal."

"Vice, I'm not sure I like all this agreement," Pitch grumbled.

Dagger looked at the hanging fetishes, and then at the tunnels. They looked like the mouths of something with retractable fangs. "We go in," she said.

"Oh, good," Saber muttered. "I've always wanted to visit an evil cave."

Dagger turned to Vice. "The Vigil's servants discuss the next exit toll with you?"

"Shit, Captain," Powder said, "You're already asking about that?"

"Doesn't hurt to be ready."

"Awful for morale, though."

"Quit moaning, Powder."

Vice shook his head. "The Vigil only considers one thing as pure evil, but it is not of this plane. And if that scourge is here, there will be no toll."

There was a moment of strained silence. As was often the case, Saber was the one to break it. "You holding us in suspense, Vice?"

"Demons," the monk said.

Pitch swore under his breath, but not with disbelief.

"Did the Vigil's servants mention demons?" Dagger asked.

"No," Vice said, "It's possible they didn't know. Or it's possible they were afraid we would not agree to go if they did."

"Aren't gods great?" Saber asked. "The world's abusive over-parents."

"Why no exit toll?" Dagger asked Vice. "Men. Demons. It's just more souls for the machines."

"No," Vice said. "Demons enter our plane of existence from one with different natural rules, where the raw material we call the soul does not exist. If there are demons in those tunnels, we can kill them by the legion and earn nothing for the Vigil. No exit."

The Armory fell silent. Dead for real this time.

"So, what kills demons?" Dagger asked.

Pitch rubbed his eyes. "Quite a bit in theory."

"Your scholarship fails you," Vice said. "Demons exist, whether you have studied their entrails or not."

"Oh, I know they exist, Vice," Pitch said softly.

"I don't give a shit about theory," Dagger said. "Both of you, start talking."

"In their world almost nothing but another demon can kill them," Vice said, "but when they come into our plane of existence, they are formed of our matter. Misshapen, yes, and stronger, more singular in will than any creature of this world but made of the same flawed material as everything else. They will bleed. They will die."

"What Vice isn't making clear," Pitch said, "is that because demons were created outside the laws of our nature, they don't feel things like fear. They have no value of life, not even their own. We can kill as many as we like. They'll just keep coming. Exterminating them isn't enough. If there are demons in that mine, and they're still inside, it's not because of some bundles of bone and leather hanging from posts."

"Then what?" Dagger asked.

"It means there's a gate," Pitch said, "and they're still coming through it. They haven't left the mine because they don't want to. They're still preparing. Building their numbers. We have to close the gate, but I've never seen one before. No scholar I know has. I don't know how they work."

"Could you close this gate, Vice," Dagger asked.

"I believe so. As could any priest."

"Well, we don't have any priest," Dagger said. "We have you, and your god's dead. Can you do it?"

"That was unkind, Dagger," Vice grumbled. "But yes."

"The idea of fighting a horde of demons in a dark tunnel has that effect. Pitch, what are you doing?"

The alchemist was divesting himself of bottle after bottle. Vials of powder littered the ground around him, along with battered tin flasks and small wooden boxes. "Getting rid of my hallucinogens, toxins for fear and for deep sleep. I don't want to throw them by accident in the dark."

"Why not?" Powder asked, glancing at the growing pile. "Don't get rid of anything that might work."

"But they won't," the alchemist said. "Demons don't sleep and I can't make them see anything worse than what they have at home. What they are."

"Maybe you could make them think they're frolicking in a field of daisies?" Saber said. "Oh, you could make them see puppies!" Dagger gave him an annoyed look, but Pitch actually stopped and considered it.

"I know you're just trying to be funny, Saber. Too hard I might add. But there's something to that. I have euphorics and sedatives. I usually save them for us. But they might affect the demons negatively."

"I have good ideas all the time," Saber said.

Pitch chuckled darkly. "No, Saber. You really don't. Dagger, I can try it."

"What's the alternative?"

"Fire. Acid. Powder's explosives. We can burn them or blow them up."

"Let's stick to that," Dagger said, and swung her hammer up onto her shoulder. "If we meet a nice demon, you can make him see puppies."

"There are no nice demons," Vice muttered.

"Acid and fire it is, then," Pitch said.

The Armory moved toward the three tunnel mouths. Vice shuddered, hacked from the back of his throat and spat a wad of snot into the dirt.

"What's the matter with you?" Dagger asked.

"I can smell them. Their wrongness," Vice said, "they are unholy. I can taste it. It's making my throat itch."

"I get like that around cats," Powder muttered.

"Vice is allergic to demons. Great," Saber said.

"It's not an allergy," Pitch said. "What limited scientific study there is about demons speculates why the holy are so bothered by them."

"And?" Dagger asked, "anything that can help us?"

Pitch was about to answer when Vice sneezed violently. Saber chuckled and handed the monk a lace handkerchief. "Here. There's snot in your beard."

"What is this?" Vice asked, holding the silken thing by one corner like it was a live scorpion.

"A dancer in Shivar gave it to me."

Vice stared at the scrap of silk with horror.

"Don't worry," Saber said. "It's clean enough."

"Nothing about you is clean," Vice said, but blew his nose into the piece of silk.

Pitch continued. "Anyway, demons represent an essential polarity to the order imposed by the gods, and by extension the servants of gods. As the gods see it, our world is theirs to protect. Demons represent a perversion of that concept of order, another way a world can be used and organized. Holiness, when not perverted by human desire and lust for power, is essentially the idea of order and peace. It's a framework upon which new life grows and thrives. Like a wooden lattice for vines in a garden. But demons represent the antithesis of that order. Even a god that views its congregants as little better than cattle would not want them slaughtered."

"Even the Farmer?" Powder asked.

"Especially the Farmer," Pitch said. "When was the last time you met somebody who raised chickens or cows who liked foxes and wolves?"

"The Farmer is a vile perversion," Vice snarled. "Humans are not cattle to be husbanded, groomed and confined for their own good."

"And yet, he's one of the most powerful gods with the most worshippers," Pitch said. "That should tell you something about people."

Vice shook his head sadly. "Your mind is an ugly place, Pitch."

"Like yours is a sanctuary?"

"Which tunnel?" Dagger cut in.

"The middle," Vice said.

"How do you know?"

"I feel it."

Saber went to the adit and peered inside, then he looked down and kicked something over in the dirt.

"I'd say he's onto something," Saber muttered. It was a human arm, flayed down to the bones and tendons. It looked like something had used a vegetable grater on it. Saber moved into the tunnel with the rest of The Armory close behind. The mine swallowed the daylight only steps from the entrance.

"Hold on," Pitch said and went back to the light of the tunnel mouth, knelt and took three vials from his rig and mixed them into a tin bowl. As the chemicals blended, they gave off a fierce blue-green glow.

"Over here, everyone," Pitch said, and liberally smeared each of their shoulders with the glowing paste until they stood in a nimbus that lit the cavern all the way to the walls and ceiling.

"I don't want to quibble, Pitch," Powder said, "but we can't exactly hide like this. At least with a torch or a lantern we could have put it out or covered it."

"This leaves our hands free," Pitch said as Saber took the bowl to smear Pitch's shoulders. "It won't ruin our night vision and we can easily recognize each other."

"It also makes us stick out like fucking beacons," the gunner said.

"That won't matter," Pitch said.

"Why not?"

"Demons don't have eyes."

Saber scoffed. "Then how they hell do they see?"

"Well," Pitch said, "I could explain how sight works with light spectrums, and that vision isn't much more than the way our brains react to and interpret... yep. There we go. Barely finished my sentence and your eyes are already glazing over."

"They are not!"

Powder sighed. "I'm guessing we're not gonna like anything we see in there?"

"No," Vice said, "you will not."

Dagger looked at each of them and took stock of their rising nerves. "Pitch," she said, "dose us up."

"What do you have in mind?"

"Make us sharp, fast and numb," she ordered. "I want us able to walk out of there on bloody stumps if we have to."

Pitch borrowed one of Saber's wide cleavers and mixed powder from three leather satchels and laid out five lines of the blend on the weapon's side. After each of them had snorted a line, they advanced into the pitch black. The floor sloped down. Iron tracks for mine carts stretched before them, glinting between the spots of rust. They heard a scrabble in the dark as something sharp rasped against the rock.

"Rats?" Saber asked.

"No," Pitch said. "They'll have eaten those. But if it makes you feel better, they're a bit like rats where they come from. Or maybe locusts are a better comparison."

"It doesn't," Saber said.

"Be odd if it did," Pitch said. "In their world the rats won the—"

With a shriek, a thing of meat, angles and jaws rushed them from the darkness. Saber lunged between Dagger and Pitch, shoving them aside with the speed of his thrust. His narrow-bladed sword skewered the rushing beast through the jaws, snapping off several of its teeth as it slid into the throat behind them. The beast snarled and chewed, trying to eat the sword and cutting its mouth to ribbons as it slithered along Saber's blade toward him. Its head was membrane smooth and shiny. Shit, Saber thought, it really doesn't have any eyes.

Dagger brought down her hammer on the fleshy body. The creature roared. Its flesh bubbled and writhed. Its mouth and neck shifted impossibly with the sound of cracking bone as it re-arranged itself to wrap its claws around Dagger's hammer. Saber slid his sword free and stabbed the demon again and again as Dagger fought to free her weapon from its grip.

"Leave it pinned, Captain!" Powder yelled.

Dagger let go of her hammer. The beast squealed under its weight.

Powder stepped to the demon and set both barrels of her scatterguns against the place with all the teeth. She pulled her triggers and the jaws and cranium vanished in a spattering of lead and gore. The beast shuddered, squeaked like a rabbit in a snare, and went still. Its flesh continued to move and twitch. Dagger lifted her hammer up and brought it down again, pasting the creature against the tunnel floor.

"Burn it, Pitch," Dagger said. The alchemist poured a vial of acid out over the creature's remains. It smoked as it ate the demon down to the rock beneath. The Armory stepped back out of the smoke, coughing and spitting.

"So, that's a demon," Saber said.

"A juvenile," Vice said. "Pray they are all this young."

"Do they all look like that?" Powder asked and nudged a twitching claw. "It doesn't really look like anything, you know, except fucking horrible."

Vice grunted. "They may be defined by our natural laws but buck against them constantly. What you see is a rebellion in flesh."

"More or less," Pitch said. "If you want a more scientific explanation, they must work with the physics and matter of the world they are invading. On other planes they may look different. Our world limits their forms to perversions of the ones we already have. They copy them to survive and breathe our air, drink our water and eat our flesh. I think this one was trying to be a dog."

"Dogs don't have," Saber counted with his finger. "Seven legs and a stump that ends in another mouth."

"Three cheers for narcotics," Pitch said. "Imagine having to look at that sober."

Dagger cut a glance at Pitch. "I said I wanted us up and ready to roll. Not stoned. What did you give us?"

"Do you feel stoned, Dagger?" Pitch asked.

"No."

"Then don't worry about it," Pitch said. "I don't tell you how to smash things or lead do I?"

Dagger raised an eyebrow. "Don't get testy with me, scholar."

"When this is over, Pitch," Saber said, "I'm just gonna have you put me into a coma for about fifteen years."

"No comas for us," Dagger said and lifted her hammer. "No afterlives either. Forward."

They crept further into the twisted warren. There was only The Armory's breath and heartbeats, the sound of loose stones shifting under their boots. They found a mine cart, its wheels rusted to the track. Dagger glanced inside, sniffed and shook her head as the rest joined her. In the cart was what was left of a miner. Several rough holes had been bored through his helmet, and his chest cavity had been opened in a few places, the edges ragged and filled with splintered bone. He still clutched a pickaxe, one end crusted with gore.

"Went down fighting," Powder noted. "Looks like they sampled him, trying to figure out what was good to eat. I wonder what they decided."

"Looks like just the gooey filling," Pitch said, probing the body cavity with a slender metal tool. "All his organs are gone."

"I used to eat cream puffs like that when I was a kid," Saber said.

"Of course you did," Powder muttered.

The tunnel beyond the cart opened up and was lined with wooden platforms and scaffolding. Bodies littered the structures. Decay thickened the air. The Armory eyed the limits of their glow as the tunnel narrowed again and headed deeper into the earth.

There was a scratching in the darkness ahead and Dagger halted them just before a swarm of meat and teeth boiled snarling out of the tunnel and blocked it with their bodies, most of them bigger than the young demon The Armory had smashed. Their many mouths and clawed limbs raked and savaged at each other even as they oriented their strange, slick heads toward the humans.

"Oh, look," Saber said, and hefted his sword, "puppies."

"Guess we're not going that way?" Powder muttered hopefully as the horde crept closer, spittle turning the dusty mineshaft floor to slurry.

"You guess wrong," Dagger said.

"I knew that."

Vice glanced behind them. "Backwards is also not an option."

The path behind had a horror mob of its own, and the scaffolding was now lined with things held together with meat, wire and bent physics. The air filled with their hissing chorus that became a roar of triumph as a demon the size of a grizzly bear slammed its way to the front, crushing and devouring the smaller ones in its way.

"Where the fuck was that thing hiding?" Saber asked.

"Why don't you ask it?" Powder suggested as the creature sniffed the air with too many wet nostrils, "It looks friendly."

"I got a better idea, Powder," Dagger said.

"Yeah?"

"Shoot it."

Powder shouldered her rifle as the massive demon sauntered closer. One of its legs was too short and its gut dragged on the ground, but it moved with a peculiar grace. She pulled the trigger, the gun barked and blazed, and the bullet bit punched through the demon's head and took a bucket-worth of meat along for the ride. The behemoth barely flinched, and a smaller demon pounced on the morsel and dragged it back to its fellows, where they fought over it while the big demon roared.

"What kind of bullet was that?" Saber asked, drawing a dagger to go with his longer blade.

"Split round," Powder said with a satisfied grin. "Basically turns into a caltrop on impact."

"Sexy. Do it again."

The demons rushed the bravos, slithering down slope and scaffold in an amorphous, fleshy mass. Odd bones occasionally poked and ripped through their skin as the natural laws of the world fought their strangeness. Dagger swung her hammer in a wide arc and spattered two of them against another. The dying were eaten by their own before they could even stop moving.

"Powder," Dagger shouted, "make another hole in the big one! Pitch, give it a snack!"

Powder slung her rifle, hefted her twin shotguns from her belt and rushed the bear demon with Pitch close behind. It lunged with one clawed arm, but they rolled under the clumsy swing. Powder opened up on its belly with her scatterguns and splashed them both with gore just before Pitch heaved in a packed paper bundle. It dissolved, smoked and then burst in brilliant white flames as the chemicals mixed and burned despite the wet of the demon's belly.

It shrieked in agony. It thrashed and lay about itself with misshapen arms, killing little demons but doing nothing about the flames. Vice lunged and slammed one armored fist into what might have been a knee. The hulk stumbled. He bashed at it with his fists until it was still and backed out of range as smaller demons swarmed over the corpse in a hungry, gnawing coat.

Saber danced with a swarm of demons, leaping back and forth with his blades whispering through their flesh, but his thrusts did little damage. The demons shrieked angrily as he tried to put them down. Dagger shoved him to one side and splattered a demon with her hammer, then spun and drove the spike on the other end through another and then ripped it loose, tearing the vile thing in half.

As before, the living pounced on the dead. Horrifying though it was, these little feasts worked in The Armory's favor. The demons' hunger prevented any organized rush.

"What is it with all the eating?" Dagger called, as The Armory formed up back-to-back. "Not that I'm complaining."

"They need raw matter to grow and change," Pitch said as he drew another pair of vials to throw, "They must have used the miner's meat for the first batch. Now they're using their own dead."

"Fuck," Dagger growled. "Any ideas?"

"Find the gate," the monk said, "it is the only way to stop this."

Pitch threw his vials in both directions. The chemicals set demons alight and herded them into manageable columns as the alchemist's acids ate bones and flesh down to puddles of foul-smelling mud. When the demons scooped the red slush into their mouths, the gunk ate at them from within and they fell, writhing in more of the same. Acrid smoke filled the air and The Armory hacked and coughed, breathing through their sleeves when they could.

Saber sheathed his dagger and elegant sword and drew heavy cleavers, trading dancer's grace for butcher's work. He lodged a cleaver in meat and used it as a crude lever to turn and control demon after demon as he methodically blocked claws and lopped off hands, feet and fanged jaws to leave them crippled, easy meals for the rest.

Powder fired again and again as she slid and dodged between her comrades, her hot lead ripped off demon legs and turned their heads to pulp. The ground was slippery, but the shattered teeth and bone beneath their boots offered some traction, like sand in wet snow.

"Pitch, Powder, Saber," Dagger shouted, "handle the rear. Vice and I will clear the path ahead."

Dagger and Vice waded into the squealing demons that blocked the way forward. Hammer and armored fists shattered their line. Vice grabbed a demon by the head and crushed it, driving his fists into the confusing flesh. He found undecided bones and snapped them. Dagger pulped and pulped.

Behind them, the bear demon roared and surged awkwardly back to its feet. It slung the smaller beasts chewing at it into the walls. The scaffolding shattered and fell, crushing dozens of smaller demons beneath it. They squealed like piglets as the splintered wood impaled and pinned them down. The crippled behemoth dragged itself toward The Armory, trailing its own guts.

"Fuck me!" Saber yelled, "Can we kill it again, please?"

Powder slung her guns and dug a bomb out of her bag. She began to strike flint against the fuse, but Pitch grabbed her arm.

"You out of your mind?" he yelled. "An explosion could bring the tunnel down on us!"

Powder shrugged him off. "Do you not see that thing? Even its wounds have teeth for fuck's sake!"

She was right. The hole they'd made in its side had sprouted mismatched fangs.

"I'm thinking!" Pitch yelled.

"Can't kill it with your brain, Pitch!"

"Well, technically —"

"Shut the pedantic fuck up, Pitch!"

The behemoth was scorched and leaking. Six mouths sprouted and moved across its flesh like roving lily pads of teeth, and when they met, they slid into one another. Flesh and bone folded together into a single maw — a slavering, thick-lipped ring filled with long, needle teeth like a lamprey that could drain whales dry. It roared. Foul breath coasted over The Armory. It stank of sulfur and rotting plums. The behemoth limped toward the human threat, and now that it was too active to be food, the smaller demons forming up behind and alongside it like an honor guard.

"Can you make that throw, Powder?" Pitch asked, pointing at the mouth.

"What am I? An asshole?"

"Light a short fuse."

"I thought it'll bring down the tunnel!"

"Just fucking do it!" Pitch said. "We have to make it roar again. Saber, with me!"

Powder clipped the bomb's fuse short and lit it.

Pitch took a big jar from his bag and inched toward the behemoth as Saber moved beside him, his blades ready to take the smaller demons that might challenge them, but the creatures hung back, fearful of getting in the behemoth's way. Two did dart forward, but the behemoth snatched them up and ate them.

Pitch threw the jar.

It broke against the side of the behemoth. The liquid hit the air and burst into blue and yellow fire, hot and bright in the darkness. It roared in rage and pain, mouth open all the way down to its gullet.

Powder didn't have to be told.

She threw her bomb into that flaming ring of teeth, the fuse nearly down to the iron. The behemoth closed its mouth in shock and gulped. There was a muffled thump and it burst outwards in a cough of hot fire and rotten-plum reek that spattered Pitch and Saber with meat, hot blood and broken teeth.

The cratered behemoth wavered.

It fell.

The smaller demons swarmed the corpse. They ripped and gulped without chewing, shoveling the pieces into their swelling bellies.

"Fucking hell," Saber muttered. Powder and Pitch could only nod.

Dagger's battle roar came from behind them, and Vice screamed a prayer.

Pitch, Saber and Powder ran to their side.

# — CHAPTER 6 —

## That's the gate?! Ew,
## it looks like a...

S aber shoved Pitch and Powder toward where Vice and Dagger were clearing the way, and then drew an estoc nearly as long as a spear and vaulted over them in a perfect jackknife that scraped his boots across the ceiling.

He landed just behind Dagger and Vice, and his slender blade whispered between the cannons of Vice's fists and feet, and the thunder of Dagger's hammer. The floor sloped ever down, deeper into the warren as they danced between each other in the close confines. Spaces no smaller than a wink between bodies were enough for Powder, her bullets cracked between leather to drop anything with too many teeth. Pitch heaved vials and handfuls of dust that burned and ignited and ate flesh in dirty puffs of hungry acid. The air stank of chemicals, gunpowder and guts.

"They're getting bigger!" Saber shouted as he turned to guard their rear. Powder kept one hand on Saber's shoulder and her gun barked from under his arm.

"That is their way," Vice said. "Each one we kill feeds one that remains."

"Pitch, can you buy us some space?" Dagger yelled.

Pitch moved to the rear of the party while the rest of The Armory formed up around him. He dug a trench in the dirt floor with the heel of his boot, took two pouches from his waist and mixed them into the ditch. The chemicals mixed, sparked and sizzled into a thick smoke that filled the tunnel.

"Back!" Pitch yelled, coughing and hacking from the noxious curtain. He doubled over, retching and Saber grabbed him by the belt and dragged him to safety just as a demon burst through the barrier, screaming as its flesh smoked down to its warped bones. It gurgled and dissolved. Others tried to follow and met the same fate.

"Fuck, that's some nasty shit," Pitch said, and swigged from a vial to soothe his burned throat. "But it won't hold long. They'll swarm it and use it up."

Their rear protected for the moment, they cut their way ahead. Claws twitched in the dirt in angry farewells, plaintive, idiot calls to come back, fight, be our meat. Even with Pitch's chemicals Dagger could feel her shoulders getting stupid, her waist and back aching with every swing. The tunnel ahead was blessedly empty but dangerously narrow. If they continued, they'd be fighting single file.

"Powder, Saber," Dagger ordered.

"I see it, Captain," Powder said.

"Yep," Saber said.

"Saber, at the back with Vice. Vice, be a wall. Saber, be where he isn't."

"Got it," Saber yelled.

"Powder, with me," Dagger said. "We'll take the unknown. I want your shotguns going off under my arms and between my swings."

"Captain."

"We keep Pitch in the middle, understood?" Dagger said. "He's got cooking to do. Let's move!"

They advanced in a shuffle. Behind them they could hear the scrabbling of claws as the demons fought through Pitch's chemical wall. In the center of the group, Pitch mixed furiously, precariously blending powder and alcohol between a pair of flasks. Their nostrils wouldn't take another dose — even he could feel his sinuses had thickened with the residue. He grinned tightly. If they lived, the hangover was going to be incandescent. They would breath knives for a month. Luckily, I've got something for that too, he thought, I've got something for everything. The liquid in his flasks glowed, eerie and delicious.

Dagger advanced with Powder's hand on her broad back and a scattergun beneath Dagger's arm like a deadly purse. Behind them Vice walked backwards, his armored fists crossed before him to meet the brunt of whatever rushed up the tunnel. Saber stepped lightly behind him, his estoc in a ready grip.

"They come," Vice muttered to Saber.

"Mmhm."

Dagger pushed her way deeper into the tunnel, her shoulders rasped against the rough stone. "Hold!" she ordered. "Powder, cover me."

"They come!" Vice called again.

"So, stop them!" Dagger shot back.

The Armory held their position as demons crashed into Vice, who battered them against the walls, floor and each other, his pliers-like armored fingers ripping and bashing. Saber's blade flickered through the gaps in Vice's brutal, economic movements and slithered into flesh again and again.

In front, Dagger knelt and Powder stood over her with a scattergun in each hand, driving her eyes into the narrow darkness ahead, waiting to give her irons a chance to speak. Dagger laid her hammer on the ground and took a sharp spearhead from her belt and screwed it into the top of the head. She stood, her beastly weapon now a halberd fit for a blacksmith with a grudge against gods.

"Moving," Dagger said, and advanced behind her spear.

Two demons rushed her, their forms at first just fast shadows, and then their squealing skin wedged together in the tight confines. They thrashed at each other, claws scrabbling for friction against the walls, ceiling, floor and even each other. Dagger stepped in and drove her hammer into the blended mass of them. The spearhead popped one swollen body like a balloon and crunched into bone somewhere beyond. She kicked the other, nearly losing her boot to its jaws.

"Powder!" Dagger yelled and stood tall, her hammer over her head. For a slivered moment she looked like a statue as Powder snugged herself against Dagger's back, shoved a scattergun under each of her arms, and cut loose blind. Lead and fire cleared the way ahead, and turned the demons into little more than bone-flecked gel against the stone and dirt.

"Dose ready," Pitch said and handed the smoking flask to Dagger, who took a gulp and passed it to Powder. Their bodies flooded with new energy, the air almost crystalline. Dagger gestured and shuffled positions with Saber and Vice to take the brunt of the rush from behind. When Vice and Saber had drunk, and Pitch had swallowed the flask's final sip, Dagger again slid into the lead. The stone walls grew rougher and showed less the traces of miner's tools and more the ragged marks of animal clawing.

"They're trying to widen the tunnel," Dagger noted. "We have to finish this fast."

They burst out of the corridor and into an atrium of stone and darkness. The air was thick and warm. The Armory had killed wet, crawling creatures with too many teeth every step of the way, idiot, locust things that pounced on their own dead and ate the leavings — but in that atrium of rough stone, a sight cut through their jade and Pitch's sedatives.

"Well," Saber said, "that's just needlessly fucked up."

At the atrium's center was a swarm of demons, far smaller than any they'd faced so far, and two larger, corpulent ones that were covered in tooth-jagged scars. They shuffled around the brood of little demons like nursemaids, shoving and herding the squalling spawn into little clumps. The baby demons nestled close to their minders and ripped small gobbets of flesh from their plump legs, backs and paunches. The nursemaid demons didn't seem bothered, rather they turned themselves this way and that so the little horrors could find new flesh to eat, like sows lying on their sides so their newborn piglets could find a nipple. The ragged holes in their bodies healed almost instantly.

The nursemaid demons turned eyeless heads to regard The Armory. They hissed a warning but did not advance.

"Is that—" Powder said.

"Yeah," Pitch said. "They're nursing."

"No, I meant that," Powder said, pointing beyond the demons to the center of the room to a pulsing boulder of sweaty fleshy that writhed on the ground. The room reeked of charnel and ammonia.

"The gate," Pitch said in a voice both awed and horrified. "I've only ever seen scholars' drawings. But that looks more like..."

"It looks like a..." Saber said.

"Leave it in your heads, both of you," Dagger said, staring in disgust.

A gate was a thing of wood, stone or iron. It was a symbol of protection, a barrier with safety on the far side. It was not a big pulsing sack with veiny, rippling flesh and a sphincter-like opening at one end. It was not supposed to squat like an obese tumor, shifting its weight to and fro in a bed of its own filth.

It was not supposed to be alive.

The gate convulsed and a shrieking eyeless horror oozed from the puckered opening on a wave of mucous, and landed thrashing and keening into this unfamiliar world.

A gate did not heave and gasp in the throes of birth.

The baby horror was already growing as a nursemaid demon rushed over to tend to it.

"This is an abomination," Vice said.

"You know," Saber said, "before today I only thought I knew what that word meant."

Powder giggled. "Don't leave Saber alone with it," she said, pointing at the pucker of the gate's business end.

"Oh, c'mon, Powder. Not even I'm that depraved."

"Tell me you weren't thinking about it."

The duelist shut his mouth with a click.

The gate shuddered and the pucker sealed itself as the mass settled with what could only be a relieved sigh. Extending from it were snarls of fleshy tubes that led to vibrating bubbles of skin.

"We have to sever the boilers," Pitch said, pointing at the bubbles. "That's where it's drawing its power."

"Boilers?" Dagger asked.

"Fine," Pitch said. "You think of a better word."

One of the nursemaid demons wrenched open a connected bubble and stuffed in pieces of dead miner, helmet, apron and all. The gate shook and chunked like it was swallowing. The sphincter rippled as it expelled a gasp of foul air.

"I think it just burped," Saber said.

"How do we close that?" Powder asked. "It's not like it's a fucking door."

"Kill it and burn it," Dagger said. "Pitch?"

"White phosphorus," the alchemist said. "It's too wet for ordinary fire."

"Vice?" Dagger said.

"I can seal the breech it came through. The Vigil will aid me. No god of our world would suffer this thing's existence."

The rest of the group looked at each other. It was unnerving when Vice talked about his dead god as if it wasn't.

As The Armory approached, the nursemaid demons gathered their young charges, shielding the infants behind their bodies. Then they turned their maws to the ceiling and screamed as one, a piercing whistle of sound that drilled its way into The Armory's ears.

"Cry for help," Dagger noted.

"Yes," Vice said and shook out his shoulders.

"But we slaughtered everything on the way here," Saber said.

"You sure about that?" Powder said.

A mass formed beyond the gate, a ripple in the darkness out of reach of Pitch's phosphorescent paint. It could have been a moving wall. It stretched across the cavern as it advanced toward The Armory, and stepped into the range of the light, breaking across the gate like a slow wave.

"I thought the miners were all dead?" Saber said.

It was a wall of men and women. They still wore the heavy canvas aprons and leather gloves of their trade. Tools dangled from their belts. They walked on stiff legs. Their hands twitched. Their eyes were blank, their mouths open and slack.

"Zombies?" Dagger said with a snort. "That's a children's story."

The miners stepped between The Armory and the demon infants and spasming gate, but advanced no further. Behind the living barrier, the nursemaid demons furiously fed human slurry into the boilers.

"Why aren't they attacking?" Powder asked.

The human wall swayed, their shoulders bumping into each other idiotically.

"Powder, cover me," Pitch said.

"Go," Powder said, one of her pistols up. Pitch stopped a half dozen feet from the human wall. Their eyes did not focus on him. They did not turn their heads. He took another step and reached out a hand.

"Pitch!" Dagger yelled.

"It's an experiment," he called back. One of the shambling miners lifted a limp hand toward Pitch and its chest caved in with a crack as Powder fired. The miner fell and Pitch grabbed its apron and dragged the corpse back to The Armory as the shambling miners closed ranks around the gap. Pitch rolled the dead miner over and a wet little something ripped free from the corpse's skull and skittered toward the miners. It squealed as it was crushed beneath a shuffling boot.

"What was that?" Dagger asked.

"Some kind of parasite, I think," Pitch said, staring down at a hole in the back of the miner's head. "Shows a primitive knowledge of human movement, bipedal walking being as complicated as it is. But they're not attacking. Perhaps they don't have a handle on the higher motor functions enough to fight. Yet. Very interesting."

"So glad you're fascinated," Dagger said.

Vice stared at the wall of miners. "Life must be preserved," he muttered.

"Since when?" Dagger asked him.

166

"This isn't life, Vice," Pitch said. "This is anima past its prime."

"Pitch," Dagger asked, "could they recover if we get those things off their skulls?"

Pitch thought for a moment. "Possible. If they're only on the outside of the skull. Saber, lend me one of your knives."

"Hurry up," Dagger said with a glance at the wall. Their shuffling had grown more animated. Their fingers twitched and their heads turned this way and that. One by one, sets of dead, staring eyes focused on The Armory. Saber handed Pitch something more chisel than knife and the alchemist slid it into the hole in the back of the miner's head. He levered open the skull like he was cracking an oyster. Inside was filled with a honeycomb of fibrous mucal strands.

"Most of the brain's gone," Pitch said. "But it's possible their souls are still intact."

"Without their brains?" Dagger asked.

Pitch shrugged. "Nobody can agree where the soul is kept. Before my time with you, I would have argued it was only a metaphor."

Dagger nodded. "If their souls are still in there, you know what happens when we kill."

"I'd say it's still better than this," Pitch said, gestured at the shuffling zombie wall. "Trapped in their meat. If I were in that wall, I'd want this to end."

"Deliverance," Vice said with a reverent sigh. "I misjudged you, Pitch."

"Not really, Vice," Pitch said. "I would have done it without checking if you weren't here."

From behind his back, the alchemist took a squat bottle with a rope loop wrapped around its neck. He poured in a fine dust from a pouch and re-sealed it. As the chemicals within mixed, they glowed with a sickly yellow light. Pitch tossed it at the wall. One of the miners reached out and caught it, clutching it to her chest.

"Impressive," Pitch said. "They're learning fast."

"Yeah," Dagger said. "Cute. Powder? Before it learns to throw?"

Powder fired. The bottle shattered. The chemicals met air and burst into gouts of liquid fire that splashed over the miners, consuming half the wall. The miners staggered. The wall broke.

"With me!" Dagger shouted and lunged forward, swinging her hammer in a mighty arc that felled three of the shambling miners. The Armory moved like farmers threshing a field of grain. The miners that hadn't burned tried feebly to fight back but the creatures bored into their skulls hadn't mastered their bodies. The Armory cut, shot, burned and battered them to spare parts. The tiny creatures that had burrowed into the miners' skulls ripped loose of their puppets in a panic and were stomped beneath boot heels like tavern roaches or else ran into the fire, sizzled and died.

Through the dying flames and smoke, The Armory pushed forward, the floor slick and tacky under their boots. Their last barrier gone, the nursemaid demons faced The Armory, their mouths slack and screaming, empty of teeth. Their hands did not have claws, their bodies were awkward and not built to fight. They were walking feed troughs, but they were all that was left. Their young charges continued to gnaw on their thick haunches and climbed their backs to rip mouthfuls from their shoulders and necks.

"We have to stop the eating," Pitch called. "They little ones are growing."

Powder fired and her bullet tore a hole through the shoulder of one of the nursemaids. It rocked back and squealed at her, but the hole filled in seconds with new flesh, making a fresh patch of scar. Four of the demon infants rushed Saber, climbed up his trousers and bore him to the ground, their teeth scraping and rasping on his leathers. Screaming, he rolled and slammed himself into the ground, crushing two. Vice picked the rest off the duelist and smashed them together until they ceased moving. He threw them too far to become a meal, then grabbed a nursemaid, held it down and drove his fist against its fleshy skull. After it went limp, Dagger brought down her hammer over and over until it was paste and mud. Powder dragged Saber to his feet and then opened up on the last nursemaid demon with her scatterguns and made half of it disappear.

"Heal from that," she spat out.

Pitch poured acid over the writhing, half-gone creature.

The Armory turned its attention to the swarm of infant demons. They shuffled and keened pathetically as The Armory pulped them against the stone. When the cavern was quiet but for the pulsing, sucking noises of the gate, the bravos stood, panting and staring at the obscene thing.

"Vice," Dagger said, "get started."

Vice knelt and began to mutter. The gate spasmed.

"Sever the boilers," Vice muttered between prayers.

Saber and Powder went to each of the fleshy tumors. After he cut though the tendrils connecting them to the gate, she destroyed them with her shotguns. The gate whined and wriggled. It tried to move, but it was too heavy. Vestigial legs poked and squirmed from under its bulk.

Pitch threw two glass jars at the gate, one filled with chalky rocks and water, and the other filled with captive fire. They shattered and the chemicals inside smoked and blazed as they hit open air. The gate shook and made wet kissing sounds with its birth opening as if gulping to breathe around the white-hot conflagration. An old-garlic reek filled the cavern. Dagger swung her hammer down on the gate. Power fired her scatterguns again and again. Saber chopped with big strokes of his cleavers. They worked artlessly until the thing was a lumpy, sizzling mess in the dirt.

"This is never gonna wash off," Saber said, fruitlessly trying to find something clean to wipe his mouth.

Dagger turned back to the praying monk. "What are we waiting for?"

Vice did not answer. His head was bowed and his lips moved. Without the sucking, gurgling noises of the gate and the squeals of the baby demons, The Armory could hear his repeated phrases, intense and plaintive. Dagger shook her head and sifted the gate's leftover meat with her boot and the spike end of her hammer's handle. She kicked a misshapen bone out of the way and toed along the floor of the mine. She bent down and pushed her fingers into the muck.

"There's something under here," she said, wiping her hand on her trousers. "Pitch, I need more light."

Pitch produced a bundle of acrid-smelling cloth. "Drive your hammer into the floor."

Dagger stood and stabbed her hammer's spiked handle deep into the ground and Pitch wrapped the head with the cloth and then took out flint and tinder. Sparks danced across the reactive cloth, and it blazed with a bright, white light. Dagger knelt and again probed the slurry, this time with her belt knife.

"There's something carved it into the stone," she said. "It was done with tools, not claws."

"Let me see," Pitch said and bent down near her. "Yes, I see it. But I don't recognize it. This might be more Vice's line than mine."

"Vice!" Dagger called over her shoulder.

The monk still did not move.

172

"Vice!" Dagger shouted even louder.

Vice tilted his face up to the ceiling of the cavern, his eyelids closed and the eyeballs behind them flitting back and forth rapidly.

"Hey, Vice, the Vigil's over here with its tits out," Saber shouted.

Vice growled and bowed his head. He unclasped his hands. "Saber, I am going to punch you in the face."

"You can punch him later," Dagger said.

"Hey!" Saber protested.

"Vice! Now!" Dagger continued. "Come look at this."

Vice got off his knees and looked over Dagger's shoulder.

"It is a ritual sigil," he said, "this is how they called the gate."

"How does it work?" Pitch asked.

"By belief, Pitch," Vice said.

"Nothing happens just because you believe it," Pitch said.

"Belief is as strong as any science," Vice muttered.

"How were those prayers going?" Pitch muttered.

"I... there was no answer," Vice said, missing Pitch's sarcasm. His tone was anguished.

"It's probably like they told us," Pitch said, "this place is hidden. Even with the demons gone."

Vice gave Pitch a grateful look and straightened his back.

"Would the sigils keep working?" Dagger asked. "Could whoever carved this do it again, even if with the gate and all the demons dead?"

"Yes," Vice said. "This symbol weakens the membrane between the worlds and calls to another. In this case, a world where these creatures are plentiful. One they have devoured."

"Who would want something like that?" Dagger asked, not out of outrage, but curiosity.

"Somebody who believed the world was better eaten," Vice said.

"It wasn't the demons themselves," Pitch noted. "They don't plan."

Dagger grunted. "How do we get rid of it?"

"Could just blow it up," Powder said.

"Do it," Dagger muttered.

"Pitch," Powder said and gestured to the sludge that had once been a gate, "can you burn some of this shit off so I can see what I'm doing?"

The alchemist poured acid from a jar over the slurry on the ground, and it sizzled as it ate the gate's meat down to smoke and crystalline dust.

"Why is that making me hungry?" Saber muttered at the smell of dissolving, quick-burning flesh.

"Because, as usual," Vice said, "your appetites have outstripped your brains."

Saber shrugged. "It's a gift."

Powder set her bag down, removed several slim sticks of dynamite and laid them in the sigil's grooves. She took out a spool of fuse and attached one end to the dynamite.

"Time to go," she said, and played out the fuse behind as The Armory made their back through the mine. They heard nervous skittering in the darkness, the sound of claw on stone.

"What do we do about the stragglers?" Powder asked, gesturing at a demon trying to hide behind a rock and hissing at them. "I don't want to waste bullets."

"We close the gate," Dagger said. "Whatever doesn't die in the blast, the locals can clean up."

"If there's any locals left," Saber muttered.

The journey back, as is often the case with walks into the unknown, felt shorter.

The Armory burst gasping and squinting into the sunlight. The fetid rank of the yard tasted like fine wine after the murk of the tunnels and the smell of burning flesh. Powder lit the fuse, and it shot back into the tunnel behind them like a firefly.

"Stop right there," a strange voice commanded and all around them was the sound of swords being drawn and rifle hammers being cocked. Dagger blinked until the half-moon of liveried soldiers blocking their way came into focus.

"Who the fuck are you?" Dagger asked.

"The Queen's guard."

"Which queen?"

"Our queen is not a witch!"

"Not what I meant."

"Do you not know where you are?" The soldier asked.

"Frequently," Saber answered, fingering the hilt of one of his swords and looking speculatively at the ring of weapons. "We're out. Job's done. We could just sell this one dear. All those miners back there. They gotta be worth an exit."

176

"Hold, Saber," Dagger said.

"What were you doing down there?" The soldier asked.

"Solving your demon problem," Dagger said.

"How?"

Dagger held up a finger. They stood. The soldiers shifted nervously.

Several moments passed and nothing happened.

"Powder?" Dagger turned to the sharpshooter. "Little quieter than your usual work."

"Captain, it's a lot of fuse. Just wait."

"You're making us look bad in front of the yokels," Saber said with a giggle.

"Shut up, Saber," Powder said. "Captain, I know my business."

The gunner turned to the soldiers. "Sorry for the delay. Think of it as a dramatic pause. Like the theater."

"What?" The guards' leader asked.

Then the ground shook and a tempest of dust burst out of the mouth of the mine. The soldiers all flinched and then retrained their weapons on The Armory. Dagger looked behind them, waving a hand and coughing.

"Your mine will need to be re-dug," she said, "but the gate is dead."

"What gate? Why would you kill a gate?"

"Dead," Dagger sighed. "Closed. Whatever. You had to be there."

"What?" The soldier asked again.

"This lot seem easily confused," Pitch muttered.

"Now," Dagger said to the soldiers, "what's this about a queen?"

"Queen Dinar S'ylin Amarenta Qual D'sine, Fortieth of her Line, Jeweled Light of the Citadel requests your presence. You will come with us."

Dagger blinked at the barrage of titles.

"How's he remember all that?" Saber muttered to Powder.

"Probably gets beheaded at dawn if he doesn't," Powder muttered.

"That would motivate me," Saber said.

"Nothing motivates you to remember anybody's name, Saber," Powder said. "That's why you end up in so many duels with husbands, wives and shepherds."

"I've always thought it was better if I can't remember their names, so they know it's nothing serious."

"It's not better," Powder said.

178

"Come with us," the soldier repeated, trying again to take command of the situation.

"Why?" Dagger asked in a bored voice. "Because you said so?"

"You're outnumbered ten to one!"

"That's a shit reason," Dagger said, "We'd only be outnumbered for the first three seconds."

"Our queen has a job for you," an older soldier called out. He was grizzled and scarred. "Paid in gold."

Dagger grunted. "You should have opened with that. How far?"

"We have a carriage waiting," the first soldier said.

"I changed my mind," Dagger said.

The soldiers shifted nervously.

"You should have opened with carriage, " Dagger said with an exhausted sigh.

# — CHAPTER 7 —

## A queen under glass, a job.

The tower was nearly as big around as the village in its shadow, and tall enough to bisect the sky. It tapered almost to a point, had neither ornament nor window, and flew no flags. Not even the weather had stained the stone, which looked like it had been cut from a quarry the day before.

The soldier who'd done most of the talking outside the mine rode in the carriage with The Armory, sandwiched between Vice, who was staring at nothing, and Saber who kept giving him suggestive, sidelong glances. The soldier shifted in a futile effort to get some space for his shoulders between an object that didn't care and one trying to care too much under the circumstances.

"That's a lot of palace for such a small village," Dagger muttered to herself.

"That's the Citadel," the guard said.

"Citadel, palace," Dagger said with a dismissive wave. "Whatever."

"That isn't the palace. You've never heard of the Citadel of Stairs?"

Saber snapped his fingers. "Of course. The Citadel of Stairs. I remember now..." Saber paused and cocked his head. "No, sorry. That was the Shithouse of Doom."

"What's the Citadel of Stairs?" Dagger asked.

"Better if her majesty explains," the soldier said. "We're nearly there."

The carriage stopped outside a low, one-story building.

"This is the palace? It looks like a tavern," Dagger said.

"It is," the soldier said. "And brothel. The finest in town."

Powder leaned across the carriage. Her tone was sly and confiding. "It's the only one isn't it?"

The soldier nodded reluctantly.

"Brothel, huh?" Saber said.

"Later," Dagger said. "If you're good."

When The Armory entered the tavern's common room, every patron kept their dull eyes on their cups. Even the odd working girl or boy sitting in a lap or rubbing shoulders was staring off into the middle distance.

The soldier ushered them through the meager crowd to a set of stairs at the back that led down into a rough-cut, well-lit basement. A dozen more soldiers stood or sat, but all turned to watch as The Armory entered. At the center of the room was a gray-haired woman with weathered, heavily lined features behind a battered wooden table. She wore a boiled leather vest over rough brown canvas. There was a pistol by her hand.

The soldier who escorted The Armory greeted the woman with a spare bow. "Your majesty, I've brought them."

"Thank you, Ghired. Please sit, all of you," the queen said and gestured to empty chairs around the table. She poured ale from a jug into five cups and served The Armory with her own hand.

"This is interesting," Dagger said, and drained off half the ale in her cup with a single swallow.

The queen grunted. "You were expecting more ceremony? A throne room?"

"That's usually how we meet with monarchs," Dagger said.

"Met a lot of those, have you?"

"One or two," Dagger said. "Generally, it's their factors who hire us."

"And I bet you thought that overcompensating stone dick trying to fuck a cloud was my palace."

Dagger nodded.

"Naturally," the queen said and chuckled darkly. "But there's not much majestic about this place, or me. Did they tell you my title? I would repeat it for effect, but I can't remember it. Don't know how they do. It's not even really my title. Nothing here belongs to anybody."

"Why are we here, your majesty?" Dagger asked.

"That's a good question," the queen said. "I certainly didn't invite you. Yet, I heard a band of armed strangers went down into that mine. And now here you are. Alive. You cleared it out?"

"That's what we do."

"Why? Who hired you? How did you even get here?"

Vice stiffened and was about to speak, but Dagger put up a hand and talked before he could.

"We don't discuss who hires us, your majesty," Dagger said. "Most seem to prefer it that way."

The queen jutted her chin toward Vice. "The one in the hood seemed about to say something."

"He doesn't speak for The Armory," Dagger said, "I do."

"The Armory. Interesting. Honestly, I don't care," the queen said. "You did us a great service, even if you didn't know it. Is your job done?"

Dagger nodded. "And what can we do for you?"

"The aforementioned eyesore. The Citadel of Stairs. Heard of it?"

"Not before today," Dagger said. "If it's not your palace, then whose is it?"

"Belongs to our jailers," the queen said with a heavy sigh. "The jailers of all who came before me. You," the queen said to Pitch. "All those jars and vials. You smell like an apothecary. What are you? An alchemist?"

"I am," Pitch answered.

"How do you conduct your experiments?"

"I don't have much time for study these days, your majesty," Pitch said with a wry smile. "I'm just a working man."

"But you're familiar with the concept?"

Pitch nodded. "A distant memory, but yes."

"These lands. My people. All are an experiment conducted by the ones who live in the tower. They both support and exploit us. Food and building materials, whatever we might need, though I don't know how they know that. We're rats in a cage. We cannot leave. Our only contact with the outside world is the occasional merchant vessel. Very few know we exist to visit, so you understand my confusion at your presence."

"We get around," Dagger said.

"Perhaps you're just another one of their experiments," the queen said.

"We aren't," Dagger said. "If you have a job, we'll take it."

"I doubt you would tell us anyway," the queen said. "Maybe it doesn't matter." The queen trailed off, lost in thought, or perhaps just a wish for better.

"Your majesty?" Dagger prompted.

"It's always something," the queen said. "The mine was just one of their games. Every tragedy, and every deliverance, comes by their hand. They probably sent you. Whether you know it or not. Maybe they want to know what a little hope can do."

"Why don't you attack?" Dagger asked, "you have soldiers and weapons."

"We're like children with sticks and kitchen pots playing war. We have weapons, yes. We've sent soldiers. We've sent mercenaries like you, who also seemed to wander here by accident, hence my skepticism. Almost everyone we've sent, everyone my forbearers sent, most never even got past the guards on the stairs. The ones who made it inside vanished."

"Did the tower retaliate?"

"No," the queen said. "At least not in a way that was clear."

"Any why don't you just leave?"

"Every ruler is taken shortly after birth to the gate of the tower. One of their... priests, I suppose you could say, comes out and blesses the child. That ruler is bound to the tower and the people to the ruler, we're told. Should the tower fall, so will we all."

"That's interesting," Dagger said. "Do you think it's true?"

"There are journals left by previous rulers," the queen said. "They write of trying to leave by land or sea. Weather turned them back. Or hostile beasts. Their food all went mysteriously bad, or their water turned toxic. The moment they stopped trying to leave, the torments ceased. That guessing game ended years before my time."

The Armory looked around the room. They noted the slumped shoulders, the general air of defeat. They'd never seen an armed group look so weaponless. Even the queen, who seemed as solid as stone, appeared to be near to crumbling.

"There were demons in that mine," Pitch said.

"Is that what they were?" The queen asked. "In any case, what does that matter? It was just another sick game."

Pitch shook his head. "Nobody would want those things loose in their land. They are beyond control. The destruction would have been immense. There would have been nothing left. If that was an experiment, it would be like trying to discover the boiling point of water by setting the laboratory on fire."

"Perhaps," the queen said. "I can tell you from experience that no cataclysm the Citadel unleashes is beyond their control. Nothing happens here that the tower doesn't have a silent hand in. Even random events can't be trusted not to be some play. I want it gone. I want my people to have lives that aren't predetermined. Ordinary bad luck. Poor fishing. Bad harvests. Disease. Not strange death at the hands of whatever the Citadel decided to unleash that month."

Dagger looked at each of the members of The Armory in turn and saw agreement on each face. She nodded.

"We can do that," Dagger said. "What are you offering in return?"

"What do you want?"

"Gold," Dagger said. "What else?"

The queen snorted. "Gold? Take as much as you like once the job's done."

"I'd see the coin first."

The queen gestured to one of the guards who, with two others, dragged a chest over and heaved them onto the table. They opened the lid. It was filled with yellow nuggets of varying sizes.

"That didn't come from the mine," Pitch said.

Powder picked up one of the nuggets. It was the size of her thumb. "How can you tell?"

"Did you see any veins of ore?"

"I was a little busy."

The queen's expression was grim. "I told you. They give it to us. That mine never yielded any metal of any sort. We hoped for something. We dug and dug. We only mined apathy, and then horror."

"Typically, we get paid in coin," Dagger said.

"We don't bother milling it into coins," the queen said. "We don't need to buy anything. Do you have any idea how many of my people want to just be simple shopkeepers? Bakers? Butchers? Our economy is a puppet show."

"Dagger," Vice said in a low, urgent tone.

"Yes, Vice. I know," Dagger said and gathered herself, knowing if she let Vice explain, they'd be there all day and the next while he preached. "Your majesty, what we did, we did in service of the Vigil."

"The what?"

"A god," Dagger explained. "A god that heard your subjects' prayers and sent us."

"I thought you didn't discuss your clients?"

"Usually. But when there's a purpose, rules change."

"My people aren't the praying sort. The Citadel is our god. Or good as. And those capricious fuckers aren't the sort whose attention you want to attract. Anyway, I've never heard of this Virgin."

"Vigil," Saber corrected, "About that—"

"Shut up, Saber," Dagger said.

Vice burst through the talk, unable to contain himself. "You stand in the Vigil's light, though you know it not. We have been sent to deliver you. Our god would have its aid repaid in something more than gold."

"You lot don't look particularly holy," the queen said with a look at Saber, who was whispering to the soldier who'd brought them. The man was blushing furiously. "How would your god like to be rewarded? I'll tell you for free, I've had quite enough of inscrutable powers. I won't deliver my people just to enslave them to some other thing's whims."

"Prayer," Vice said. "Faith. To stand witness. That is all. These are the currencies of the watcher of the world. It is not the heretical bondage that you have suffered under. "

"You get rid of the tower," the queen said, "And I'll build this Vigil a temple. Hell, I'll build it five."

"Good enough," Dagger said, "but—"

"The Vigil requires no holy places, your majesty," Vice broke in. "Only the one each of us carries in our hearts and minds."

"Your god comes cheap," the queen said with a grin. "Deal."

"Can you tell us anything about the inside of the Citadel?" Pitch asked.

The queen shook her head. "As I said, nobody has ever been inside and come out. The tower's servants, the ones we've seen, are either guards or priests, though we've not seen one of those since I was just a girl. I'm not even sure they're human."

"Any idea what they might be?" Dagger asked. "Generally, we like to know what we're fighting."

The queen shrugged. "At a guess? Creatures created by the tower. The journals I mentioned say other bands like yourselves were sent in, some several times your number. But whether it was a lone adventurer or a small army, and they tried every time they had visitors who looked like they could handle themselves, they were never seen again."

"You haven't sent The Armory," Dagger said.

"I bet they were confident too," the queen said with a sad smile.

"We have certain advantages. Now, your majesty, we'll need a place to get ready."

"You're standing in it," the queen said, "Do you need anything?"

Dagger looked around at The Armory.

"Is there an apothecary?" Pitch asked.

"We have one, though the inventory may be limited."

"I'm very resourceful, your majesty," Pitch said.

"Gunpowder and bullets," Powder said.

"I'll have my guards leave their supply. Not like they need it."

Then the queen nodded at Dagger, and gestured to her guards who formed up around her and led her from the basement. When they were alone, The Armory took council.

"This bullshit doesn't have to be our problem," Powder said. "We could probably just go around and tell people about the Vigil. They'll pray."

"You would lie in the Vigil's name?" Vice asked.

"If the job is to win prayers for the Vigil, and they pray, it's not really a lie, is it?"

"It's a job," Saber countered. "We said we'd do it. We go back on our word, and we'd have to fight our way out. Her soldiers are nothing special, but there are enough of them. We could die. I know we'll come back, but does anybody really enjoy it? Do you, Powder?"

"Probably more than I'd enjoy raiding some kind of wizard tower from hell," the sharpshooter said, folding her arms.

"You're gonna make hell jokes after being knee deep in demon guts?" Saber said.

Vice threw back his hood to reveal his craggy face and gray beard. His eyes looked like lanterns at the bottom of a dry well. "The Vigil's servants sent us to win new believers. That job is not done."

"You heard the queen, Vice," Dagger said, "these people aren't believers. They're broken."

"Salvation can turn an uncaring head to the heavens."

"Maybe," Dagger said.

"Either way," Pitch said." The queen is paying a lot of gold. And It's interesting. This Citadel... it's strange behavior for tyranny."

"How do you mean?" Saber asked.

"This place has a hierarchy," the alchemist said. "The queen has armed soldiers. Somebody supplied their weapons. Gunpowder just doesn't fall from the sky. Those were steel swords. Powder, what's your opinion of their guns?"

"I'd need a closer look, but it's odd. Why would you arm a population you want to keep under thumb? The powder and bullets they left are sound."

"Of course," Pitch continued, "we could be part of this Citadel's experiment and not even know it."

"You suggest this Citadel could control the Vigil?" Vice asked the alchemist.

"No," Pitch said, "I'm suggesting the prayers may not have come from these people."

"Fine," Dagger said. "Reservations noted. Any of them strong enough to keep us from doing this?"

"We do this in the Vigil's name," Vice said. "We could double or even triple the number of faithful. That is heavenly wealth."

"A monk and an economist," Pitch said with a grin.

"We hit the tower tomorrow at noon,' Dagger said. "Get some food and rest, see to your tools. Pitch, go shopping. Saber, brothel."

"No," the duelist said with a sigh.

"No?" Dagger said, shocked.

Saber shook his head. "They all look too sad."

194

# — CHAPTER 8 —

## Have fun storming the castle!

The Citadel bisected the sun-blazed, azure sky with alabaster, but its shadow was so big, so absolute, that The Armory approached in a shaft of dusk. The street opened into a wide, cobbled thoroughfare as the last village buildings fell away and Dagger called a halt.

She turned to Pitch.

"I want clear, sharp and fast."

"The apothecary had a few interesting compounds," Pitch said. He shook a vial hard until the liquid glowed. He uncorked it and cupped his hand around the mouth, huffed from the fumes, then handed it around. The rest of The Armory took several strong, snorting inhales. The air brightened and even the Citadel's oppressive shadow lightened.

Dagger shivered appreciatively. "Oh, yes."

Her muscles, knotted and sore from the fight with the demons, unpicked as golden, cleansing fire pulsed up and down her spine. Even Vice's perpetual scowl lifted a degree or two.

"And now," Dagger said through deliciously gritted teeth, "this bullshit."

Six long flights of stairs with five wide-open landings led to the Citadel's massive iron doors. On each landing stood a pair of guards. On the first were two hulking figures draped in sheets of steel and leather. Each held a halberd big enough to behead the moon.

"The first two are mine," Dagger said from the fire in her belly.

"Aye, Captain," Powder said, checking and re-checking the brace of loaded pistols strapped around her torso.

Pitch squinted past the first two guards. "Boss, wait a moment."

But Dagger ignored him, and left the rest of the band had no choice but to form up behind her as she marched up the first set of stairs. As they climbed, the tower swallowed the sky and became a frozen, stone wave poised to crash over them.

Dagger stepped onto the landing and the sentinels faced her with the creak and screech of leather and steel. Each was half again as tall as her and twice as broad. She hefted her hammer and waited to see which of the two steel-clad hulks would swing first. In her leathers she'd be faster. She eyed their glinting shoulders. Well, she thought, I did tell Saber to wait until we were sent to kill giants.

Something sailed over her head and shattered against the first of the two guards. Its armor smoked as acid ate through the metal and leather. If there was a living thing beneath the steel, it did not scream, but fell with a crash, thrashing as its armor was planed away to whatever lay beneath. The other guardian only watched. Perhaps it was afraid of touching the corrosive chemicals, or perhaps it was only a detached curiosity. When the first had stopped moving, the second turned to face Dagger. It lifted its halberd and was about to swing when a gunshot cracked and a hole punched through its chest plate. It staggered as the slug ripped out through its back. It did not bleed. There was a moment of delay, then the guardian lurched as if it had swallowed something the wrong way.

It shivered.

It fell.

Dagger spun to face her crew, her expression livid.

197

"What did I say?" she grated through bared teeth.

Pitch stepped right up to her, his face in her sternum and his chin jutted up at her pugnaciously. "And what's with this single combat shit? Since when do we solve problems like that?"

"I solve problems like that all the time," Saber said mildly.

"Saber," Pitch yelled, "you fight idiots on fields and in alleys who assume you carry that many blades because you're overcompensating."

"Well, no. It's because variety is the spi—"

"I know, Saber," Pitch interrupted, "I see your variety leaving every inn we stay at."

"Oh. Do they look satisfied?"

"Yes, and vaguely ashamed of themselves. Anyway," Pitch continued, "since when do we fight fair, boss?

"I lead, Pitch," Dagger said in a dangerous tone. She leaned down until she and the alchemist were nose to nose. "I take the first risk."

"Or maybe I just put too much fire crystal in that vial!" Pitch shouted.

Dagger's anger dipped. She fought to keep it there. "Did you?"

"I'm yelling at you, aren't I?!"

Dagger clenched her teeth. "Fuck's sake, Pitch."

"I figured we'd need a little more aggression since we were going to face the tower of fucking doom, or whatever this overgrown pile of rock is! And clearly, I fucking overdid it!"

Dagger frowned. "You going to stop yelling?"

"Maybe. Yes," Pitch said, mastering his tone with some effort. "Anyway, there's something odd here."

"There's something odd everywhere," Dagger said. "Everything we do is odd."

"Yeah, but... just show her, Powder."

Powder handed a telescope to Dagger and then reloaded her rifle.

"Look at each of the landings, boss," Pitch said.

Dagger put the glass to her eye. On the next landing was a pair of lithe swordsmen. After that was a pair of thickset, shirtless fighters, their fists wrapped in chains and their faces covered by steel masks. Beyond them were two men behind a barricade with a series of bottles and jars balanced across the top. And far past them, on elevated stone perches above the doors to the Citadel, were two sharpshooters. Their rifles were already trained on The Armory.

"What the fuck?" Dagger muttered, riding above the waves of chemical rage in her chest.

"What does all that look like to you?" Pitch asked.

"Like shitty versions of us," Dagger admitted.

"Almost like we're expected," Pitch said.

"Any idea how that's even possible?" Dagger asked.

"In a larger sense? No," Pitch said. "But as to what to do about this? That seems obvious."

"What do you suggest?" Dagger said, fighting to unclench her teeth.

"Ooh, I have an idea," Powder said and took aim at the distant barricade with the men that looked like they could have been Pitch's colleagues. She fired. One of the jars atop the barricade shattered and burst into flames. In rapid succession the other bottles burst in a technicolor conflagration that swallowed guards and barricade both.

"That was a very good idea," Powder said as she reloaded.

"What about the gunners? We don't want to get much closer," Dagger asked her, her augmented temper now fully under her thumb.

"We're out of range," Powder said.

"Of rifles? Are you sure?"

"I'm sure we're out of range of their rifles," Powder said with a wink.

As if to argue with Powder, one of the snipers fired. Something bounced and careened down the stairs past Dagger and whacked into Vice's shin. He growled in annoyance and looked down at his greave. He bent and plucked a deformed lead slug from the hard leather. "Ow," he muttered.

"See? Out of range," Powder said. "they clearly don't know how to compensate for bullet drop or muzzle velocity. Anyway, their barrels are too short. It's like somebody taught them to shoot yesterday."

But even that small attack on one of her people sent the fire thundering in Dagger's blood once more. She controlled it with effort. "Let's go. Saber, Vice. Take lead on the swordsmen."

"Be our pleasure," Saber said and turned to the gnarled monk. "Oh, I'm sorry, Vice. You probably don't plan to enjoy it, do you?"

"My shin hurts," Vice growled.

"Well, you got shot. Kinda."

Vice and Saber rushed up the stairs with the others close behind, and the waiting swordsmen drew their blades to meet them.

One of them swung at Vice, but the monk of the dead god caught the blade and struck it with his other fist, snapping it off near the hilt. He kicked the swordsman's legs out from under him, dragged the man to the ground and stomped him into the stone. Saber parried a thrust meant for Vice's back and forced the second swordsman back. They danced with their blades for a step or two, the edges glinting, until Saber closed the distance and forced the grapple, their hilts tangling. The guard shoved Saber back, but the duelist danced to the side, spun around the confused guard and then stepped back with his sword pointed at the man's eyes in a stylized pose.

With a crack, half the guard's head vanished in a puff of red mist.

"I had him!" Saber shouted at Powder.

"And?" Powder said, reloading her pistol.

"How come you didn't shoot Vice's guy?"

Powder shrugged. "Vice did his job. You were fucking around. If I wanted to watch you have fun, I'd peek through your keyhole at night."

"I hate you."

Powder blew him a kiss.

"These guards are not good," Vice said.

"No," Dagger said. "They aren't. Powder did say it was like the sharpshooters were given their guns yesterday."

"Correction, sharpshooter. Singular," Powder said, shouldered her rifle and fired. A limp shadow slumped from its perch to land in a heap before the great doors. Powder sighted again and swore.

"What?" Dagger asked.

"The other one's hiding. I can't get a clear shot," she said, fired again and cursed. The sharpshooter popped up and fired back. It whined past them like a big mosquito and then plinked down the rest of the stairs. Powder returned a shot. "We get any closer," she said, "and that prick might get lucky."

"Fuck's sake," Dagger said and ducked slightly as another shot whined past them.

On the next landing, the masked figures with chain-wrapped hands waited patiently. Powder fired and there came a little puff of dust from the stone above the sharpshooter's perch.

"This is fucking stupid," Dagger said. "And boring. Fall back."

They returned to the first landing where they were firmly out of killing range.

"Sorry, Captain," Powder said.

Dagger looked at the armored giant guard Powder had shot. She knelt by the body and prodded among the armor plates with a short knife. She grunted, cut a pair of straps and lifted off the guard's chest plate. She lifted it by the straps and held it like a shield. It was nearly as big as she was if she moved in a crouch.

"Behind me," she ordered.

They advanced behind Dagger and her breastplate barricade. Bullets plinked off the steel, and Dagger grunted and shifted as the bullets' impact grew with every step she took.

As they mounted the steps to the landing with the masked brawlers, they shuffled forward, their hands out to grapple. They went straight to the shield as if they thought it had come to life, and started idiotically pounding at it with both hands like they were driving railroad spikes. Dagger pushed back, swore and growled under her breath. "Somebody do something about these idiots."

Vice stepped out to meet them, but Saber and Pitch dragged him back behind the breastplate. Powder peeked out with a pistol and fired twice. The brawlers fell and The Armory advanced past the two newest corpses.

They climbed the next set of stairs to where the barricade was still burning with chemical fire. Sweat poured down Dagger's face. The sharpshooter fired again and punched through the metal. Dagger grunted and dropped to a knee. Her grip slipped and the breastplate tipped forward. Saber lunged and grabbed one of straps, but it was too heavy. As it fell, he was catapulted swearing over the top, up the last set of stairs and into the Citadel doors with a hollow bang. Powder stood tall and fired both pistols at the sharpshooter's position to force them behind cover as Pitch and Vice dragged Dagger up to the door by her leathers. Powder peppered the sniper with covering fire until they all stood beneath the protection of a stone overhang. Saber lay in a dazed heap.

"Saber, get up," Vice muttered.

"Dagger?" Saber groaned as he rolled over and felt his face for breaks. He spat out a gobbet of blood.

"I'm fine," Dagger grated. "Just pissed off. The steel slowed the bullet. It didn't get through," she picked the flattened metal slug from her armor and threw it disdainfully down the stairs. As Pitch prodded at her ribs, the sniper continued to fire down, bullets cracking ineffectually against the stone a few feet away.

Dagger gently shoved the alchemist back. "Pitch, I'm fine."

Pitch scowled. "You would say that if you were crawling up here lubricated by your own blood."

"What do you want to do about him," Saber asked Powder as she reloaded her pistols.

"Maybe Dagger can set up the shield again to toss you up there," she grinned.

"Very funny."

"It really was."

"We don't have to kill everyone," Dagger said.

"Out of character for us," Powder said.

"We're at the door already," Dagger said. "Who cares? Let them waste the bullets."

"What if he warns somebody we're here?" Saber asked.

Pitch shrugged. "We just fought past guards tailor made for us. I'd say surprise isn't on our side.

Dagger nodded. "Pitch is right. But when we're inside, we'll find a way up to that perch. Then I'm going to beat that shitty gunner to death with one of my boots."

The doors to the Citadel towered over them on steel hinges bigger than Dagger. She set her hands against one of the doors, took a deep breath and shoved.

It swung open as if it weighed nothing at all.

The Armory slunk into a central hall so large its edges vanished into shadow. The only light came from a low stone monument on a dais at the center of the hall, covered in spiraling patterns of too-bright candles. Along the curved wall to their left was a gradual set of stairs that circled the room and rose up beyond the reach of the monument's light.

"So. Up?" Powder asked, training her rifle on the place where the first bend of stairs became a blind spot.

"It is a tower," Dagger said and took point upon the stairs.

As they climbed, they couldn't help but stare at the blazing monument. As the dark reaches of the tower revolved and they climbed gradually higher, their attention shrank to that single luminous point. The floor filled with shadows like water in a well and the ever more distant light seemed to grow brighter. They lost perspective. Was the floor falling or was ceiling lowering to meet them? Or were they just spinning around the light endlessly?

But eventually, The Armory reached the top and Dagger climbed the final steps onto a walkway with the rest close behind her. At the end was a doorway filled with a perfect blackness. When Vice — who had brought up the rear of the climb — stepped off the stairs, the room lurched like a carriage brought to a stop too fast, and The Armory rocked with the aggressive tilt and clutched the wall for balance.

"What the fuck was that?" Dagger asked.

Vice muttered a prayer under his breath. Powder and Saber looked around as if they could shoot or stab physics. Pitch tapped Powder on the shoulder.

"Your glass?"

Wordlessly, Powder handed over the telescope and Pitch trained it on the glaring blaze of the monument far below.

"There's runework on the monument," Pitch said. "I can't quite read it, but there's no mistaking the patterns."

"What's that mean for us?" Dagger asked.

208

"I don't know. Yet. There's something familiar about it, but I can't quite place it. I should climb back down and check."

"Vice, go with him," Dagger said. "Powder, Saber, we'll hold the doorway."

As Pitch and Vice turned to descend, the steps rose to meet them, rolling over and over each other in a wave of stasis that went nowhere. The alchemist and the monk looked like trick dancers walking in place.

"Fuck," Pitch said.

"What the hell is happening?" Dagger asked.

"Fuck, fuck, fuck!"

"Fuck what, Pitch?" Dagger asked.

Pitch threw up his hands in disbelief. "I've never seen it except in books. It's supposed to be bullshit."

"What is?" Dagger said. "Pitch, you keeping us in suspense? And stop trying to walk down the stairs, you're giving me a headache."

Pitch and Vice stepped back to flat ground.

"It's Temker's Clock," Pitch said, his voice a bit shrill. "I've only ever seen diagrams, but it's just a fucking theory! It's never been done before."

"What's Timmy's Crock?" Saber asked.

"Temker's. Clock," Pitch said. "It's an alchemical concept. From when the craft was more closely allied with magic, before the schism away from faith toward science. Temker was a disgraced priest from a religion that used labyrinths as a form of ritual meditation. He was obsessed with clocks. In his drift from faith, he blended those mystic practices with alchemy. He posited that light and timed revolutions in the right repeating patterns could break one free from time."

"Free from time?" Dagger asked.

"The stairs, think about how slow they ascended. Their angle. Even their width and their number. All of it was part of Temker's Clock. Every step we took, we were winding it."

"And you didn't think to mention that?"

"I didn't see it!" Pitch said, as angry with himself as the situation. "It's not supposed to be real. Temker was an even shittier alchemist than a priest. At the academy, they taught it as a cautionary tale not to allow one's preconceptions to pervert the search for truth."

"So, what does that mean for us?" Powder asked.

"It means there's only forward," Vice said. "There is always and ever forward. No other directions exist."

"Vice is mostly right," Pitch admitted, "if Temker's Clock was successfully applied here, which it looks like it was, it means the Citadel exists outside time, or at least everything inside it does. If that's the only entrance, it means whatever enters and climbs the stairs is broken free from time. Every living thing, maybe even every object, permanently in a state of timelessness."

"So?" Saber asked.

"While we are in the clock's grip, time won't pass. Not for us."

"So?" Saber repeated. "That's good, right?"

"No, Saber. It's not good," Pitch said, looking defeated. "We've been in here for half an hour. Maybe. By our reckoning. Meanwhile, the outside world could have marched along by years already. Decades. And if the Citadel itself isn't affected..."

"It still doesn't sound that bad," Saber said, "we'll wrap up this job quickly and get out of here."

"Saber, everything you do is governed by your perception of time. Everything. Every heartbeat. Every blink. Every memory. Worse, if the structure of the Citadel itself is not outside time, but everything inside it is, then it could crumble to dust over decades, but to us it would seem like five minutes. The floor you're standing on could vanish before you take your next step."

"Feels pretty solid to me," Saber said, stomping on the floor with both feet.

Pitch glared at Saber. "Why do you even have ears?"

"For nibbles," Saber said.

"Do you think about nothing else?"

"Stabbing."

"I give up."

Dagger gave them both a level stare. "If you two could talk this place to death, it would already be rubble. Worry about next when next happens."

They stepped through the doorway and into a glow that had been invisible from the other side, and they blinked as their eyes adjusted. The doorway vanished behind them, and when they turned again, they were in a long corridor. Guttering torches lined the walls and broken, twisted doors with barred windows lay on the stone floor. Pitch grabbed an empty torch sconce and the metal snapped free from the time-degraded stone and nearly dissolved in his hands.

"This is what I meant," he showed the others his handful of rust, "not everything in here is affected by the clock, perhaps just living things. This is eons of neglect."

"It looks like a dungeon or a jail," Powder said, nudging one of the fallen doors with the toe of her boot.

Dagger walked into the nearest cell. Against the far wall was a bucket and a low table. Mounted to the wall was a snarl of rusty chain restraints, decorated with several manacles at intervals among the links. The chains were woven through with wires that led to a leaking metal box with a hand-crank.

"Something was imprisoned here," Dagger said and lifted up one of the manacle-studded chains. Rust gave way and a manacle fell to the ground and broke. "Something with a lot of arms."

"Something they had to shock to keep under control," Pitch said, pointing to the leaking device with the hand-crank. "That's an electrostatic generator. Diagram perfect. But like Temker's Clock it's just a theory. A way to produce low current electricity."

"Torture?" Saber said.

Pitch shook his head. "The current wouldn't be high enough for that. But either way, whatever or whoever they had here, time set it free. All it had to do was wait."

"So, where's the jailer?" Dagger mused. "Who was maintaining this place?"

"Nobody has for years, looks like," Pitch said. "Perhaps they're dead."

They left the cell and continued down the corridor. As they passed door after door, they saw that not all were shattered open. Some still had occupants. In one was a glass case filled with some viscous liquid. In others, humans and creatures they did not recognize met The Armory's curiosity with hopeless, dull eyes that suggested, even if the mercenaries had swung wide every door and offered them their freedom, they would still not escape.

At the end of the hall were metal double doors, streaked with rust and buckling bands of steel. The lock had been burned out by something. The bravos opened the doors on screeching hinges onto a hall the same size as the one through which they'd entered.

And heard the sounds of fighting and machinery.

214

"Oh good," Saber said, "some shit that isn't dead."

"Hold," Dagger muttered, and raised up a hand.

The hall held scattered pockets of glowing light with no visible source, as if there had been others but they'd gone out. The floor was crumbling and had given way in some places to large pits, and Dagger edged forward to peer into one of these drops. Below the floor were whirling gears, their teeth gritting together and stuttering as they turned. They whined and slowed down as they got stuck for a moment on some unseen debris, and then cracked free and spun back up. Several spiral staircases at the far end of the hall moved, spinning up into the ceiling perpetually like drills. At the center of the room, four human warriors fought with ten figures carved from some rough-hewn timber, as if the Citadel's firewood pile had come awake with a grievance about the forest it had been stolen from.

The human warriors were panting. Fatigue was slowing them down.

"Go," growled Dagger. "Keep the human ones alive. They may have answers."

The Armor rushed out onto the floor, taking care to avoid the yawning pits. The floor cracked and gave way under Pitch, who would have fallen if Vice hadn't grabbed him by the collar and dragged him clear. Once upright, Pitch hurled a clay sphere at the nearest wooden soldier and the ceramic shattered. The human warrior it had been fighting shied away as the wooden man caught fire, blazing and spinning. The wooden fighter bumped into two of its fellows and sent them tumbling to the ground. Dagger swung her hammer down onto one of the fallen golem's chests, cracking it in half. Vice leaned away from a golem's swing, grabbed the wooden limb and turned, sticking out his foot. As he spun with the golem's momentum, he pulled hard. The wooden soldier was too heavy and clumsy to stop itself, and it tripped over his foot and stumbled past him. Its feet clunked on the stone and it fell into one of the holes where it met the gears beneath with a grinding noise. One of the spiral staircases stuttered, stopped for a moment and then began to revolve again as the golem was ground to sawdust.

The human warriors rallied at The Armory's aid and leapt back into the fight. Two of them tackled one golem and bore it to the ground. They severed its arms and legs, using their swords and axes like pry bars. Saber chopped and danced around another, but while his estoc kept him elegantly out of range, it did little more than chip and glance off the wood. With an angry swear he dropped the slender, thrusting weapon and drew his cleavers. When the golem lunged, he ducked and hacked its legs at the knees, rolling clear as it dropped. It fell and immediately began to crawl after him, but he jumped over it, spun in the air and landed on its back to ride it as he chopped away its head and arms at their joints.

Powder fired from a distance, staggering the wooden men as Dagger, Vice and the other warriors ganged up on the rest and dismembered them, tossing their hewn pieces through the holes in the floor. More gears stopped and choked, jammed with bits of wooden warrior and one of the staircases ceased to spin with a coughing grind.

Saber swore as he picked up his dropped estoc. "Poor baby, look what they did to your point."

"Next time we'll let you cower in the background," Powder said.

"But that's your job," the duelist said, sheathing the weapon.

"Shut up," Powder said and knelt by a wooden golem's torso. She began digging her bullets out of its knotty flesh.

217

The wounded, exhausted human warriors stood panting, and eyed The Armory warily.

"Who are you?" Dagger asked.

"That double dealing bitch," the lead warrior said, still trying to catch his breath. "She told us we had the contract."

"The queen?" Dagger asked.

"Yes."

"That's the way with rulers. Don't take it personally."

"Don't get in our way."

"Or save your asses again?" Dagger said. "Don't worry. Next time we'll just watch you lose a fight to some tree stumps."

One of the other warriors whispered in their leader's ear.

"He wants to know what that is," the man said, pointing at Powder.

"That's a woman," Saber said, "though I can understand your confusion."

Powder whipped a deformed bullet through the air. It hit Saber in the side of the head with a solid sound.

"Ow!" he yelled and rubbed his head. "Don't waste those! We might be in here a while."

"Worth it!" Powder crowed.

"No," the warrior said, "her weapon. The one that shoots fire."

Dagger turned to look at Powder with a raised eyebrow. "You mean the gun?"

The warriors looked at each other. "Where do such strange weapons come from?"

Dagger frowned. "Everywhere. You've never seen a gun?"

"Let me handle this, boss," Pitch said. "Tell me," he asked the warriors, "what year is it?"

"1194. It is always summer in these lands, but it is the Season of Frost in the Kingdom of Karlwhyte."

"I see," Pitch said. "Thank you."

"We do thank you," the warrior said. "but we'll go our separate ways. If we meet again, well, the contract is ours to complete," the warrior saluted with his sword and led his band away through a side doorway.

"Pitch, what was that about?" Dagger asked. "You know what the year is, and it's not 1194."

"The exact answer doesn't matter much anyway," Pitch said. "The Karlwhyte Empire's ruler was idiot who forced his people to use a calendar that began with the day of his coronation."

"Where's Karlwhyte," Saber asked, "I've never heard of it."

"That's because it's barely a footnote in history," Pitch said. "Karlwhyte fell two hundred years ago."

# — CHAPTER 9 —

## A 12 out of 10 on the
## weird-shit-o-meter.

They stood for several moments in the wake of Pitch's words.

"That's why he's never seen a gun," Saber said. "They hadn't been invented yet."

"Then..." Powder said.

"They could be among the first hired to destroy the Citadel," Pitch answered. "If not the first."

"Temker's Clock?" Dagger asked and Pitch nodded.

"The Citadel has removed itself from time," Vice said. "Only the gods are capable of such artifice."

"Apparently not," Pitch said.

"Alchemist," Vice said with a rare smirk, "can you say for certain this place is not the work of gods?"

"No," Pitch said, looking like he was trying to swallow a razor blade, "I can't. I also can't explain why we seemed to be speaking the same language as a two-hundred-year-old kingdom."

Dagger turned to regard the revolving staircases and Powder moved up beside her.

"Up or down, Captain?" Powder asked as she walked over to one of the constantly drilling spirals. The staircases, now that she was close to them, weren't actually moving up and down but perpetually curling their way up into the ceiling. "Never mind, Captain. Left or right look like the only options."

"Unless we want to follow those guys," Saber said, thumbing at the doorway into which the four warriors had disappeared.

"They're not the job," Dagger said. "Vice?"

"Yes?" The monk was standing off to the side, staring at nothing with a troubled expression. Of all of them, he seemed the least fascinated with their surroundings.

"Can the Vigil's servants move us through time?"

"Possibly."

"Can you ask?"

"I have been trying to reach them."

"And?"

Vice shook his head.

"What are you orders, Captain?" Powder asked.

"Forward. Always forward. We have a job to do."

"Wait," Saber said, "what if we just work our way back to first room? The queen said agents of the Citadel were able to go in and out. There must be another way back. Powder can bomb the clock thing into oblivion. Boom. Done."

Pitch thought about it. "You know, Saber, that's not a bad idea. One problem."

"Of course there is," the swordsman muttered.

"We can't be sure exactly how long we've been here. If we simply destroy the clock, we might find ourselves only minutes from when we left, or it could be decades. Centuries, even. We could be stranded in a time hundreds of years past our own."

"Pitch," Dagger said, "do you have any paper?"

"Of course," Pitch said, producing a notebook and charcoal pencil.

"Start charting our way through here, best you can."

Pitch took a moment, nodded, and sketched their path through the Citadel thus far. As maps went, it looked more like a stack of river stones. He shook his head.

"Is that going to be any use?" Saber asked.

"Probably not," Pitch said. "But we might be able to avoid where we've already been."

The Armory moved to the revolving staircase near Powder, stepped aboard, and rode its slow revolutions up, up, up into the next floor of the Citadel of Stairs.

They emerged under a dark sky filled with stars.

"You weren't kidding about the time thing," Saber said. "It was noon an hour ago."

"This is bullshit," Powder said. "That's not how stairs or buildings work. It's not how reality works, for fuck's sake."

"Maybe we're on the roof?" Saber suggested hopefully.

"Definitely not," Dagger said, pointing first at the ground and then at the sky.

They stood on one of hundreds of overlapping, uneven steel platforms that had been riveted haphazardly together with treacherous gaps between as if they'd been installed as the workers went. The Armory's steps were muted on the metal. The very air around them seemed to swallow sound. Above them was an endless black expanse decorated with glinting stars, and the steel flooring stretched ahead, longer than it was wide. It ended to either side perhaps a hundred feet in both directions. Behind them, where the staircase should have been, was more of the same. The spiraling stairs, even the opening they'd entered through, were gone.

Pitch was looking up at the black sky. "These aren't our stars," he said finally.

"What do you mean, our stars?" Dagger asked, "Stars are stars."

"No. I've never seen these constellations," Pitch said and pulled a loose rivet out of the floor. He walked to the edge of the platform and hurled the bit of steel. It flew for a moment, then paused with a hiccup, before continuing to drift at a much slower pace until it was out of sight.

Pitch peered down over the edge and grunted with surprise.

"You'd all better have a look at this," he said.

Dagger knelt near him. "Well, that's interesting."

The plates under their feet were riveted to bones.

They looked over the edge at the curve of a pale rib, big as a building. The far end of its curve vanished from sight into star-filled darkness. In one direction, the ribs ticked off the distance toward a broken stump of an arm and then a skull, face down and the size of a fortress. In the other, a pelvis. Below the bones, as above, more blackness yawned, dotted with bright, winking pinpricks.

They were on the back of a titan, interred in the sky.

Saber rubbed the back of his neck. "We're going to lose our fucking minds in here."

Powder patted his shoulder.

"Another question occurs," Pitch mused with a sly grin.

"Please don't," Saber said a bit plaintively.

"Is the skeleton really that big? Or have we shrunk?"

"Oh, fuck you," Saber said and stepped back from the edge. Pitch chuckled under his breath.

"There's something ahead," Dagger said, squinting in the direction of the skull. "Maybe it's another door."

"I don't think so," Powder said, her telescope at her eye, "unless doors move."

"Of course, doors can move here," Saber said. "This place follows the rules even less than we do."

They picked their way along, eyes firmly on the plates. Staring anywhere else, like into the winking, diamond-studded expanse of the sky, caused a kind of vertigo, as if one could fall up and into forever. The plates were rusty and pitted, like they'd been stolen from someplace that had rain and wind.

"Blood," Vice noted and pointed down. Under their boots were dark streaks.

"Something was dragged across this," Pitch said. He knelt and rubbed a finger against the stain. "It's relatively fresh."

"And heading in the same direction as we are," Dagger said.

As they neared the distant shadow that was not a door, it took shape in the starry half-light. Something — it looked like a very tall man in a cloak — was moving busily around a low structure. Chains dragged behind the figure. Dagger gestured The Armory to a halt.

Whatever the figure was, it hadn't noticed them yet. But the structure was clearly visible: It was an arranged pile of corpses, their armored parts interlinked in patterns. Limbs seemed to form language, though not any that could be spoken. Heads were arranged in trinities, balanced upon tripods of legs bound together by wire, string and intestines. One of the steel plates had been ripped free from the floor and driven horizontally into the mass embrace of the dead.

It looked like an altar.

The figure tending it turned its cloaked head to regard them. It did not behave as if threatened. It bound a severed arm and hand missing most of its fingers into place, stepped back to gaze critically at its work, and then turned again to face The Armory, its face still hidden. The cloak was a patchwork of skin and cloth, stitched together with stolen sinew. It lifted something to the shadow of its hood.

"Have you come to add to my work?" it said in the light voice of a young male human. Its tone was cheery, friendly and unmarred. "Welcome. Welcome."

"Who are you?" Dagger asked.

"You could not speak my name even if I told it to you, just as I could not speak yours before I made my translator. It was the same as these primitive soldiers. They babbled and mistook my silence for reticence, for hostility. They believed the height of their knowledge to be the height of all knowledge, that they were superior. Fools. You may call me the Craftsman, if you'd like, though that too is not quite accurate. You could think of me as a traveler, if the distances I have crossed could be conceived of by your minds."

Dagger nodded. "And what are you doing?"

"Trying to make a phone call," the craftsman said. Below its cloak, it seemed as if it had more arms or legs hidden away. It kicked a length of chain out of its way. The end of the chain had a broken steel base plate that looked like it had been twisted free of something.

"I think we found that escaped prisoner," Pitch whispered to Dagger, but she held up a hand for him to be quiet.

"A what?" Dagger asked the Craftsman.

"Phone call," the Craftsman said. "A word from your world, yes? A means of communication. Do you not know it?"

"Afraid not," Dagger said.

"Hmm," said the Craftsman, "I am forced to work with the memory of language I learned from the medium of my work," it gestured to the pile of arranged corpse parts, "perhaps an older word? Very well, though it will be less accurate. I am trying to send a telegraph."

Dagger shook her head.

"Still no? Judging by your more primitive appearance, an even older word would be better..." the cloaked figure paused a moment. "Ah, I am trying to send a letter."

"With corpses?" Dagger asked.

"How else?" The Craftsman said.

"Is this an altar to your god," Vice asked, stepping forward.

The figure's hood nodded. "God. Yes. This word. My medium used it as well, though with less reverence. In fact, all of my medium used it when they still walked and made the noises I now make with my device. This I learned in those moments before: You believe you are aided by beings more powerful than yourselves, yes? A strange idea."

"Oh, you have no idea," Saber said and nudged Vice playfully. The monk looked like he was about to swat Saber off the platform like the screw Pitch had thrown. The duelist wisely sidled out of range.

The Craftsman continued as if nobody but it had spoken.

"One of my medium called for one named Jesus Christ. Another for Allah. One begged for something called Basic Human Decency. Do you know any of these gods?"

"No," Dagger said.

"There were others," the Craftsman said. "In the tower before I escaped. They screamed their questions. I arrived disoriented, and so they were able to capture me. They kept me chained to a wall and tortured me with their nascent understanding of pain. Electricity! Can you imagine? Pumped by hand. It was almost amusing. So primitive they were, in method and question. At least my medium here, these who have been reconfigured, they were more advanced. Their weapons hurt."

The Craftsman lowered its hand and walked around the altar, chains dragging behind. It reached out to adjust and move the pieces and tighten twines of wire and gut. It tried to force the limp parts to balance differently. The patterns in the pile shifted as it did, and the jointed parts formed new, strange glyphs. As it did, the edge of the cloak slipped a little. The Craftsman looked as if it was wearing armor or made of armor. Its fingers were like needles of glass.

231

"It is frustrating," the creature said. "Your kind are too soft for me to work with properly. I am too sharp. I cut when I touch. My kind. My kind would be better. We hold our integrity after cessation. If I could work with such, I would already have made contact. I would already be going home."

"Sorry to hear that," Dagger said. "Have you a seen a way out of here?"

"There is a door at the far end," the Craftsman said absently as it continued to tinker. "Near one of the feet. The left. Left is the word my device suggests I use. Feet. Door. Your language takes an eternity to convey even a single idea. They tortured me not with pain, as they believed, but with wasted time. Boredom."

"Boredom's a bitch alright," Dagger said. "Thanks for the directions. We'll just be on our way. Good luck getting home."

"No," the Craftsman said. "Stay. Help me send my letter."

"Not that way," Dagger said, gesturing to the pile with her hammer.

The Craftsman stood to its full height and turned to The Armory. "No? No. I see. You will fight. A concept that my medium also believed in. Conflict. One suggested we would go to war.

232

What is war? Is it also one of your powerful helpers? One of your gods?"

"Yes," Dagger said, "one we know well."

"You are not agitated. You are calm," the Craftsman said. "Why is this? My mediums were afraid. They made loud noises. They made threats in the moments before they joined my work. They did not converse as we do now. You do not behave as they did. Why?"

"Experience," Dagger said.

"And chemistry," Pitch said.

"Yes. Chemistry..." The Craftsman almost seemed to taste the word. "A framework of reason pressed upon the chaos of the world to give it shape, meaning, to help one understand. Yes. A primitive science."

"Wait," Powder said, and stepped around Dagger.

The gunner took something from her bag and approached the Craftsman, who towered over her. "This will let you signal somebody far away. If it works, will you let us pass without joining your work?"

"Perhaps," the Craftsman said, leaning down to peer at the cylindrical object in her hand. "How does it function?"

"It uses light."

"Light. That is clever. I have not tried light. There is not much light here."

"Just from the stars," Powder said.

"Stars, you call them," the creature said. "You see them as just lights, but they are distant worlds. How does your device work?"

"I have to light it first. With fire."

"Fire?" the Craftsman said.

"It's a way that we make light and warmth."

"Yes. My medium was very warm once. I could feel them as I could feel you. You are also warm. Your world must be very cold."

"Sometimes," Powder said and gestured for the Craftsman to take what she held. It reached out one segmented arm. This one ended in a bundle of delicate little appendages of different shapes, sizes, and perhaps purposes. Powder placed what she held in it — a thin, steel tube with a short fuse dangling from it. Powder took out her striker and flicked it, sparks dancing against the end of the fuse until it caught. The Craftsman flinched.

"So bright," it said. "It has been a long time since I have seen something so bright." Its hood leaned down to the hissing fuse.

"Yeah," Powder said, stepping back slowly, "very bright."

The fuse reached the metal tube. Powder leapt back and covered her eyes with one arm.

"Why are you —" the Craftsman said but was cut off when the device burst into a thousand sudden sunrises. The creature reared back, covering its cowl with one arm. The hand that held the flare was scorched black and crispy, and the device it spoke through fell to the ground.

Powder, eyes still shut and sighting by ear, dropped her hands and popped up her scatterguns. She cut loose with both into what might have been Craftsman's chest. The Craftsman flexed the body within the cloak but made no sound. Dagger rushed up behind her and yanked Powder back out of reach of the Craftsman's flailing arms as several more burst from its cloak. She swung her hammer low and crushed what Dagger hoped was a leg.

The blow ripped away the cloak.

The Craftsman was a collection of limbs and razors with no torso, almost like a long, glass sea urchin. The Craftsman's face — if that's what it was — was a blank ovoid somewhere near the top of its various spindles, blank except for dozens of tiny holes. It spread its limbs and gestured at The Armory in a silent battle cry.

Dagger backed away and the rest of The Armory formed up around her.

They circled the creature. The Craftsman spun its sharp limbs, and the chains attached to them flailed dangerously. The only sound it made was the skittering of sharpness upon metal.

Pitch heaved a jar, and the Craftsman smashed it from the air, but the acid inside splashed its limbs and ate several down to nubs. The Craftsman hunched and tucked the smoking, crippled appendages close. Other limbs took their place.

Vice and Saber moved in as a pair. The monk caught scalpeled strikes upon his gauntlets, picking up a dozen razor cuts as he trapped limb after limb and smashed them between his fists. Saber fared a little better, his entire craft was based on moving between slim, sharp things — but even he was bleeding in several places as he tried over and over to find a soft target for his thrusts. There seemed to be nothing of the Craftsman but limbs, and its eyeless head towered out of the duelist's reach.

When neither fighter could finish the Craftsman, they coordinated their attacks, occupying its limbs and dividing its attention. Dagger rushed between them, getting stabbed twice as she swung her hammer where the Craftsman's limbs met. She let the weight of her hammer carry her forward with total abandon, and at the last second let go. Her weapon struck the center of the Craftsman with a sound like cracking ice and pinned the creature to the metal floor. The Craftsman lay flailing as it tried to get out from under the heavy steel.

Saber looked down at the struggling creature in shock.

"It's fast and big," Dagger said, "but it's got almost no weight of its own. No mass."

"One side, Captain," Powder said, and aimed at the Craftsman's pocked face with a pistol. The gun barked, and the creature's head caved in along one side. The Craftsman shook and went still, silver ichor pouring from the wound.

Dagger cautiously lifted her hammer off the creature. It did not stir.

Saber grimaced and picked up the device through which the Craftsman had been speaking. "It's kinda wet," he said. "What's this made out of, anyway?"

"Let me see it," Pitch said, taking the contraption from Saber, who wiped his hand on his thigh. Pitch turned the device over and over in his hands. It was slightly ovoid and organic-looking, hollowed out with a hole at both ends. Stretched over one was a veil of strings or fringe. Pitch peered at them. "Interesting."

"What is it, Pitch?" Dagger asked.

"A human femur," Pitch said, knocking on the device gently with one knuckle. "A thigh bone. The marrow's been scraped out." He stroked the damp fringe on one end with his index finger. "And these are vocal chords," he gestured to the pile of bodies. "Several sets. Probably taken from the bodies. To allow it to speak, I would guess, though I have no idea how."

Saber swore. "He could make a bugle out of a neck, but couldn't find a way out of here?"

"I'd argue the "he" designation," Pitch said, "but, yes."

"Then we're fucked," Saber said wryly.

"It never said it couldn't get out of here," Powder countered. "It said it wanted to contact someone." She examined the altar. The metal plate that formed a sort of shelf had a human head on it. Powder picked up a weapon discarded near the pile: It was shaped like a rifle, but made of a light material she'd never seen. The helmets on the disembodied human heads that formed the base of the altar had glass visors and were made of the same light material as the weapon.

"I've never seen a gun like this before," Powder said, and pulled a lever around the gun's trigger. A glass tube popped out of the side and skittered away, lost forever between gaps in the metal floor. All around The Armory, space and stars revolved. There was not even wind to disturb the quiet and their voices all felt too loud even though the very air seemed to swallow any spoken word. Powder turned away, aimed into the starry blackness, and pulled the trigger. A beam shot from the end without sound or even a hint of recoil. She racked the lever and another tube popped out of the side.

"Oh, I'm keeping this," she muttered.

"You're going to trust your life to an untested tool?" Dagger asked.

Powder aimed at a steel plate a few feet away and pulled the trigger again. The beam burned a smoking hole in the sheet of steel. They all stared at it in shock.

Saber shook his head. "They had weapons like that, and this thing killed them?"

Vice grunted and crossed his arms. "You heard it speak. They panicked. They were not ready. They were not warriors." His tone held notes of both judgment and sympathy.

"They were armed," Saber argued. "They had armor."

"And still," the monk said with a sweeping gesture, "here they lie. In pieces."

"Perhaps they were explorers," Pitch ventured. "Maybe these suits were for something other than fighting."

"Like what?" Saber asked.

"Warmth? Who knows," the alchemist said.

"Does it matter?" Dagger asked, cutting through the debate. "We're not here to solve the mystery of the corpse pile. We have to move on. It said there was a door ahead. Powder, leave that thing here, I'm not having you get run through when it clicks on empty."

Powder sighed and laid down the strange weapon. "You're no fun, Captain."

Saber removed the human head from the altar and put it on the ground, then went to the body of the Craftsman. Kneeling, he used a cleaver to sever the ovoid head. He picked it up, dripping silver across the ground, and placed it on the altar.

"Why did you do that?" Pitch asked.

"Don't know," the duelist said, "seems poetic. Didn't it say if it could use its own kind, it would have already made contact?"

"Your leaps of reason shock me, Saber," Pitch said. "It's like you do it without thinking."

"You have your science. I have instinct."

They moved down the wide expanse of steel plates to the place where it forked along the skeleton's left leg. At the end was a faint shimmer in the air. As they neared it, Powder looked behind them.

"Captain," Powder said in a tense voice.

Something new had appeared in the starry void — a negative blackness that blotted out the faint light where it sat. It nearly filled the sky and was made of sharp angles, some of which glittered back at the bouncing starlight.

"What the fuck is that?" Saber asked.

"It could almost be a ship," Pitch said, "but I don't see any sails."

The shadowy void seemed to grow. It was several times larger than the place they stood.

"Or if there was even wind out here," Powder noted.

"Time to go," Dagger said, and grabbed the duelist by the collar. "I think your little leap of reason worked a little too well."

241

"That happens sometimes," Saber said.

An even greater blackness opened in the side of the ship like a doorway or a hatch.

"Through the door! Now!" Dagger grated, shoving her crew one at a time through the shimmering portal until only she was left on the metal-plated skeleton in the emptiness of benighted space. She looked a moment or two longer at the vast sky ship.

"Go then," Dagger muttered to it. "Collect your dead."

She went through the door.

# — CHAPTER 10 —

## Among abandoned mechanisms.

The Armory stood again on familiar stone, surrounded by walls of familiar rules lit by torches in iron sconces burning with familiar fire. Behind them the black door onto space still yawned. In the distance tall, narrow shadows were crossing the uneven steel to the altar and the dead Craftsman.

"Seal it," Dagger ordered, and grabbed one side of the heavy double doors. Vice helped her, and the rest of The Armory grabbed the other door, straining and shoving until the heavy, iron-banded wood met in the middle and closed away the stars. Dagger dropped the crossbar in place and made a sound that might have been a sigh.

"We have to get out of here, boss," Powder said, her voice shook.

"Pitch," Dagger said. "Might be time for another dose."

Pitch produced the same vial from earlier and freshened it with a pinch from one of his pouches. "We'd better be quick about it, though. We don't have much more of this. After that we'll have to rely on our will. Which is a problem."

Dagger stared at him. "Why?"

Pitch shook the vial to activate it as he spoke. "We've been experiencing this place for however long now. The drugs just keep the worst of the tension at bay, but our bodies are still aware of and affected by it. When they wear off, there may be a cumulative effect." He indicated the vial. "We are essentially borrowing sanity."

"Borrowing sanity," Saber said, snorting hard, "I like that."

At the far side of the room was a brass cage with an open door. There was no other way out of the room. The cage was paneled in gleaming, polished wood and red velvet, and there was a brass plaque covered in buttons on one side.

"Maybe it's bigger in there than it looks?" Powder asked.

Dagger grunted and led them inside the cage. It was not bigger than it looked.

And the gate shut with a cheerful ding.

"Oh, kiss my ass," Saber muttered.

Dagger pushed a button and the brass cage shot straight up. As their stomachs hit their boots, wind that smelled of mold, dust and machine grease rushed around them. They clutched the walls for seconds that stretched on far too long, and then the cage halted with a deafening screech. The Armory bounced off the walls and each other like marbles in a jar.

"They should call this the Citadel of Fuck You," Powder said, crawling out from under Vice with difficulty.

"It is starting to feel a bit personal," Pitch said as he checked his rig for broken vials.

Dagger went to the panel and pushed button after button. Each time some unseen mechanism whined, and the cage hummed with repressed effort. Saber looked up.

"Vice," he said, "give me a boost."

The monk made a stirrup of his hands and lifted Saber to the ceiling. The duelist drew a stout knife and pried at a panel. It fell open with a bang and a shower of dust. Coughing, Saber grabbed the edge and hauled himself up and out.

"I think we can climb," he called down. "There are cables. This cage must be lifted by pulleys somewhere. But the shaftway leads up."

"You assume," Pitch said, "for all we know that isn't up at all. Could be down. Or sideways."

Saber poked his head back through the panel. "Can you climb and ponder the nature of reality? Or you want to wait there until you grow moss on your balls?"

"You're usually the one who ends up with something growing on his balls, Saber," the alchemist said.

"And when that happens, do I whine about how bad your medicine tastes?"

"Yes."

"Just give me your hand."

Dagger boosted up Pitch and Powder, who then reached their hands down for Vice. Finally, Dagger jumped up and grabbed the edge of the hatch and hauled herself out.

They were in a dark shaft that stretched above them to what might as well have been eternity. Several cables attached to a winch on the roof of the cage thrummed with its weight as they shuffled around. Dagger grabbed hold of one, braced herself on another, and climbed. Vice went next, then Pitch, while Saber and Powder brought up the rear.

They climbed and climbed. After a time, Pitch swigged desperately from a vial and paused, gasping as he held himself in place.

"Pitch?" Dagger asked.

"Don't mind me, boss. Just a little something extra. Not built for this sort of work."

"We have you, alchemist," Vice said. "You will not fall."

Vice and Dagger climbed down next to Pitch, and each wrapped one arm around the panting, exhausted scholar. Powder and Saber climbed up until his feet rested on their shoulders. They twined their limbs around the cables and rested as best they could. Pitch sagged with relief and let them carry his weight.

"I'm sorry, boss," Pitch said.

"Never mind that," Dagger said. "If we all pulled the same kind of weight, there wouldn't need to be five of us. How many times have you kept us going?"

Pitch nodded and fell silent, but Dagger could see his jaw clenching with frustration. "Saber, Powder," she said, "climb around us.

See if there's a way out up there. Vice and I have Pitch."

"Yes, Captain," Powder said.

The sharpshooter and the duelist reached for another cable and climbed for dozens of more feet, their hands shaking.

"Wait," Powder said, wrapped her body around the cable, and took a foot-long, fat cord from her pocket and sparked it alight. Warm, red fire dashed itself against the dark walls of the shaftway. She held the other end in her teeth as they climbed on. Saber squinted and winced as sparks fell from the makeshift flare and landed on his back and shoulders.

After several more agonizing feet, Powder stopped.

"Think I found it."

Saber grabbed onto another cable and climbed up next to Powder. In front of them was the suggestion of a doorway with a narrow sill. A golden seam ran down its center. There was light on the other side.

"Help me with this," Powder said.

With Powder's help, Saber stepped across to the sill, thrust a knife into the seam and levered it open enough for them to slip through.

They were in a sparsely lit room full of tables separated from each other by low walls. The air was filled with the funk of moldering paper, and somewhere water was dripping. The only light came from big squares on the ceiling, many of which had gone dark.

Powder went around one of the low walls and beneath the table, she found a coiled stack of strange black rope. One end led to a machine with a blank, glass face and the other vanished through a hole in the floor. With her knife she sawed both ends of the cables free and dragged their length in until she had a few dozen feet wrapped around her arm.

"What is it?" Saber asked.

"Some kind of rope?" she suggested. It was coated with something, but inside was a tight bundle of metal filament. "There's wires inside. It was a bitch to cut."

"Will it hold him?" Saber asked.

"Give it a hard tug."

They grunted as they wrenched the black rope between them. It didn't even stretch.

"Good enough," Saber said.

They secured one end of the strange rope to a handy steel ring inside the shaftway and dropped the other down into the darkness.

Powder looked down into the shaft, took a deep breath and let it out slowly.

"I'll go," Saber said and took the burning cord from her.

"Are you sure?"

"I'm good," the duelist said, his mouth set tight. Powder could see his hands were still shaking.

"Saber?"

"Yeah?"

"Don't fall."

"Powder," Saber said with a tired grin. "I'm touched."

"Close as you'll ever get to me touching you."

"Oh, I don't know," Saber said as he clamped the cord between his teeth, "thish hash been in your moush. Itsh shtill wed."

"Asshole," Powder chuckled as the duelist took hold of one of the steel cables and stepped out into the shaftway, sliding down the cable in bursts until the lumpy shadows of the rest of The Armory were in view.

"Saber?" Dagger grunted.

Saber took the burning cord out of his teeth. "We found a way out. It's just a few more feet. Use this to secure Pitch," he said, gesturing to the black rope they'd tossed down into the darkness.

Dagger gave the alchemist a worried look. "We'll climb first and pull you up after.

"I'm fine," Pitch said, his face twitching and his jaw sawing back and forth.

"What did you take?" Saber asked him. Even in the dim light of the flare, Pitch was a white as a sheet.

"Too much," the alchemist said. "Heart's pounding. I'll need to rest once we get up there, but I'll get up there."

"Stout fellow," Saber said, as he and Dagger wrapped the thin, black rope around Pitch's waist a few times and then tied it off. Dagger gave the rope a hard yank while Pitch still had hold of the steel cable, but it felt sound.

"Let go, Pitch," Dagger said.

The alchemist took a deep breath and unclenched himself from the cable. He dangled, his legs kicking. "This is undignified."

"A bit," Saber said. "You look like bait on a hook."

Pitch looked down into the shaftway as if there might be a giant fish eyeing his twitching legs with interest. "Saber?" he muttered.

251

"Yeah, Pitch," the duelist replied. "I know. I'm an asshole."

Dagger and Vice climbed up with a huffing Saber leading the way. At the doorway, Powder helped them to cross into the strange new room. Dagger and Vice then turned and grabbed hold of the black rope, pulling the dangling Pitch up hand-over-hand and hauling him across the threshold.

"This is not a place of our world," Vice said, looking around the room. He went to one of the tables and picked up a device covered in buttons. Each had a letter of some alphabet on it. "Pitch, do you know these letters?"

But Pitch was sitting down with his back against a wall, his breath coming in small gasps. Dagger held up a hand to Vice and the monk fell silent.

"Pitch," Dagger asked, "you going to be alright?"

"I... just... need... a minute," he fumbled in his clothes for some vial or jar or packet, but Dagger knelt down and covered his hand with hers, stopping his search. He looked up at her with a question on his drawn face.

"Just take your time," she said softly. Then she turned to the others. "We could all use a moment. Saber, Vice, Powder, clear this place. Then we'll rest."

They nodded and fanned out through the room, their gazes coasting across the various objects of curiosity as they listened for footsteps and kept an eye out for fast-moving threats. When they found nothing but dust and strangeness, they returned, and there The Armory sat in the silence.

It was just an hour of calm. But it felt like a banquet.

***

After a while, Pitch nodded. "I'm ready. My heart rate's slowed down. Show me what you found, Vice."

Dagger nodded and helped him to his feet as the others stood and Vice brought over the strange device with its buttons and letters. Pitch took and it and turned it over in his hands.

He shook his head. "I don't even know what it's made out of. It's not wood or metal. Too light."

One of the glowing rectangles on the ceiling flickered like a firefly and went dead. A layer of dust covered everything, and the floor was carpeted in a rough gray material. They walked between the cubes. Each was identically furnished: a table on which rested a box with a dark glass face, and a flat device with letter-adorned buttons.

At the end of the row of cubicles, they found room with a much larger, long table. Chairs were arranged around it at intervals, each empty but for the dust.

"What is all this shit made out of?" Powder nodded, rapping on the table with one knuckle.

Dagger was staring at the far end of the room. "Look," she said and went over to a large white rectangle propped on an easel. It was covered in writing and diagrams, all rendered in bright red. Pitch leaned close. Symbols spiraled their way up the sides in a language he couldn't speak and a system of calculation he didn't recognize, but the pictures were clear.

"It's the Citadel," he said. "Look. Look at how the design repeats and overlaps."

Four towers were drawn on the white surface, arranged into floors and linked boxes. Each tower's layout was slightly different, but the outside structure was the same. Scrawled notes crept up and down, with arrows pointing to different rooms inside the diagrams.

"What does it mean?" Dagger asked.

"This is a home of the gods," Vice said. "The ones who built the tower. We are staring at the plans of celestial entities."

"I'd argue the gods part," Pitch said.

"Pitch," Vice growled, "your stubborn refusal to —"

"No," Pitch interrupted. "Not because it's not possible. Obviously, gods are possible. But this many diagrams... I don't think this is about planning."

"What else could it be?" Vice countered.

"I'm not arguing with your faith, Vice. But have you ever seen the Vigil's servants write out notes or plans?"

"No," the monk admitted.

"No. Exactly. Gods don't plan. They think, and it becomes so. This is study. Analysis. You don't take notes because you already understand something. You take them because you are trying to. See these?"

He gestured at a row of symbols. "I think these are numbers. See the way these symbols repeat many times but in different configurations? And these others are must letters, there's more variation in the characters."

Dagger swept her hand through the dust on the table and looked at the gray furring on her palm. "Whatever it was, they gave up a long time ago."

"It does look that way," Pitch said.

"Do these notes indicate any direction or a kind of map, do you think?" she asked.

Pitch shook his head. "They're too crude. Whoever made them knew enough that they didn't need an exact representation of the tower. Anyway, I can't understand the language. But they suggest that the Citadel has a definite verticality."

"So?" she said. "It's a tower. Up is the only direction that matters."

Pitch smiled wryly. "You make that sound like a small thing, Dagger. We guessed we had to keep going up. But now we know that as long as we go up when a direction presents itself, we should eventually reach the top."

"Assuming what we want is at the top," Dagger said.

Pitch nodded. "That is a blind spot."

"Any indication from the drawings how far we have to go?"

"None at all, boss."

Dagger swore under her breath. "Okay. Let's see what else these scholars were hiding."

The Armory left the room and continued along the low hall. In a tiny antechamber they found a vat and several dirty clay cups. Saber gave one a sniff and laughed.

"What?" Pitch asked.

"Coffee," Saber said. "They were drinking coffee." He opened the vat and peered the inside. "Very, very old coffee."

"Humans then," Dagger mused. "Pitch, what do you make of that?"

"Only a little more than I can make of that," he said, pointing to a framed picture on the wall. The image was of a kitten fighting to cling to a branch. "The letters are the same as on the devices on the tables with all the buttons. And the notes in the meeting room."

"What's the kitten supposed to signify?" Dagger asked.

"Perhaps it is a metaphor?" Vice suggested. "A reminder to hold on no matter what."

"Come look at this," Powder called from outside the room. The Armory followed the sound of her voice to the other end of the hall. They found her staring at a rip in the fabric of reality with glittering, shifting edges that flashed shades of purple and yellow. Through it was another world with a set of gradual stairs that headed down from the rip toward a circular platform lined with columns. Their tops vanished into the sky, and their bottoms fell away into an unfathomable darkness. The sky boiled with fast, dirty gray clouds, and in the distance something massive and hidden disturbed them with its passing.

Powder took out her telescope and trained it on the platform. Then she passed the glass around. On the platform was a figure sitting in a dejected hunch. Thrust into the stone by its side was a greatsword.

"The stairs head down," Dagger noted. "Pitch, you said we should always go up."

"It's just a theory," Pitch said "In reality we can't count on perceived directions as being accurate. We've already seen how little sense this place makes. And I don't see another way out of here."

Dagger grunted. "I'll go first. Wait a moment, then follow."

She stepped through the rip and onto the stairs. When she glanced back, the portal and the room behind were gone. Behind her the stairs continued up for an uncountable distance and disappeared into the rushing clouds.

Dagger grunted in mild surprise. "Well, fuck."

With only two options, Dagger walked down the stairs to the columned platform. As she got closer, she realized it could only be one thing: an arena.

Perhaps this waiting warrior could offer directions.

***

Back in the room, The Armory watched as Dagger glanced at them once, but her eyes were distant as if she was looking beyond them. Then she turned and descended the stairs.

"Going next," Saber said, and moved to walk through the cosmic rip in the wall. Instead, he smacked into what felt like hard air. The view was a moving painting for all that he could step into it. He struck at it with his sword, but the weapon bounced off.

"She's not waiting," Pitch said tensely. They all shouted for Dagger, but she didn't seem to hear them.

"She has seen something, but it is not us," Vice rumbled.

"We have to get to her," Powder said.

"Well," Pitch muttered tapping at the see-through, solid wall, "we're not getting through this way.

They watched helplessly as Dagger descended the stairs, ever closer to the hunched figure in the arena that rose and drew the greatsword from the stone. Its tip had a cruel barb.

Then the view through the rip blurred, faded briefly to a wall like all the others in the room, and then changed to show a ruined cityscape snarled with staircases. Rows and tilts of steps wrapped and twisted around each other, coiling about the buildings at impossible angles and in directions no living being could logically, or safely, walk.

"My turn," Vice said, stepping forward.

"Hang on a second, Vice," Pitch said.

"A test in every moment," Vice intoned.

"No," Pitch grated. "What's that even mean? Just wait a minute, you fucking lunatic!"

But Vice went through the rip and the alchemist's lunge failed to reach him. Pitch wasn't even sure he'd have been able to drag the monk so much as an inch.

"Vice, you asshole!" Pitch yelled as he slammed against the now obdurate view and tried to push through. Saber and Powder grabbed him and pulled him back. They watched as Vice, just like Dagger, turned to look back without seeing them.

Vice looked out onto the stair-snarled city, its buildings rotting under the weight of time. There was no path behind him. No strange room. No Armory. Vice stood under a sky made of stairs. The platform that held him was one of many, he could see them out there suspended among the steps. He breathed deeply of musty air that held not one hint of a living smell.

"A labyrinth within another," he said.

He sat down, crossed his legs and closed his eyes. He clasped his hands beneath his chin and wound his fingers together in shifting patterns until he found the one he wanted. The metal on his hands rasped. The sound was a comfort.

Any sound louder than his heartbeat was a comfort.

***

Pitch, Powder and Saber looked at each other and at Vice, watching helplessly as the rip in the wall shifted again and Vice disappeared.

"I don't care what we see next. Don't you two fucking go anywhere," the alchemist said from between clenched teeth.

"We're here, Pitch," Saber said. "We won't."

"Can you feel them?" Powder asked.

"It's faint," the duelist said, "but the tickle's there."

"The tickle?" She asked.

"That's what I call it."

"You would," Powder said.

"What do you call it?"

"The tug."

"And that's better?!"

Pitch rounded on the duelist and the gunhand. "Can you two stop fucking bantering for five seconds?"

They watched the wall, waiting for the next scene.

# DAGGER

## Yeah, how 'bout no?

There was no sound but the wind that rushed around Dagger as she descended the railless steps. It butted at her and tricked around her ankles like a cat, and so she walked as slowly and heavily as she could. Somewhere behind her was her crew, trapped in another aspect of the Citadel.

Alone.

Bereft.

She had to get back to them. But first...

The sky was a boil of clouds resting on the giant stone pillars that seemed to be the entirety of the landscape. As she studied them, one of the distant monoliths gave up its structure to time's force. It fell, shuddering and dissolving into a black expanse so far below she couldn't hear it hit the bottom, if there even was one.

She walked the last few steps to the edge of the arena and stepped between two of the columns. Stairs led down to a flat area and the seated figure she'd seen was standing now, with its barbed greatsword in both hands. Dagger stopped.

"You've returned," the warrior rumbled in two voices, "it has been so long."

"You know me?"

"I know conflict. It is all," said the figure. "It rests slumbering in the heart of every visitor to this circle. I have waited and waited. For you. And here you are. Again."

"Uh huh," Dagger muttered. "I'll ask again. We've met before?"

"I have met you a thousand thousand times."

"And what happened?"

"Fallen. All fall. You will fall again."

"No," Dagger said.

"No?"

Dagger sighed impatiently. "I don't have time for this."

"Time is all you have. We are the recipients of a squandered wealth of ages, of eons."

"Coin or time, if there's nothing to do with them, they're worthless," Dagger said.

"A contemplative fighter," the warrior said. "A rarity."

Dagger peered around the warrior to the other side of the arena. There was another set of stairs that led up and vanished behind a column and a cracked obelisk of black stone. She wondered if the warrior was a god or just the child of one.

"Are you a giant?" she asked.

"Are you a gnome?"

"Just let me pass. I'm not here to fight. I need to get back to my crew."

"But you have come to the arena."

"Not by choice."

"Choice," the figure snorted. "Choice is a dream we never wake from, a single step in a staircase we cannot fully see until we have finished walking it."

"You sound like somebody I know," Dagger said, wishing Vice was here to distract this overgrown, stabby poet so she could sneak behind him and cave in his skull.

"Is he also a wise man?"

"He might be," she replied. "He talks like you. Like he's unwinding a ball of yarn."

"Come, warrior. Fellow contemplator. Fight. Spend what's left of your coin of time. We can be, for some moments, as two reformed misers tossing their gold into the ocean. Let us stretch a moment into a lifetime."

"You've clearly had too much time to think," Dagger muttered, and wondered how much of any of it was real, and how much the Citadel's creation. Was she even still inside its walls? Or had it opened a door into an ending world? Could she reach those distant places? How long would she have to walk?

The giant brought his sword up into a guard stance. "When you are ready."

"No," Dagger said and began walking around the edge of the arena.

"No?!" The warrior thundered.

"Nope," Dagger repeated without stopping. "Not interested."

"You can't refuse!" The warrior shouted but did not pursue her or even move more than a step or two from his spot in the center of the killing floor.

"Eh," Dagger shrugged. "Sure seems like I can."

"There... There are rules!" the warrior cried. "I have waited a thousand years for a worthy opponent!"

"Not my problem."

The warrior's shoulders slumped. "But how will you ever know which of us is better?"

"Don't give a shit," Dagger said.

Dejection gave way to anger. "Coward! I name you coward. If you turn your back on me, I'll strike you down," the giant said, hefting his great, hook-tipped sword. His knuckles cracked as he tightened his grip.

"Doubt it."

"You doubt my word?"

Dagger had nearly reached the far side of the arena.

"Listen, big guy," she said, "you're telling me you've waited on this platform in full view of two sets of stairs for a thousand years?"

"Yes. Such is my dedication."

"And you didn't leave?"

"I—"

"You just sat here that whole time? Waiting."

"Yes. That is my purpose."

"Says who?"

"It has always been so!"

"Right. One of those. You like rules."

"What?"

"Rules. Fair combat. Valor and honor," Dagger couldn't keep a tinge of disgust out of

267

her voice. "You want to compete. Not fight. Well, I wish you good luck with whoever shows up next. Maybe you'll get lucky in another millennia."

"No! Face me!"

Dagger reached the far side of the arena. The warrior had not taken a single step toward her. "Maybe think about leaving?" she said, as she put her foot on the first step. "This place is falling apart."

Behind her came a crash. She glanced over her shoulder. The giant had dropped its sword and sat down with its face in its armored hands.

"I... " it mumbled into the cup of its fingers. "I cannot."

"I figured," Dagger said. She began to climb the stairs, but stopped after a step or two, muttered "shit" under her breath and turned back.

"Hey!" she called to the giant.

He lifted his face from his hands. "You'll face me after all?"

"Hell, no."

"Why do you taunt me then? To simply leave would be kinder."

Dagger rolled her eyes. "Fuck me, I've met bards who're less dramatic. C'mon. Let's go."

"Go? Fight?"

"No, dopey. Leave. Come with me. You want to wait here forever? I'm gonna find a way out."

"You would bring me with you?"

"That's the idea," she chuckled. "You're the size of a house. You'd be useful in a fight, and where I'm going there's gonna be a shitload of that."

"Worthy opponents?"

"Yeah. Sure. Whatever. So, get up. Quit moping. I don't have all day."

The giant paused, considering it. But finally shook his head. "I must stay. It is my duty. I have to guard the way."

Dagger gestured around the quiet. "Says fucking who? Do you see anybody else?"

The giant was about to answer, and then paused and looked around.

"I cannot remember."

"Then whoever they are, fuck 'em and feed 'em fish. Let's go."

The giant looked hesitant but got to his feet and grabbed his sword. He walked tentatively closer to Dagger, the massive weapon resting on his shoulder. "Are you... are you sure?"

"I'm sure waiting here's a shit idea."

Dagger turned back to the stairs and the giant's heavy footsteps followed. When she'd gotten to the fifth stair, she heard a thunderous ring of falling metal. She spun, her hand going to the haft of the hammer.

The giant was gone. In its place, on a patch of stone just past the pillars, was a pile of empty armor. The giant's sword lay beside it, and as Dagger watched, armor and sword rusted over and began to flake away on the wind.

"Shit," she muttered to the swirling rust. "Guess you were right. Sorry about that."

She turned and walked up the stairs.

# VICE

## Nice labyrinth. Shame if something happened to it.

Meditation brought Vice no clarity when the sky was a staircase filled with stone-platform clouds, and so eventually he opened his eyes. He saw a flash of movement on a distant set of stairs. He narrowed his eyes.

People.

They were little more than specks moved around the distant snarls of elevation and descent, and they were too far away for his voice to reach them, but if they hadn't been he might have asked why they were running.

He walked to an ascending staircase, the only one attached to his platform.

"Pitch said always up," he whispered. "If this place is still within the tower, perhaps this holds true."

Vice set his right foot upon the stairs.

The world spun and inverted.

Vice crouched and put one hand down to steady himself. He looked above him and saw the platform on which he'd been standing when he first arrived. There was now no direction to go but down. But was it truly down? Or was it really up? The idea of stepping backward onto the ceiling twisted his perception so thoroughly that feared he might take a single step and fall up into the sky. With breath and moments, he mastered himself.

He climbed the stairs to another platform and then another, and in doing so adjusted to the abrupt rips of perspective. He walked sideways and upside down. Direction as a core concept lost all meaning.

"This is absurd," he muttered, stopping on a platform with a single small house made of stones. Inside he found a table and one chair. On the table was a clay carafe and matching cup. The jug was full of the clearest liquid Vice had ever seen. He poured a cup.

"A moment of grace woven like a knot into the chaotic pattern of the world," he said, and sipped.

It was a delicate honey wine that tasted like sunlight and blackberries.

Vice went outside the hut and looked into the distance past the uncountable stairs and platforms. He wondered where the light was coming from in this twisted place where the singular law of direction seemed to be that there was none. He couldn't see even the hint of a sun. Then he heard steps, moving fast and getting closer.

A tattered man in a panic sprinted down, or up, a set of stairs onto Vice's platform and then dashed past the surprised, drinking monk.

"Wait!" Vice yelled.

"No!" The man shouted back as he dashed up, or perhaps across, another set of stairs and away.

"Why are you running?" Vice shouted after him.

"Why aren't you?" The man called back.

Vice thought about that. It was an interesting question. He smiled. Why not run? Why stand still? There was much to ponder in this place. A bubble of gratitude rose from within him, through his chest and then burst out in a giggle. He looked down into the cup suspiciously.

"Uh oh," he said, and giggled again.

His suspicion turned to anger.

"I am drunk," he said to the empty platform. "From a single sip. Like some novice!"

He clung to his anger, which was difficult when half of him seemed keen to dance with joy at the strangeness of this place. He flung the cup over the side. It stopped in the air for a second, and then shot to the left in a perfect, straight line and out of sight. He heard it shatter somewhere. Shaking his head to clear the moonbeams, he stared hard into the distance. There was an indistinct curtain there, a constant downward haze on the horizon. It almost looked as if it was raining, but the largest, dirtiest drops he'd ever seen. He screwed his eyes down to a squint.

It wasn't rain.

No.

Falling stones.

Then an entire platform shot up past his own, trailing a breaking staircase and a pair of screaming people who looked to Vice as if they were standing upside down. He ran to the edge and watched as the platform continued to rush toward the sky, tearing through other staircases and shattering platforms as it went with the roar of stone hitting stone.

"Why aren't you running indeed," Vice whispered.

This labyrinth was falling apart.

The monk felt a brief spike of fear, and he turned to look at the stairs branching from his platform. Fear told him to run, but with breath and effort he brought his pounding heart to heel and clasped his hands.

"I watch and observe," he whispered. "I do not panic. I run when I choose. I stand when I like. I do not react to the world's random conspirings unless I choose to do so. Vigil! Watcher in the Darkness! See my vigil. Action without purpose soothes only a scared piglet squealing for its mother in the lonely dark. If these are to be my final moments, they won't be filled with screams. I will not mistake panic for purpose."

He sat. He would watch dispassionately as this world crumbled.

"If it is to be now, let me not wish like a child for it to be later. I will not buy trivial moments with mindless choices. I will not turn my face."

His heart calmed. The aggressive joy of the strange liquor faded.

Finally. There was the peace he'd been seeking.

# PITCH, POWDER AND SABER

## At play in the fields of WTF.

"Now what, Pitch?" Saber demanded as the rift flickered and closed behind Vice.

"How should I know?" The alchemist shot back, clenching and unclenching his fists.

"Well, I sure as shit don't."

Pitch looked at Powder, but the sharpshooter could only shrug. "Do we go on without them?"

"Machines," Pitch said under his breath. "This place is a mass of untended machines."

"So?" Saber asked. "The fuck does that even mean?"

Pitch, filled with a new energy, pointed at both of his fellows.

"Quick! Look around," Pitch said. "Don't leave this room, don't walk through any strange doorways. Something has to be powering this gate. Find it."

As he said this, the hazy rift reformed to show what might have been an idyllic forest clearing. As the three watched, the vegetation rotted and the limpid pond at the center filled with scum and fallen leaves. Behind the canopy of degraded trunks were patches of stone. It wasn't a vast forest, but a garden. A faun staggered from between the trees and approached the pond. Its tongue hung from its mouth with thirst, but before the faun could reach the water, it keeled over and died. It decomposed at speed. Its fur fell away to reveal gangrenous muscle and pitted, corrupt bones.

"This is the shittiest job," Saber said.

"Worse than the one in Rinlek?" Powder asked.

"For the last time, Powder," Saber said with exasperation, "they only looked like babies, it wasn't my fault, and they were fucking cannibals."

"Oh, right," Powder mused, "I forgot about the whole babies eating babies thing."

"One of them ate a fucking cat right in front of me!"

"Kid have no impulse control."

They searched the workspaces and narrow corridors, their steps muted on the rough, hard carpet. They found room after room down narrow corridors with nothing but more blank, dead machines and dust.

Then Saber found a locked door with a small square of glass in the center. It was too opaque to see through, but when he pressed his ear to it, he heard a faint humming on the other side — not a human voice in absent song — but a steady noise that reminded him of distant factory din. He tried the knob, but the door was locked fast.

"Pitch, Powder!" he called. "Over here."

"Let me take a look," Pitch said after he'd run over, and the duelist moved aside. Pitch knelt to stare into the lock. It was a tiny thing he'd never seen the like of — the opening little more than a slit in the metal. He knocked around the lock plate.

"It's not steel."

"Is that good?" Powder asked.

"Well, the door is metal," Pitch said, "maybe tin? I can't tell without testing it. Ordinarily, I could pick it, but I've never seen a lock as slim as this before. I'm not sure I have anything slender enough."

"Saber, wanna give it a shot?" Powder asked with a suggestive glance at his crotch.

"I don't know, Powder," Saber replied. "A battering ram kinda seems like overkill."

Powder laughed. "You're disgusting."

"Now, now, Powder," Saber said, "Pitch said no more banter. I can hear something on the other side."

"I know," Pitch said. "I hear it too. Some kind of machine."

Saber stepped back and kicked the door near the lock.

"You can see it opens out, right?" Pitch asked irritably.

"Oh," Saber said.

"Step back, both of you," Powder said.

"What are you going to do?" Pitch asked. "Shoot it?"

"No," the gunner said. "You're being too intelligent about this."

"There's no such thing as too intelligent," Pitch said.

"There is if you're dithering over a decision instead of making one."

Powder took a small iron bomb from her bag and uncoiled a long fuse. She considered the door and then the hall behind them. She cut the fuse to length and shoved one end into the bomb.

"Pitch, can you make me something sticky? Fast setting?"

"Putty or glue?"

"Glue."

Pitch produced a wood mixing bowl and set a piece of tree gum in the center, adding liquid from a vial and a pinch of white dust. He stirred the mixture into an acrid paste and Powder dipped one side of her bomb with it and stuck it to the lock.

"Count to thirty," Pitch told her.

The gunhand held it against the metal and counted until the bomb was stuck fast, then herded Pitch and Saber ahead of her as she played out the thin fuse along the ground. She gestured for them to kneel behind a wall.

"Do we really need to take cover?" Saber said. "It's just a little bomb."

"Just get down, Saber. I'm not gonna pick shrapnel out of your ass. Again."

She lit the fuse.

A moment later the lock, and much of the door, was a twisted, blackened wreck.

They entered the room and Pitch stamped out a few burning papers. If the deserted worktables

280

and corridors of the strange, colorless rooms behind them was a desert, this was an oasis. Every surface was stacked with pages, each covered with printed words in the same inscrutable alphabet and scrawled with handwritten notes in red and blue. Against one wall was a massive black glass window. Beneath it was a table covered in buttons.

Pitch collected a small stack of papers and shuffled through them. He put them aside and turned his attention to the table beneath the screen.

"What is it?" Saber asked.

Pitch grunted. "It's all got the same language as everything else in here. I can't read it, but judging by the buttons, I'd guess it's a control panel of some kind." He knocked one knuckle against the table, and it made a hollow sound. He ducked under it and found a pair of thick rubber cables.

"Those are like the one we cut to use for your rope," Saber said. "But much thicker."

"You cut something in here?" Pitch asked, his tone reproachful.

"We needed a rope. For you."

"Fair enough," Pitch said, and followed the cables along the sidewall to a cabinet under a worktable on the other side of the room. He opened the doors to a machine painted a vivid red. The cable ran to it and on the machine was a single switch. Pitch sniffed the air. Then he leaned in and sniffed at the machine.

"Don't know this scent," the alchemist said. "It almost smells a bit like coal oil."

"What do you think it does?" Powder asked.

"Well, if it's coal oil, or something like it, it's fuel..."

"Then what?"

"One way to find out." Pitch flipped the switch and the machine sputtered into life, trundling happily in its cabinet home. Pitch watched it.

"It doesn't seem to do anything," he muttered. "Maybe they just liked the vibration or the sound?"

"Uh, Pitch," Saber said, "turn around."

The glass window against the wall had lit up. On it was a scene like a moving painting or a tapestry. Pitch got up and peered into it, and then put his hand against the glass. It was a moving picture, but not a portal like the one Vice and Dagger had vanished through. It was solid.

The glass showed a gold-hued forest glade — the grass, the trees, each leaf and even the pond at its center, all were a burnished hue of dull yellow stained green in some places. It was an exact copy of the rotting forest they'd just seen.

"Is that gold?" Saber asked.

Pitch shook his head. "Brass. See the verdigris?"

On the screen, a mechanical faun crept out from between the brass tree trunks, crossed the yellow, metal ground, which was etched to suggest individual blades of grass, and bent down to mime at drinking from the pond. A key sprouted from the faun's back like a fairy's wing. It turned very slowly, then paused and stuck. The faun stuttered, stopped and then began moving again when the key did. It turned from its pantomime drink and left the way it had come.

"Like a big version of some children's toy," Powder said.

"And it's winding down," Pitch said. "Saber, stick your head out and tell me if the portal's showing the same thing as the screen?"

"Why would it be?"

"Just go look."

Saber left the room and came back a moment later.

"Okay, that's weird," he said.

"Same scene?"

"I could have walked through. Want me to go steal the faun?"

"What? No. Why?"

"Want me to shoot it?" Powder asked.

"Why in the— " Pitch said, before noting their sly grins, " Oh, for fuck's sake. Focus. We need to get Vice and Dagger back. And I think this is how."

Pitch pushed a button on the far-left corner of the panel and the screen shifted again, this time showing a snowcapped tower. The top had already partially collapsed, and as they watched another stone fell from it and then another, crashing down the side of the tower and falling into the abyss that surrounded it.

"Saber," Pitch said.

"I'm going," the duelist said, and darted from the room and back. "I can see the tower."

Pitch pushed the last button again, and the brass glade reappeared. They watched the fawn totter back out to drink.

"It's the same scene again?" Power asked.

"I think it's just repeating itself," Pitch said. "Everything we've seen. Remember what the queen said about the tower's experiments?"

"So?" Saber asked.

"At the academy, sometimes students would resign, often with their experiments still running. It was a big place, not much oversight. But the students knew who'd left what. And sometimes we'd watch as the work of some failed student ran way past schedule. Sometimes it even worked."

"Worked?" Powder said. "What do you mean, worked?"

"Unintended outcomes were sometimes better than the intended ones."

"Like what?"

"You know that tincture I use to keep us sharp?"

"Yeah."

"It's supposed to blind you."

"Pitch, what the fuck?" Powder cried. "If you fucking blind me I'll—"

"You'll what? Shoot me?" Pitch smirked. "Obviously, it's perfectly safe. Anyway, sometimes an experiment spawned an unintended discovery. Other times, they just fell apart. Slowly. Like this place."

285

Pitch pushed another button, and then another. And another. The screen flickered through scenes, some ordinary, some so strange that in the brief moment they were on the glass they burned themselves into the three mercenaries' brains.

"There!" Powder shouted.

Pitched went back to the last button he'd pressed.

In the glass was Dagger, walking slowly down a narrow staircase in the sky, her hammer balanced on her shoulder like she was taking a country stroll over the abyss that yawned beneath her feet. The clouds on the far side of her rippled as something very large and fast moved within them.

Saber dashed out of the room.

"Dagger!" He shouted through the rift in the air. The narrow staircase was close enough for him to step onto it. Dagger stopped, glanced behind her and then resumed walk slowly toward the rift. Her pace was agonizing, almost aggressive in its leisure.

"Hurry!" Saber shouted. "I don't know how long this stupid magic door will hold.

But Dagger would not speed up. She did make a gesture in front of her mouth, but it was too far for Saber to see what it was.

"Dagger!" Saber shouted again.

She waved her hand at him.

"What?" Saber shouted.

The clouds on the other side of Dagger rippled, bulged, and then something burst out of them with a roar like thunder.

Dagger glanced behind her and broke into a sprint up the stairs. From the clouds unwound a black, serpentine body. The front end opened up in a mouth of triplicate jaws lined with dull, strangely human molars. It bore down on Dagger.

"Run!" Saber shouted through the rift.

"I am fucking running!" Dagger yelled back as the beast closed in.

"Powder!" Saber shouted behind him, "Rifle. Now. Biggest fucking bullet you got!"

But Powder was already there. A rifle barrel reached past Saber's face and came to rest on his shoulder. He stood tall and firm, closed his eyes and covered his ears. The sky serpent was closing in on Dagger and its dull teeth were gnashing as it screamed. It shattered the staircase behind her as it closed in, and both Saber and Powder's hearts leapt in their throats.

But the stairs held.

Dagger ran and ran as brick and mortar fell down into oblivion at her heels.

Powder aimed into the monster's screaming throat and fired.

The bullet ripped past Dagger's shoulder as she leapt for the rift, and Saber, deafened by gunfire, opened his eyes and reached out ready to grab her.

Powder's bullet ripped into the serpent's mouth and burst out one side, trailing purple mist. The creature snapped its jaws shut with a deafening crack and reared back in pain as Dagger burst through the rift and tackled Saber as Powder stepped delicately out of the way.

The beast collected itself to lunge again, and a ripple blinked across the skin above its mouth as several bright red eyes stared into the rift. It roared and shot toward them. A gust of wind that reeked of mold and dust blew across their faces.

"Pitch!" Powder shouted. "Shut the door!"

"It's not strictly a door!" Pitch called back.

"Fucking close it!" Dagger yelled, still on top of a wheezing Saber.

The rift shifted just as the beast reached them. One moment they were faced by jaws, the next by the brass mechanical fawn bending down for yet another drink, this time much slower and with a palsied step as its mechanisms wound down.

"Where's Vice?" Dagger said as she rolled off of Saber, who made a theatrical gasp for air. "Oh, shut up," she muttered at him as she got to her feet and pulled him up after.

"Hopefully, he's next, Captain," Powder said. "Pitch has a handle on the machine. What the fuck was that thing?"

"Didn't stop to ask," Dagger said.

"Why were you just strolling along if you knew it was there?" Saber asked.

Dagger gave him a steady look. "It's nearly blind. Only responds to sound and fast movements."

"So it didn't know you were there until I... " Saber trailed off as he connected the dots. "Oh."

"Yeah," Dagger said. "Oh."

Saber looked down at his boots. "Sorry."

"Let's just find our fucking monk."

# — CHAPTER 11 —

## An unexpected rescue.

I t would be peaceful, Vice thought, to watch the world end. Fitting.

When he fell — and he would fall — he decided he would not scream. He would go silently to that place in the sky and there he would continue to watch, to keep his Vigil in both heart and mind as that eternal rest crumbled as well. It would not be quick, but he would be there to see the machines of his heaven fail by degrees. Without him below there would be nobody to harvest for above. Perhaps he would don a gray robe. It would be peaceful. Quiet. He knew the other servants would not judge him for his failure — they had all failed as well.

And the rest of The Armory would be free from this eternal cycle. He hoped they would not be too upset about that. Dagger's hammer would rust when she grew too weak to lift it. Saber would slow down, perhaps forget his appetites. Powder's sight would fade, her trigger finger would grow arthritic. Pitch's mind would crumble with the years. Perhaps, as he neared the end, even he would learn to pray. Maybe before that happened, they would even earn enough gold to live in comfort while they fell apart.

But as Vice thought of all of that, a pain grew larger and larger in his chest, a pain he tried desperately not to understand.

"Vice?"

The voice came from behind him, but the monk did not stir. It was just a quiet thought made loud by meditation, memory and forecasted remorse, a fleeting and returning blink of a familiar sound when he was faced with the end.

"Vice!"

It sounded like Saber. The mind was an absurd little animal: Who would want to hear Saber's voice at the end? It could not be. Vice had stepped through. He was lost to the world. The Citadel had swallowed and defeated him like a whale of purpose.

"Fucking hell, Vice! Why are you just sitting there?"

With an irritated growl, the monk humored a hallucination just as irritating as the real Saber and turned around. There was the dissolute duelist, standing in a rip in the world, the rest of The Armory with him.

"You aren't real," Vice informed them.

Saber rolled his eyes. "Your god's bullshit. I fucked half your order. I fucked your mother. I'd fuck you too if you were five minutes younger. Are you just gonna sit there until you grow roots out of your asshole?"

Vice blinked.

"Vice," Dagger said gently as she shoved Saber out of the way, "time to go. Die later."

Vice could see from her expression that she understood why he was just sitting in acceptance. He got to his feet and stared at his comrades for a few moments more, peering at each of their faces and testing his heart against these phantoms. They did not waver.

Then he sighed and stepped through the rift.

Behind him a platform trailing a sets of stairs like streamers smashed down where he'd been sitting. He turned at the noise and they all coughed as a cloud of dust and grit blew through the rift. His platform groaned and shrieked with the sound of stone grinding against stone.

Then it shuddered and fell.

"Ah," Vice said, a bit wistful.

"You look disappointed," Saber said.

"I would not expect you to understand."

"You sure?" Saber said, staring out at the crumbling world on the other side of the portal. "Might have been nice to be done."

"And we will be," Dagger said, "one day. But not today."

But Vice was still staring at Saber. Even his hood looked shocked.

"What?" Saber said, "Yeah, Vice, I feel it too. I just don't walk around moping all the time."

"I do not mope," Vice grumbled.

Saber threw his arm around Vice's shoulder. "It's okay, Vice, it's a very dignified mope."

"Saber."

"Fifty poets, a hundred painters and a thousand bards could not hope to mope with even half your gravitas."

Vice sighed heavily but did not throw off the duelist's arm as they walked through the strange cubicle-studded room to where Pitch was examining the controls.

"Can this thing get us out of here?" Dagger asked as she entered the room.

The alchemist nodded at Vice. "How was wandering oblivion?"

"Quiet," the monk said. "Peaceful."

Pitch chuckled as he looked back down at the rows of buttons on the table. He began to push them, one at a time and in order, making notes in his book as he did. The scenes in the glass shifted one by one, each stranger than the last. There was even one that appeared to be underwater. They all stared, mesmerized by a scene even they had never witnessed. There was a thunderous, roaring splash from the other room and the air filled with the reek of salt. Briny water sloshed around their ankles.

"What the hell?" Pitch said and got up to check, but Dagger lunged past him and pushed the next button. The roaring stopped.

"I don't want to drown, Pitch."

"But I," he began, and then stopped. "No, that's fair."

The next scene was somewhat familiar. A stone hall with a stone floor.

"Looks more like it," Dagger said. "Drier, anyway. What do you think, Pitch?"

He shrugged. "It could be any where or when. But it's the least strange of all the options."

"Good enough."

They filed out to the rift.

"All together this time," Dagger said.

"Should we hold hands?" Saber asked.

They stepped through the portal in a tight clump and found themselves on a narrow platform in a chamber so vast that a gentle wind caressed their faces. At the far end a single set of stairs with no railing, leading up.

Powder whistled long and loud. Somewhere in the unseeable distance were the faint sounds of battle — screams of men and beasts, the clash of steel and claw, rushed footsteps on stone.

Saber gestured to the stairs. "Should we go up? Or up?"

Dagger led. What happened next was a blur of bottled time and violence.

For what might have been one hundred years or one hundred minutes, The Armory battled in the Citadel of Stairs in a stasis of conflict. They charged down hallways and dashed through tunnels in creeping, tactical retreats. Up was the same as down. Left and right became irrelevant. Turning around meant nothing. To backtrack was to go forward. One dimly lit path was the same as another. They fought men. They fought beasts. They killed things that were both and neither. They witnessed horror and wonder in such variety that there became no distinguishing one from the other as Pitch's rationed chemicals muted terror and triumph alike. Sometimes the ceiling became the floor, other times they battled sideways, and any misstep could send them hurtling to be smashed against the walls. There was no escape. No hunger to mark the time. No daylight. The top of the Citadel was as distant as never, and as close as a minute into memory.

In blinking moments between battles, Pitch stitched their cuts and sealed them with thread or glue. They camped in abandoned jail cells and moldering throne rooms. Pitch and Powder scavenged chemicals and old metal to make bullets and bombs. Powder fingered the new bullets and thought they want us to fight forever. Saber sat, his humor spent, his hand cramping around the hilt of his weapon as he carelessly let its point rest upon the ground. Vice prayed so much the words lost meaning. Pitch looked down at his notebook map of the Citadel, muttering about wasted time. With a disgusted grunt, he used a few of the disjointed drawings to kindle a fire in the helmet of an ogre they'd felled moments before.

Even Dagger gave a small sigh when she was able to set down her hammer, but as she looked at the drawn faces of her crew, her hand clenched around the haft once more.

"We fight forever," Dagger said as if one of them had voiced their thoughts. "We struck that deal long ago." She got to her feet with a grimace. "So, straighten up. Forget the end. It doesn't exist for us."

"Captain," Powder said with a nod, and reloaded her weapons. Saber massaged his hands and sheathed his blades. Vice rose from his knees. Pitch was the last to get up. He looked down at his pages of his notes, and then tore them in half and tossed them into the fire.

And so, they strode out to find the next battle, each hoping it would be the signpost that might hint at the true distance traveled.

A battle came. Then another. Eventually even the Citadel of Stairs ran short of sameness, and a turn that looked like the last thousand they'd taken showed a difference as welcome as spring thaw. In a narrow and winding corridor of stone, the torches grew sparse and guttering, poorly tended and dim.

"Different," Pitch noted.

"Never thought I'd be happy to see less torchlight," Saber said.

At the end of the corridor, a spiral of steel stairs led up, and for once in what seemed like a generation, that direction felt like something other than arbitrary perspective. They climbed past floor after floor of stone landings where they could see men and beasts just like them, trapped and slavering in bloody, ceaseless battle. The stairs steepened, and the spiral tilted and became a ladder. The hand and footholds were deeply grooved and gleaming, and while so much of the tower seemed to be in disrepair, the ladder shone as if newly built. The shaftway closed in around the stairs as they climbed.

"Maybe it leads to the roof," Saber suggested.

"Or the basement," Powder countered. "At this point how would we even tell?"

"If it leads to the roof we could just jump off," the duelist suggested.

"At this point, I'd push you," Powder said.

"Kinda sweet under the circumstances."

They paused often to rest, twining their arms and legs between the rungs to hang and ease their aching limbs. Finally, Dagger saw a grid above them and a hatch. She dragged herself through it, stepped from the ladder and stood tall.

The walls and floor were new steel. The room was lit by glowing orbs in wire cages. It had only one door with a small glass window. She wondered if they'd ever been meant to find their way into this place and considered the tower's nature. She could not decide which possibility bothered her more: That they'd not been meant to find this, or that they had, and it was just one more boring, eternal twist in this weird, tangled labyrinth.

As the rest of The Armory dragged their way up from the ladder, Dagger peered through the window in the door. Beyond was another corridor. Like the one they'd entered through, it was lined with doors, but unlike that battered hallway, none of these doors were shattered.

Dagger leaned back from the window and looked up. There was a sign above the door in a language she couldn't read.

"Pitch, any idea what that says?" She asked.

Pitch peered at the sign for several moments. "Pictographs. It could almost be ancient Couju, but that's a dead scholar's language, and this is..."

"What?"

"It looks like what might have happened if the language never died."

"Want to explain that?"

"Living languages change as they're used," Pitch said. "They evolve. Accents change and meaning with them. Words fall out of use and new ones are invented. A language only dies when it stops being spoken. Couju fell hundreds of years ago. The ones that escaped the cataclysm learned other languages where they settled and eventually abandoned their own. It wasn't useful anymore. We only have a few books in Couju. We don't know what it sounds like."

"Can you read it?"

Pitch peered closer. "That word could be box, well, or lock."

"Pitch, it's one word," Saber said.

"Couju's grammar and meaning are contextual. The pictographs to either side that I can't read would provide the meaning of this one. The books we had at the academy were all histories. Not a lot of use in modern alchemy. This is the one shape I kind of recognize."

"Box, well, lock," Dagger muttered. "Box, well, lock."

"Prison?" Powder suggested.

Pitch nodded. "It's entirely possible."

"The whole place is a prison," Dagger said. "Pitch, we entered through a dungeon."

"Was it? It certainly looked like one, as we understand them anyway. But what if it wasn't a dungeon at all?" Pitch said.

"What else would it have been?" Dagger asked.

"Think of what we've seen, the automations, the crumbling systems. So much of this place is like an observatory. And think of how the queen described the Citadel's actions. Experiments. Yet not one sign of an authority figure or anyone who runs this place. The walls are holding all this in, and Temker's Clock is still functioning on the living creatures who entered, probably because nobody has found their way back to break it. This place is full of untended mechanisms run wild, so if this part looks this well-maintained—"

"—then things are about to get nastier," Dagger finished.

"That would be my guess, boss, yes," Pitch said.

"Well, we know what's behind us."

"Forward always," the rest of The Armory muttered, more or less in unison.

"Quit stealing my lines," Dagger said with a smirk, grabbed the handle of the door and pulled. It would not open. She swore.

"Pitch? If you would?"

Pitch peered into the lock. It was large and circular.

"Never seen a key that would fit this, but that's nothing new," said the alchemist. He took a metal funnel from his kit and slid the slender end into the hole. Into the funnel he poured a measure of acid, and they waited while the liquid smoked. On the other side, something clanked and fell.

Pitch pulled the door open, and Dagger stepped through first, hammer ready. They crept their way to the first door. Above it was a metal plaque with more of the same writing as above the entrance, and to the right was a large window that looked into the room.

It looked empty.

"Maybe they haven't gotten around to putting anybody in the cells yet," Dagger suggested.

The glass vibrated and Dagger flinched back with her hammer up. The glass thrummed again, more violently this time, as some force inside the room threw itself against it. The glass held as the smashing continued, and Dagger cautiously put her palm against the transparent barrier.

"It's not ordinary glass," Pitch noted.

"Thanks, Pitch," Dagger said dryly.

They moved on.

The next cell was more obviously occupied.

Inside was a single human man, then the air in the cell shivered and there were four of him, then two, then so many that the cell was filled with duplicates of his face and staring eyes. There was no space between their shoulders. They jockeyed to press their faces against the glass, to knock, beg and gesture for The Armory to open the door and free them. They jostled and quarreled, three of them eventually getting into a brawl that absorbed the rest. The copies flickered and fought and then vanished until there was only one left, squatting on the ground with his head in his hands, his fingers rubbing his scalp.

In the next cell was the head of a hound the size of a wagon. Its neck ended in a ragged, bleeding stump from which the blood was still seeping, covering the floor and running to a drain at the center. Whatever had been used to sever head from body had been dull and heavy.

The giant hound's tongue lay dead, lolling between its jaws. When The Armory got close, one of its entirely too human eyes rolled to regard them, and the tongue flopped and licked the glass.

In another cell was a shiny black orb draped in heavy chains. It shivered, and as it did so, the chains rattled silently around it.

The corridor stretched on, but The Armory was grateful for the oddities in the cells — they interrupted the monotony of the hallway. Without them, there would have been no way to gauge distance or difference, and every step would have seemed as meaningless and infinite as the one before. Then, with a gasp, Vice shouldered past Dagger.

"What the hell, Vice?" Dagger muttered as the monk ran ahead. He did not answer. The Armory could but follow to make sure that whatever he faced next, he would not do so alone. The cells blurred as they ran.

"Vice! Slow down!" Dagger called.

The corridor opened into a rotunda with a single cell, far larger than the rest. Vice dashed to it and pressed his hands against the glass. He fell to his knees and stared up at the cell's occupant — a figure twice even Dagger's height, so tall that it brushed the ceiling. It seemed to have two forms, and either both existed at once, or it phased between both so quickly that they appeared to. The figure was hooded and draped in floor-length robes of plain gray, but it was also a stone watchtower. A colorless fire burned at its highest point, creating a nimbus around both the hood and battlements.

The Armory stopped in a loose semi-circle around the prostrate monk.

"What is it, Vice?" Dagger asked. The monk only kept his imploring hands on the glass and his head bowed.

"Vice?" Dagger tried again.

"The Vigil," Vice murmured with awe.

"That's what the Vigil looks like?" Saber asked.

"What did you expect?" Pitch said.

"Oh, don't act so casual. You've never seen a god either." Saber shot back.

"Definitely not one in jail," Powder muttered.

"I didn't know they made jails for gods," Saber said.

Dagger appraised the cell's occupant as Vice clasped his fingers so tightly that his arms shook. He spoke furiously under his breath, and no matter what was said to him, refused to open his eyes, answer, or move. They waited as the prayer, or whatever it was Vice was muttering, continued. And continued. If Vice took a breath, he managed to speak at the same time.

"So... we live here now?" Saber asked.

"Quiet, Saber," Dagger said and laid her hand on the monk's shoulder. "Vice?"

The holy man did not answer.

Dagger took a deep breath and tried again. "Vice, talk to me. Do you really believe this is the Vigil? Think. That can't be possible."

"I can feel it," Vice whispered. He tilted his head back until his hood fell away. His face was pained and full of longing as the monk, who none of them had ever seen beg for anything, pleaded with his eyes at the figure on the other side of the glass. Then he leapt to his feet and hammered at the door with both fists but couldn't even scuff the steel. With an effort, he gathered himself and finally laid hold of the handle and yanked as hard as he could. The door held. The Armory had seen Vice break plate steel with his fists and rip chainmail like it was cotton gauze.

Vice turned from the door and rounded on the alchemist. "Pitch! Open it!" he shouted. "Open it now!"

Pitch backed away. "Now, just wait a second, Vice."

"Pitch!" Vice howled, and advanced on the alchemist. His face was bright red, his eyes were bloodshot. Tears streaked his cheeks.

"Vice," Dagger stepped between them, "calm the fuck down!"

Vice only growled and turned to redouble his efforts, tugging and wrenching and thrashing against the door's handle.

Pitch looked around the room. Inside the cell, the towering figure/watchtower did not react. The alchemist raked his eyes across the floor to where it met the cell wall and up along the boundaries of the ceiling. Finally, he saw a brass plate by the cell door that somehow none of them had noticed, and on it was a button. He pressed it.

*Why are you here?*

The voice spoke in all their minds at once. It was so dry it made them thirsty. Vice fell back from the door.

"Watcher, I have come!" The monk said.

"What in the fuck?" Pitch whispered, his hand still on the button.

*I am the Watcher in the Darkness. Again, why are you here?*

"We've come to destroy the Citadel," Dagger answered.

"We've come to free you," Vice said.

"No," Dagger said, "we didn't."

*Admirable. Honest. Perhaps. You are killers. But there is nobody left to kill. Time dragged them along like a dead knight with a foot trapped in the stirrups of his charger. They have all been pounded flat beneath hooves of time.*

"You know what happened here?" Dagger asked.

*I see all. I have watched your bloody march through this place. I have watched the deteriorated systems try in vain to slow you down. I know that you are not liberators, but that does not mean you cannot liberate.*

"You watched us?" Dagger asked.

*Yes.*

"And you know who we are?"

*You are wedge and fire, the finger on the scales, the knife in the back of power. And you are prisoners. As I am. But you know it not.*

"What?" Saber asked.

*I see you all so clearly. Your newness to this place marks you like motes of light in perfect darkness. The one of stone. The dancing fool. The worshipper of the new gods called Science. The distant killer. The faithful one. You are catalysts, counterweights. You are fate's flung stone.*

"That sounds impressive," Saber said.

"You're the dancing fool," Powder muttered.

"Obviously."

*You are change made flesh. But you are trying to change a dead thing already beyond the grip of time. You are maggots on a corpse.*

"I like 'fate's flung stone' better," Saber said.

*And you are not funny.*

"I'm also not locked up," the duelist countered.

*Aren't you? Do you feel free, dancing fool?*

Saber was about to speak but closed his mouth.

"Watcher," Vice said, "what would you have us do?"

*Free me. I will guide you from this place. We will destroy it together. I have watched long enough. I will act. And you will help me. In exchange, I will free you from this place.*

The Armory stood in something like shock, feeling a bit like squatters who'd finally found the landlord in the attic, mad as a rat in a tin shithouse and chewing on the walls.

"Vice, what do—" Dagger said, but Vice suddenly flinched as if slapped. He stood and unclasped his hands. The exultation fell from his face, and he backed away from the glass with an expression of fury and revulsion.

"Vice, what's wrong?" Dagger asked.

The monk fled the room and down the corridor at a fast walk.

*Do not run, my little watcher. You have found me, faithful one.*

Dagger gestured at Pitch.

*It is unseemly to flee from the tru —*

Pitch took his hand off the brass plate and the Vigil was cut off midsentence. A weight settled across them in the silence of the prison hall. The jailed god moved closer to the glass in a flicker, and The Armory backed away as the Vigil's gray watchtower fire burned brighter.

"Stay back from that glass. Pitch," Dagger said, "and don't touch that button until I say. Saber, go get Vice."

"Me?" Saber asked in disbelief.

"He likes you."

"No, he doesn't."

"Captain," Powder said, "Vice doesn't retreat. This doesn't need a lighter touch, it needs yours."

Dagger sighed. "Fine," she said and left the rest of her crew staring up at the god on the other side of the glass.

When Dagger caught up to the monk, he was at the end of the corridor, staring down into the hatch with the ladder as if it were a wishing well.

"Talk to me, Vice."

"That... thing," the monk said, his voice thick with grief, "that is not the Vigil."

"What do you mean?" Dagger asked. "You were so sure you nearly broke your hands on that door. What changed?"

"It wants vengeance. It is angry. The Vigil is dead, Dagger. Gone. The Vigil would never seek retribution. It would never beg for freedom, especially not when it could watch. That was why we were created. We are the hands, but The Vigil is the eyes. We choose our acts carefully. To intervene is sin, but a sin taken gladly depending on consequence. Every moment I am with you, I am defiled further by active change. But it is all necessary. To keep a memory alive, to give our faithful a place to go at the end, I take on that defilement. Gladly. But this thing..."

"Maybe," Dagger said. "Maybe not. If they only captured the Vigil, it may have been a prisoner the whole time."

"Nothing can hold the Watcher in the Darkness, not even time," Vice said. "Nothing. The world is the Watcher's prison, as it is all of ours. That is not the Vigil, Dagger."

"Are you sure?"

"Wouldn't you know your own father if you met him?"

"No."

Vice sighed. "Perhaps that was a poor example. But—"

"Vice, how long has it been? Your faith..." She trailed off before she could finish delivering a hard truth.

"Say it," Vice said miserably.

"Your faith is defined by grief."

The monk nodded sadly. "It is. But Dagger, the Vigil, the true Vigil, it would..."

"It would what?"

"It would be horrified by us. By me. By what we have done to preserve what's left of the faith. It would know the ways we have perverted its teachings to persist. It would never even speak to me. It would condemn me with silence."

"Gods forgive."

"Not mine," the monk said. "What we do is antithetical to the Vigil's teachings. Killing on its behalf? Slaughtering hundreds to feed dying, celestial machines. It would know my guilt. And this creature does not."

"Maybe. But it saw what we did to get here."

"Dagger, if the Vigil had been alive, it would never have allowed us to do what we do. We would never have had to!"

"Even if it was locked up?" Dagger countered. "Think of what we've seen in here. This place, this prison, it has power. Vice, believe me, being locked away changes you forever. It changes the rules. It writes new ones that are impossible to forget."

The monk did not answer. He stared at his feet.

"But whatever it is," Dagger continued, "it might be our only way out of here. We might need it."

"What do you mean?"

"It seems to understand this place. It says it can see beyond its cell."

"Maybe. But if it is not the Vigil then it is something else."

Dagger took a deep breath. "Vice, I am going to ask you to do something you won't like."

"I like nothing that I do. I do it because it is needful," Vice said. "I do it for the refugees of our faith."

"Then this won't be any different," she said. "Talk to it. Get it to help us. If it isn't the Vigil, it thinks it is, and if it has a fraction of the power it claims, it can cut us a way out of this timeless shithole. Vice, we can finish the job."

Vice thought for a moment, his features contorting with the enormity of what he was being asked.

"What you ask..." Vice paused to gather himself. "What you ask would never be possible with the true Vigil, the true Vigil would see the lie, would see my soul and know my mind."

"Then it's simply a means to get out of here. One more ugly, needful act. If it's not the Vigil, you won't offend it by lying. I'd do it myself if I could, but I can't. None of us can. Only you. We can't talk to it like you can."

Vice knelt for a moment and clasped his hands. He began to pray again.

"Vice, we don't have time for this!"

But Vice ignored her. She waited while minutes, if that's what they really were, ticked by uncounted.

"Very well," Vice finally said in a sick voice. "I'll talk with this false creature."

"You better lock that shit down first, Vice," Dagger said. "It has to believe you think it's your god."

"And if it's some mad creation like everything else in this place?"

"Then, Vice," Dagger said in a gentle voice, "let's hope you learn to lie better than Saber in the next five minutes, or we'd better hope we're far worse than it is."

Vice nodded sadly.

# — CHAPTER 12 —

## How much is that god in
## the window?

Vice walked like a man going to the gallows. Pitch met them halfway down the corridor.

"Can you do it?" Pitch asked, having already guessed the plan.

"Be quiet, alchemist," Vice said, turning the last word into a derisive snarl.

"Vice," Pitch said, "this is just about getting the job done. Not desecrating your god."

"You could not desecrate the Vigil if you tried. Do you know what you're asking me?"

Pitch stared at the outraged, grieving monk for several moments. "Yes."

"Impossible," Vice said and walked back to the window to face his false god.

Pitch muttered under his breath: "I'm asking you to make a rational fucking decision."

"Easy, Pitch," Dagger said. "Whatever your feelings, he's saved our hides more times than any of us."

"Dagger," Pitch said, "one day they'll all be gone. The gods. All of them. Because people will finally have the answers, not them."

"Not the time," Dagger said. "Now, quit being a cunt. Unless you want to take over as resurrectionist?"

Pitch snapped his mouth shut and went to the button. He looked at Vice, who took a deep breath and nodded. The alchemist held the button down.

*You seem troubled, my little watcher in the darkness.*

"I thought you dead," Vice said.

*Only imprisoned. How do my followers fare without my guidance? Do the machines run down without me?*

"Well," Vice answered, though he was surprised at the question, "well enough. Your acolytes and I have cared for them. In our way."

*How?*

"We," Vice began but paused, "we have had to improvise. Your acolytes had their suggestions. Without recourse, we have followed them."

*You are evading the question.*

"We..."

*Ah. I see it now painted in your mind. You have slaughtered multitudes in my name. You have stolen others from their afterlives. This was never my way, but you know this. The pain you feel is great.*

"You were gone!" Vice shouted. Grief cracked his voice. The fearsome battle monk with the iron hands sounded like a wounded child. "No, it is not your way. But there was little choice! Should we have abandoned those who believe?"

The rest of The Armory looked at each other with discomfort. None of them had ever seen Vice in this state before, and none of them thought it was a very good idea to scold a god, even a false one.

*You are right.*

Vice blinked. "I am?"

*Ways change. They must change. This place has taught me that. I see you. Your faith was tested, but you held. Your faith is being tested again now. Will you continue to hold? We will speak together now, just you and I. Tell the god-hater not to remove his hand from the button. The cell will silence my voice without it, but I will speak only to you. Together we can put to rights what has happened in my absence.*

"Yes," Vice said.

318

The dry voice left The Armory's minds as Vice's shoulders rounded under the weight of what only he could hear. The monk gesticulated but did not speak out loud. He swept his hands to indicate the room or perhaps the tower itself. He seemed to be painting some picture of a larger world. After a few more minutes, Vice clasped his hands and bent to one knee. Then he turned and came back to the group.

"We good?" Dagger asked him.

"The..." Vice paused for a split second on the word as if it was a hard-to-swallow bite of food, "...Vigil will help us. It can see most of the tower. It can help us chart a course through the maze."

"To a way out?" Saber asked.

"Not yet," Dagger said.

"Uh, why the fuck not?" the duelist asked.

"The job's not done, Saber."

Saber threw up his hands. "The job also wasn't supposed to rip us out of time! Do you even know how long we've been in here?"

"That's not the point," Dagger said.

"It kind of is, though, isn't it? There was gold waiting for us. Who knows what's happened out there since we've been in here? Maybe the queen's dead. We could be keeping a deal with a ghost."

Pitch nodded. "There is something to that, Dagger."

"Doesn't matter," Dagger said. "We took a job, and that job is over when it's over. Don't forget the promise we made to..." Dagger trailed off and glanced at the god in the cell. "Anyway, this is about more than gold. Forward is the only way."

"We don't even know which way forward is in this shithole," Saber said.

*You dither in petty argument! The Vigil's voice boomed in their minds and half-buckled their knees. Are you warriors or children? Free me and your task becomes simpler. Though still, not easy. My power is muted in this place, but I have some.*

"Pitch," Dagger gasped as the god stopped speaking and its mental weight lifted, "see if you can get the cell open."

The alchemist ran his hands along the locking mechanism — a shadowed recess that seemed to go on forever. He lit one of Powder's cord flares and tried to shine a light into the keyhole, but the darkness not only swallowed the light, it dimmed it by proximity. Pitch dropped the brightly smoking brand between his feet and took a pair of metal picks from his pocket. He gently probed the void, then snatched his hand back like he'd been burned.

"What happened?" Dagger asked.

"The lock ate one of my picks," the alchemist said.

"Oh, good," Saber muttered.

*God-hater. You are the one called Pitch.*

Pitch leaned back from the door and looked in through the glass at the vastly shifting form of the Vigil that might be.

"Yes," Pitch answered.

*You are an... alchemist. A student of science.*

"That's correct."

*But science alone does not bind me here. It is a different force. One I understand better than you, I think.*

"Perhaps."

*Your denial clouds your beloved reason, god-hater. It amounts to the same thing, does it not? You are outside the door and I am imprisoned. Still, which of us is really confined? Who decides which side of a door is within and which is without?*

"An interesting philosophical question," Pitch said, "but in this case, I think the answer is obvious."

*Perhaps. Perhaps your cell is just larger. In any case, muting wards line the cell — that is magic —*

*but the devices that power them feed off the pain and despair of confinement, as much of this tower does. That is your science at work, hand in hand with the forces you reject. The lock exists in several times and existential planes at once, each a fixed and perpetual point. You would need their key to open it, or more than a thousand pairs of hands and picks.*

"Which we don't have."

*No. But consider: A jail cell, as I am sure you have found at least once in your life, is only as good as its door.*

Pitch nodded thoughtfully. "And a door is only as good as its hinges."

*Just so, god-hater. Our ways and means are not so different.*

Pitch examined the hinges carefully and then mixed two different powders into a vial of liquid. He corked it and shook hard, blending and filling the rest of the vial with smoke. With his sleeve covering his nose and mouth, he gently poured the mixture over the hinges. Metal smoked and melted, and when the hungry acid had finished its feast, Dagger thrust the spike on the end of her hammer into the thin seam of the door and levered it open, skipping back as it fell with a shuddering clang.

The inside of the door was deeply carved with sigils in repeating patterns that covered it from edge to edge. They all stood back as the Vigil left the cell, flickering rapidly between watchtower and robed figure. It hovered an inch above the ground.

"The world believes you are dead," Dagger said.

*Yes. Vice has told me, though I suspected as much. But it was never my way to involve myself directly in the events of the world. I stand Vigil, yes? But as I told Vice, it is possible the time has come for those old ways to change.*

"Based on what we've seen here," Dagger said, "quite a lot is possible."

*Yes.*

"Holy Watcher," Vice said, choking out the words as Dagger winced at his tone, "we came here to destroy the Citadel's hold. Can you show us how to reach the top of the tower?"

*Yes. That serves us all. I can see the way. I can see many ways. Though the word "see" is imprecise, it may serve best for your understanding. Tell me, how does the tower appear to you?*

"Like a series of rooms, regions and times, even worlds, connected by doors and stairs," Pitch said. "It seems to change at random. There must have been a functioning system once, but from what we've seen, it is breaking down. It has become random."

*Your limitation is fascinating. I see a multitude of towers at once, imposed over each other again and again. All exist simultaneously. What your eyes perceive and minds process as a move between rooms is actually a step between entire towers.*

"I see," Pitch said, and scratched his chin. "Yes, that would make as much sense as any explanation. But Temker's Clock would only affect time. They must have other such devices. We have seen a few of them."

*They have many times many. How do these devices look to you?*

"Like broken down machines and untended experiments."

*As you have seen in what Vice tells me is left of my afterlife, so it is here. Devices — be they magic or machine — must be maintained. They have life spans just as you do. But even toward the end of a life, weakened by time and inattention, a device or a being may still effect change, though its purpose and power might become warped.*

"So," Dagger said, "which way do we go?"

*As in any tower, no matter how many are imposed over each other, which are the most important directions?*

"Up and down," she said.

*Exactly. But the ones who created this place have altered such distinctions.*

"You are remembering," Vice said, awe and hope creeping back into his voice.

*That word is imprecise. The room they kept me in obscured much. It dampened my sight, but as their devices fell to disrepair, a fog lifted. Outside the cell, it has lifted even further. I see. Come. Follow me.*

As the god led them past the other cells, their occupants battered themselves against the glass windows. They thrashed and slammed — the sound of their impacts were bare whispers against the magic and science used to lock them away — but none of them were able to so much as crack the glass.

*They cannot escape any more than I could. Be glad of that. Some of them are quite savage. More so now that they have gone mad with eons of confinement.*

"I have no doubt," Dagger said.

The Vigil paused in front of the first cell The Armory had seen, in which something invisible was again assaulting the glass. The slamming and pounding intensified, and though still intact, the transparent partition bowed out even further, nearly into a bubble.

*Especially this one. This one must never be allowed to escape.*

The glass flexed again. The wall and floor buzzed with a faint vibration.

"What is it?" Pitch asked.

*I could not hope to describe it to you. There are no words in any language that can. I could implant that knowledge in your mind as a kind of image, but your reason would melt like snow in the rain.*

The thrashing within the cell intensified as if whatever it contained could hear the Vigil speaking of it, as if it wanted to make the same promise right back.

*If we had the time, I would ask you to help me destroy it. For now, leave it. The cell will not fail, as mine did not. They did at least that much right.*

The Vigil continued on, leading The Armory to the hatch through which they'd entered the floor of cells. It stopped and the robed figure brought its sleeves together as the flame atop its watchtower form blazed into a blinding bonfire. Vice staggered at the sight and fell to one knee before he could stop himself, his face a mass of conflicted anguish. A single tear fell down his cheek.

"Steady," Pitch said, laying a hand on the monk's shoulder fully expecting to be rebuffed, but the monk suffered the comfort.

*It is alright, my little watcher in the darkness. I see your pain. Be strong. I am here now. I am clearing a path. Both for you all to move forward and for your pain and doubt to be assuaged.*

Vice huffed. It might have been a choked sob or a suppressed gag.

The metal floor and stairs creaked and groaned. The Armory looked around nervously, waiting to dodge back from some trap or chasm, or leap to the relative safety of the corridor if the ground gave way. Instead, the metal around the hatch ripped loose and reformed, and the ladder that led down twisted up like a snake, uncoiled, and burst through the ceiling with the shriek of metal on stone. Rubble rained as the staircase bored its way toward the top of the tower. The roar became deafening for a few seconds and then settled into a low rumble. Finally, it stopped, and the Vigil seemed to sag. It dropped its sleeves, and its watchtower fire dimmed again. The ladder was again a tightly spiraled staircase.

*It is done. Now climb.*

"The stairs are too small for you," Dagger said, looking up at the god's blazing fire.

*I do not need them. Climb.*

Dagger nodded and led the way. The Vigil rose into the air next to the staircase, keeping pace with The Armory as the crew climbed past anonymous, empty stone. The walls offered no hint of progress, and the ground below soon faded. The sound of their endless steps lulled their minds, and The Armory found themselves locked into a worry greater than any they'd felt at the horrors and dangers they'd faced thus far. What if this was just another trap: To climb these stairs forever?

"How much further?" Dagger panted out the words.

*I apologize for the distance I have created. It is necessary.*

Dagger paused her climb. "You're making it take this long to reach the top? Why?"

*Your minds are fragile things. They need rules and boundaries. Time. Distance. They are crutches, but for the wounded or the weak, crutches are necessary. Time and distance are two constants that let you establish equilibrium with your material world. To do away with them is to unpick the fabric of your perception and your minds along with it. This distance allows you to adjust gradually. We are climbing through towers innumerable in their variation, through layers of dimension. If I had taken you directly, your minds would have broken from the strain of trying to see so many worlds and planes at once. You have single minds. It is dangerous for a single mind to be forced to see the overlapping nature of this place. My mind, if such a word can even apply to me, has no such limitations.*

"I see," Dagger said, and glanced at Pitch to see if he'd heard and could confirm the claim, but the alchemist only shrugged and made a *yeah sure* gesture.

The Armory pushed on. They climbed for a year. They climbed for minutes. Finally, when it seemed as though time might finally grind itself into irrelevant dust, the Vigil's satisfied voice boomed in their minds.

*We are nearing the top. Be ready.*

"For what?" Dagger asked.

*They have mounted a defense.*

"Because we've been really unprepared so far," Saber muttered.

*I apologize for my presumption. Next time I won't warn you.*

"I wouldn't go that far," Saber said.

*Your jokes and my created distance are similar, don't you think? I did so to ease your minds, you chatter like a wind-up bird to do the same.*

Saber chose not to reply.

They emerged from the staircase into a narrow alcove that, in scant feet, would open into a grand hall, the path through it more bridge than floor with a deadly drop to either side. The distant walls were curved and made of constantly spinning stairs. At the far end was a force of beasts and men. Some were already fighting each other, but when The Armory stepped out into the echoing hall, the petty skirmishes stopped, and every head turned their way. Something that looked like a giraffe draped in raw meat warbled a war cry, or perhaps just a plaintive demand to be put out of its misery. It would have been pathetic, if its head didn't split into several fleshy lips that exposed a pink throat studded with teeth made for rending. The other creatures that stood in The Armory's road were similar things that looked less grown than assembled. The human warriors among them, at least, carried familiar weapons and wore armor.

"Fuck," Powder muttered, looking up and then glancing over the edge of the bridge, "no cover and no high ground."

*High ground, I can provide.*

"How do—"

The Vigil grabbed Powder by the shoulders of her leathers, lifted her up, and flew her in revolving patterns toward the advancing monsters and men.

*Can you shoot from here?*

"Fucking hell!" Powder yelled, legs kicking, "next time warn me!"

330

*The one with all the stabbing implements seemed offended when I did.*

"He's an asshole!"

*I will remember. He is an asshole. You are not. Shall I put you down?*

"Shit, no! This is perfect. Just hold me steady."

The Vigil paused a moment, waiting for something.

"Please?" Powder asked.

*Your courtesy becomes you.*

Powder sighted down her rifle. The fanged giraffe thing that looked like it was wearing its own insides — and those of several others — warbled at Powder and the Vigil as they passed overhead. Powder fired and the giraffe's head exploded, splattering those around it with dental shrapnel and blood.

"This is fine," Powder said, "can you keep your flight pattern random, in case one of them has a gun or crossbow, but pause on my word?"

*I will. But you need not speak. Watching is my way. I will know when you want to shoot.*

As Powder dangled over the battle in the god's grip, the rest of The Armory rushed to meet the force standing between them and ornate, towering doors at the far end of the bridge. Trapped and battered heroes who had come before The Armory looking to solve the truth of this place fought next to the Citadel's creations. Did some shadowy factor of the Citadel's construction approach them with a better offer? Or it may have just been futility that drove them: a common acceptance of their fate to be just another threat encased in a glass of time. As they stood in The Armory's path, bravos shoulder to shoulder with the horrors they'd sworn to wipe out, distinctions ceased to matter. In front of their makeshift army was an enemy, and only five strong.

But they'd never faced five like this.

Dagger and Vice led. The monk, boiling over with rage at deceiving even a questionable version of his dead god, caught a swordsman's downward cut with one hand. As the surprised warrior tried to snatch back his weapon, Vice snapped blade and arm, dropping both as he met the next threat. His fists drew great, rending swaths of blood from something that bubbled beneath its skin with poorly connected muscles and bones. Its teeth broke on his armor, his fists brought it low, methodically, as if Vice was grinding wheat between wheels of stone. Dagger laid about her with her hammer, until another armored giant shoved through the throng toward her.

"Have they got all the fucking giants," she muttered, as the figure swung a sword as tall as it.

Dagger rolled under the cut, and it continued past her, too heavy to stop, and scythed through two hyena-like beasts. Dagger leapt out of her roll and drove the head of her hammer into the armored giant's face as it tried to recover for another swing. It reared back, its visor dented and cracked, and Dagger swung low, smashing through both armor and the knee it protected. As the giant staggered and fell on its shattered leg, she leapt into the air and brought her hammer down on its head. After it fell, smashing something else to pulp under its weight, Dagger dented it into immobility where its armor was designed to bend. She left the giant face up, helpless as a turtle on its back, staring up at the sun.

"Dagger!" Saber shouted as he ran toward her, "boost!"

Dagger knelt. Saber stepped on her knee and then her shoulder as she straightened mightily, catapulting the much slimmer man into the air over the fray. He sailed over the force's slapdash front line, revolved in the air, and landed in the midst of men and monsters with a short, curved sword in one hand and a long knife in the other. If Vice and Dagger were blunt instruments of raw power, then Saber was an unseen blade on a moonless night. His weapons found flesh between thin gaps in fang and armor. He redirected slashes and thrusts in the thick of the scrum so that they found homes in allies' chests instead of his. Fanged mouths on long necks, tentacles, and broadswords tried for him, and missed as he ducked, spun and sidestepped. His heart soared, his mind went blissfully quiet. He noted with a distant pleasure that the rough surface he danced upon was a porous stone that absorbed the blood and gave him perfect footing.

At the rear of the battle, Pitch threw back his coat to allow full access to the wide bandolier that decorated his chest with vial after vial. These he threw with a practiced accuracy. They broke against shoulder and skull. They were snatched from the air by foolish jaws. Green and blue fire burst out in waves and raged across skin. Steel and flesh sizzled as acids ate them away like scalding water washing wet paint from a wall. He created barricades of unnatural flame that gave Vice, Dagger and Saber avenues to fight between and boxed their foes together so that groups of five became clumsy single files of grain, ready for the scythe.

Far above the battle, Powder's keen eye and steady hands picked out the greater, larger threats and riddled them with bullets. The lead slugs were crosshatched. They went in small, warped with the impact, and punched out in large, wet holes that coughed insides out onto the ground or propelled beasts and men over the edge to the meat grinder of the revolving stone-stair walls.

She thought about going low. To swoop just over their heads.

The Vigil was already in motion.

They dipped sharply in the air and Powder's heart hit the back of her teeth as her boots dangled inches from grasping hands and tendrils. She slung her rifle strap in the crook of her arm and drew her scatterguns. Both spoke at once, and a hail of lead and fire chewed several of the things below down to their poorly manufactured bones.

Dagger fell under the weight of four of them, one man with a sword and a trio of beasts connected by membranous threads. She caught their weight on the handle of her hammer, but the sword scored her side and rasped across the leather. Three of her ribs creaked, and dimly she was aware of being bitten by a fang or a blade. The beast-trio screamed in her face, spattering it with spittle that reeked of a cannibal's garbage trough. As it kept her pinned, the warrior picked up a spear and took his time, lining up its point to drive between her and the beast, and into her heart.

Dagger kicked out trying for something's ankle, but the beast snapped at her face every time she tried to summon the strength to push. One of the beast's heads creaked with a tearing sound and its neck grew, bringing its jaws ever closer to her nose and mouth. The growth must have hurt. It sobbed in a child's voice, even as its jaws closed in. The warrior, a man Dagger could see now through the grates of his helmet, grinned and held off his spear thrust to let the beast have the coup de grace.

It cost him his life.

Something fast and covered in sharp metal hit the side of the warrior's helmet, caving in the steel. The face inside crumpled up and burst red from its eyes, mouth and nose. Then another iron hand reached over, grabbed the warrior's helmet by the face grate, and twisted until it faced the other way.

Vice had arrived.

But Dagger was still pinned beneath the beast-trio's weight on her hammer, and the growing neck had almost reached her with its snapping jaws. She was able to turn her head from first snap, as the beast wasn't quite close enough. It whimpered. Another centimeter and it could start biting chunks from Dagger's face.

Something flickered through the space between them.

The beast seemed to hiccup and wore almost a look of shock as one of its heads fell and smacked into Dagger's nose on the way down.

Only Saber could have moved that fast, made a cut that precise.

With two more delicate slashes, the duelist severed the membranes that connected the beast trio, and it howled as it fell to pieces. Vice and Saber mopped it up, blunt and sharp, rendering the creature into pieces.

Free of the weight, Dagger raged to her feet and swung hard for Saber's head. The swordsman ducked and rolled between her legs to run through the fighter behind her as she broke the chest of the one who'd been about to stab him in the back. Vice push-kicked something like a mastiff with too many legs and a mouth in its side so that it met Dagger's backswing and was smashed to the ground to squall and buck, its spine in two halves. Dagger used her hammer like a broom and shoved it over the edge.

To the rear of this force something moved. It had been hidden until then, but trundled out onto the bridge on dozens of small, mechanical legs upon which was balanced an orb of lumpy, pulsing flesh. Driven into one side, the flesh growing out of and around it, was a grunting machine that belched gouts of black smoke. The Vigil and Powder were about to fly above it. The fleshy sphere struggled as if trying to hold something inside, then split open like a flower in the sun. From inside burst a swarm of snarling larvae of metal and wing that shot toward Powder and the god that held her in flight.

The have artillery, Powder thought, just before the blast hit her and the Vigil.

She felt some of the impact like punches and other like jaws as the larvae latched onto her armor and skin. As she fell from the Vigil's grip, she was dimly aware of their chewing and the twinges of pain as their teeth got through her leathers. Powder had only one thought as she fell.

God's got a fucking weak grip.

She hit the ground and slid for several feet, senseless. Those half-metal maggots not killed in the impact continued to gnaw at her idiotically. The machine or monster that had launched them beetled its way slowly toward the fallen sharpshooter.

She did not rise.

"Form up!" Dagger shouted when she saw the gunner fall. The Armory made a blunt wedge with her at its point. Overhead, the Vigil hovered but did not intervene. It flew circles around where Powder had landed like a vulture.

*You must reach her fast, it intends to absorb her. To use her to... reload.*

"Then do something!" Dagger shouted.

*I am the watcher in the darkness. I do not directly intervene.*

Dagger shot Vice a dirty look over her shoulder and saw genuine awe and hope on his face, as if the god's inaction was the strongest proof yet that it might truly be his lost deity. With a disgusted growl, she brained a human and then kicked aside his broken form to face the next. As The Armory battled its way slowly along the bridge, two human warriors at the back detached and headed toward to the easy meat of Powder's limp form.

The trundling meatball on metal legs was closer still.

The rest of the force held their position, keeping The Armory divided.

Instead of rushing to meet them in ones and twos, the tower's opposition made of themselves a barricade of shields and sharp limbs. The humans had sheathed their swords for spears. Dagger's heart sank even as her blood raged in her ears.

"We have to get to her," Dagger yelled.

"We have to get through that," Saber countered. "Pitch, can you throw anything?"

"I'm out of the smaller vials," the alchemist said through clenched teeth, "We're all too close for anything else."

The fleshy orb was nearly upon Powder, who had not so much as twitched since she'd fallen. Dagger screamed and swung her hammer overhand at the phalanx of men and monsters, but the group split and her hammer hit the floor between them, cracking only the stones under their feet. One of them thrust a spear at her face, and Saber ducked in to parry it up and over Dagger's head as she dragged back her hammer and reset for another swing.

"This will not stand," Vice growled. He pushed past Dagger to the front of the wedge and pulled his cloak around him and his hood down over his head. "Pitch, I would blaze with righteous fire."

"Are you sure?"

"Do it."

As Vice stalked forward, Pitch threw a clay orb at the back of his cloak. It shattered into green and yellow flames that rushed across Vice's cloak, his shoulders and head. A spear thrust out from the phalanx and took him high in the chest near his shoulder, but it only made him pause a moment. He brought down one arm, snapped the spear in half, pulled the blade from his body and thrust it into the face of a squealing wild boar with four human arms instead of legs. Then he crashed through the rest, laying about with his armored fists as the flames spread to them. They screamed as he struck them.

The phalanx wavered.

Burned.

Broke.

"Now!" Dagger shouted.

Her hammer held crosswise, and Pitch just behind her adding force to her push, she shoved four of their adversaries off the edge of the bridge. Saber engaged the others with sword and cleaver, chopping through spear shafts and

341

into the hands that held them. He left them that way, ineffective and diminished, howling over their missing pieces. He had no time for mercy, no interest either.

But The Armory was still too far. The two warriors reached Powder's limp form, and the wad of meat on metal legs was upon her. Several delicate steel arms extended to grab her by the boots and hold her down. Its flesh unseamed along the top just as the two human warriors raised their spears to finish her. The wad twitched as if just noticing them. It had other ideas about just who got to finish the fallen sharpshooter. Two very human, very wet arms shot out of the seam along the top, grabbed the two warriors and dragged them inside it. It rumbled back and forth with a whirring, grinding noise, convulsing with some internal struggle. After a series of metallic clicks, it finally settled back.

It turned from Powder to face The Armory.

*Beware,* the Vigil said. *It has reloaded.*

The waddling artillery dumpling tilted its organic chassis forward, its machine legs spreading out to compensate as its weight changed. Danger to Powder or not, Pitch took a chance then and threw a clay globe at it. The little firebomb bounced off and sailed over the side to explode harmlessly somewhere below them.

"Rush it before it can fire!" Dagger shouted and charged the device, her eyes locked to that faint seam that bisected it, ready to dive to the side should it open.

But they were too fast.

The Armory fell upon the contraption with blade, fist and hammer. They hacked and bashed at its rubbery body, but the weird creature just rocked back and forth as its little metal legs scrabbled to keep it upright.

Pitch ran around it to Powder, dragged her clear and checked her vitals as he plucked off and stomped the maggots still chewing on her. The rest of The Armory managed to slide the meatball around, but there was no other effect. Its clawed legs had a wide base and a solid grip on the stone.

Dagger called a halt to the futile beatdown.

"This is stupid," she muttered, and looked up at the Vigil. "Since you're just gonna watch, got any ideas?"

"Dagger," Vice hissed, and then doubled over his spear wound.

"No. Let your god pull its fucking weight," she growled.

343

*What weight do I need to pull, Dagger?* the Vigil asked, still hovering somewhere above them. *Do you need me to lift it up and shove it over the edge for you?*

Dagger paused and looked at the artillery dumpling.

"You gotta be shitting me," she sighed and then went around behind it, grabbed it by two of its meal legs and lifted. It came up easily, and even gave a tiny, gratifying little squeal as Dagger tilted it further. Its seam opened and the two wet arms re-emerged, but Saber chopped them both in half and kicked them over the edge. Dagger kept pushing, kept tilting, and as the dumpling neared the edge of the platform, it finally fired its payload. The barrage of metal-and-flesh maggots spattered and died against the stone platform. With a roar, Dagger shoved it the last bit and it toppled over the edge. It hit the bottom with an anticlimactic squelch.

The Armory stood panting, weapons ready and eyes cutting through the air for the next threat, but they were alone on the stone bridge.

"What did I miss?" Powder asked, her left arm across Pitch's shoulder, her right arm bound to her body with a length of cotton.

One obstacle remains, the Vigil whispered urgently from above them. *Be ready.*

"Whatever," Dagger muttered.

As if in answer, a sound between a roar and a squeal filled the air.

"Oh, calm your tits," Dagger yelled without looking, "we'll be with you in a second." She turned to Powder. "You gonna live?" she asked as Pitch poured a tiny vial down the sharpshooter's throat.

"For the moment. Arm's broken," the sharpshooter said, and gagged at the taste of Pitch's medicine with a wan grin. She gave the alchemist a grateful look. "How long's that stuff gonna last?"

Pitch grinned. "Probably right up until you really need it."

"Great."

Pitch went to Vice next, and waved aside the monk's protest as he pasted a thick salve over the wound in the monk's chest. It sizzled and cauterized the wound, leaving even the stoic Vice gasping with pain.

"Try not to use that," Pitch said, gesturing to his left arm.

The squealing roar came again.

*You must hurry,* the Vigil said.

"Oh, must we?" Dagger asked. "Why? It's probably just more tentacles and teeth. It can wait."

The Vigil did not answer. Its silence almost seemed reproachful.

Dagger turned toward the sound they'd heard. At the far end of the platform was a roaring, round pustule that was mostly mouth and grasping tentacles.

"I fucking knew it," Dagger said under her breath as she stopped and installed the spike in the head of her hammer.

It shrieked at them in defiance even as it slowly retreated, but it had nowhere to go. Dagger thought about all the monsters they'd felled in the Citadel, any of which could also have been sent in on the same errand as The Armory. She'd assumed they were creations of this twisted, breaking place, but maybe their roars were not challenges, but pleas to stop or attempts to explain. Then she put that idle contemplation in the box in her mind where she kept all the things that don't matter, and marched slowly toward the monster, the rest of her crew at her sides.

The beast lunged, its jaws distended, wide enough to swallow Dagger whole, and its teeth shot forward on a neck of extra, wet skin.

Dagger lunged into the bite, but instead of finding her, its jaws closed on her hammer, wedged vertically into the roof of its mouth. Howling, the creature tried to close its jaws around her, and only impaled itself further. It tried to yank back its extendable jaws, but Dagger dug in her heels and Vice grabbed her belt with his good arm to anchor her.

Pitch tossed a vial past the creature's teeth and down its throat. When the contents hit the volatile acids of its stomach they detonated, and the beast heaved a gout of purple-tinged smoke that reeked of ignited bile. It slumped. Dagger's hammer was the only thing holding it up. She grabbed her weapon's haft, kicked it loose, and dead horror sloughed bonelessly to one side and oozed off the platform to hit the spinning tower walls below with a thunderous, wet smack. Distantly, there was a sound of bone and meat being ground to pulp.

"Any more? You had the high ground," Saber asked the Vigil, panting and blood streaked.

They all turned to look at the doors ahead, even the Vigil.

*Beyond they wait.*

"I didn't bring enough acid for that," Pitch said, eyeing the gargantuan portal.

*It is unlocked.*

"How do you know?" Saber said.

Vice muttered something under his breath.

*My little watcher in the world knows. Tell them. I permit it. There is no need for subterfuge. I know you believe I am not your true Vigil, but whether I am or not is irrelevant. I am. That is all that matters.*

"They seem to have given..." Vice paused and clenched his teeth.

*Say it, my little watcher in the darkness. Speak the truth. You are bound to by my teachings, after all.* The Vigil sounded triumphant and amused.

"The Vigil keeps watch. It is the great watcher in the sky," Vice said, though speaking the words almost seemed to hurt him.

*I am reborn, though my little watcher in the world fights not to believe it. Though none of you ever believed, he did despite his best efforts. Even as he mourned. And now his faith pains him.*

"You are not the Vigil," Vice said between his clenched teeth.

"Vice!" Dagger hissed.

*Stop. There is no deceiving me. My gift is sight. I watch. More than that, I see. And I ask, am I not the Vigil? If you believed your Vigil dead, and here I stand, then it seems you must rejoice. Welcome me into your heart.*

"Let's just get these doors open," Dagger said, eyeing the phasing figure of the counterfeit god.

*That will be easy.*

And it was. The doors opened at a single push, without groan or creak.

The Armory and the Vigil entered.

# — CHAPTER 13 —

## The king and all his court.

T he room was just like the area where they'd found the Vigil, built of steel. But time had painted these walls with rust and glass tanks lined the walls instead of cells.

In each floated a dormant body — some male, some female, some humanoid, and many something else. All wore rich, red brocade robes. Those figures with vaguely human forms wore gold crowns fixed to their waterlogged skin or chitin by struts driven into the skull. Those without heads to wear them had their crowns attached with spikes, wire, or simply clutched them in an appendage. Their eyes were glassy and staring, their limbs slack. Some of the tanks hummed, lights blinking along them in sharp, alternating reds and greens. In others the lights had gone out, and the bodies they held were faded, their skin was sloughing loose, their royal robes turned funeral shrouds.

*Rulers in waiting*, the Vigil noted as The Armory passed the tanks, though none of the bravos had wondered aloud, and none asked the god-that-might-be to clarify.

At the far end of the hall, steel walls phased back into familiar stone. Most of the torches were dead and The Armory and the Vigil moved from one bright pool of light to the next. At the far end, sitting between a pair of gilded pillars, was a slumped man nearly swallowed by an ornate throne. He wore the now-familiar red robes and blood trickled down his face where the gold crown had been fixed to his skull. Limp fingers held a chain that ran to the collar of a monster the size of a horse slumped at the throne's side. It had too many legs and eyes, and had been stitched together from lions and lizards. A clutch of tentacles fanned away from its backside in place of a tail.

It was dead as stone.

The robed figure raised his head with a great effort as The Armory approached.

"Again?" he asked and shook the chain in its fist, but the dead beast did not twitch. He tugged again, halfheartedly and without looking, the way a hopeful drunk checks a bottle emptied hours ago. His robes were damp as if he had just crawled from a tank to take the throne.

"Again and again and again," the figure on the throne whispered.

*He is the one,* the Vigil's voice was a force in The Armory's minds, *End him and the Citadel falls!*

"He doesn't look all that dangerous," Pitch said. "Or powerful."

*He is a lynchpin! A cornerstone!* The Vigil's dry thunder in their minds sounded almost panicked, desperate.

"Rulers don't usually look dangerous, Pitch," Dagger said.

"Why don't you do it?" Pitch asked the floating god.

*I... cannot. I...*

"Right," Pitch muttered. "You just like to watch."

The dull-eyed, damp-robed little king looked up at the Vigil with faint curiosity. "Oh," he said, "you freed one of them. That was foolish. They're never grateful. You'll see."

"One of them?" Dagger asked. "What do you mean?"

"Again, again, again," the king muttered, ignoring Dagger. He pawed among his robes in slow motion, looking for something. "Ah," he said with satisfaction and lifted an antique pistol. He stared at the ancient weapon, as if trying to remember how it fired.

"Powder?" Dagger asked. "A little mercy here."

Powder drew a pistol with her left hand.

"Again?" The little lost king asked as he lifted his waterlogged eyes to Powder and sat back in his throne, the pistol falling from his fingers. "Well. Be about it. I will see you again."

Powder fired and the king slammed into the backrest and curled into a ball, nearly vanishing among his damp robes.

*Fine work,* the Vigil said, its voice calm again. *It is ended. The job, as you would say, is done.*

"What did he mean, again?" Pitch asked. "He said he will see us again."

Nobody had an answer. Even the Vigil was silent.

"Nothing? Just the ravings of a mad old king?" Pitch asked the god. "What did he mean?"

The Vigil said nothing, and Pitch spat on the floor in disgust.

"So, it's done," Dagger said. "Now what? Since it's your song we're dancing to."

*Now I show you the way out.*

Pitch was examining the empty tank closest to the throne. There were others in line behind it, but in the next two, the lights were dead, and the kingly figures suspended within were rotting.

"What happens when another of these things is decanted?" the alchemist asked.

*To you? It matters not at all. Your job is done. Come.*

"That wasn't what I asked," Pitch said, but again the Vigil ignored him.

They followed the god to the wall behind the throne. The Vigil's beacon blazed, and a door opened in the stone. The god led them down another spiraling stairwell and at the bottom was a doorway that teased dim light. They went through it, and into the hall through which they'd entered, where the light of Temker's Clock waited. Pitch hurried over to the clock and furiously poured over its glyphs and sigils. He knelt near the base where the glyphs seemed to fuse altar stone to floor and busily ran his hands across them, the last words of the strange king blazing in his mind.

"Powder," he called, "do you have one of your bombs? Once we break this, time should resume. The tower will fall."

*No.*

They all turned to the god. It was looming over them.

"No?" Dagger asked. "This was the job. To break the Citadel and set this realm free. Don't you want to leave this place?"

*You will leave. But the Citadel will stand.*

Dagger set her hammer down and rested her crossed arms on the haft. "We were paid to do a job. We always do what we're hired to."

*Easily remedied. Here.*

The god extended its hand, and its watchtower form extended a drawbridge. Balanced on the palm, and the end of the bridge, was a leather bag the size of Dagger's head. Gingerly she took and pulled the strings open. The bag was filled with unadorned gold coins.

"What's this for?" Dagger said.

*I mean to hire you.*

"We already have a client," Dagger said.

*Have you never switched allegiances? Don't claim ironclad principles to me. I have seen within you.*

At first, Dagger said nothing. The god was facing her, but behind it, she could see that Pitch was still crouched by Temker's Clock, his hands hidden. She stepped closer to the floating god. "What do you have in mind?" Dagger asked.

*I cannot be sure I will survive if the Citadel falls. But here, here I am whole. I am myself. My powers are growing. They will soon be limitless within these stones. Here as time repeats, I remain what I am, but if I pass through those doors, nothing is certain. And your world may not abide my presence. I choose certain life.*

The Vigil pointed at Vice.

*He is sure I am an aberration. An accident. He grieves, but he also hopes, despite himself. He longs for the moment that will restore a distant memory, a memory not even his, of his world to rights. In any case, my nature is irrelevant. You have placated me to secure my aid, but I have done the same to you. We needed each other then, but I do not need you now. I may indeed be a false, created thing, but here that does not matter. For that I am sorry, my little watcher in the darkness, though I tell you a truth you need.*

"Do not call me that," Vice spat and turned away.

*I too grieve your loss, but you must go and leave me here. You'll only lose more if you don't.*

"Lose more?" Dagger said. "We didn't lose."

*Your monk did. Look at his face, his hope gone, his faith in tatters. You have been paid. Within these walls you cannot gauge my power, and neither can I. You cannot force me from the Citadel. You cannot destroy it from within. You cannot destroy it from without. Leave. I have seen enough to understand the power you enjoy in the world outside these walls: Life everlasting, as long as you fight and kill. But I promise you, here you are beyond the reach of that power. You will die. Your loop will close.*

"Our loop?" Dagger asked.

*In here, you believe you are singular, but that is a fault of perspective. Just as there are many towers, there are many versions of you within each one. In all you battle to the end. In all you free me. In all you attempt to stop me. And in all, you die. All those versions, trapped forever. Repeating. It is a poetic parallel of your existence in the world beyond these walls, but far more limited. If you leave now at least one of those versions — the only one as you five will ever need comprehend it — can go on marching along time's tunnel as expected. To you there will be change. You will continue. Do not concern yourself with those others. You will never know them, and if you met them, they would be as strangers to you. Do not march to death in this version as you have, as you will, in all the others.*

"We don't march toward death, we flaunt it," Dagger said. She turned to the rest of The

Armory and clenched the haft of her hammer. Nobody threatened The Armory. Nobody but she set their course. Pitch got up from the altar with slumped shoulders and went to Dagger's side.

"Boss," Pitch said, and tentatively touched her arm. "let's go."

"You want to give up, Pitch?"

"It's practical," Pitch said and gave her arm an urgent squeeze at odds with his defeated body language and tone. "Vice is badly hurt, Powder's broken arm will need proper treatment. We're fucked up."

"That's never stopped us."

Pitch nodded. "And we've seen what this thing can do. If it's not a god, it's sure as shit close. Think of it as a tactical retreat. We don't do lost causes. What are we, heroes all of a sudden?"

*The god-hater speaks true. Go. Leave me to my vertical kingdom of time. I will continue to provide for the island. Somewhere in some version of this place you will rescue me again and again. Somewhere in time you will win over and over and be presented with this same choice. I tell you again: in each, those that have already happened and those yet to happen, you make the same one. You fight. You die. Your loop closes and another takes its place. I beg you now, choose differently.*

"Nothing is certain," Dagger said.

*No? Will you test that? You can leave this place now, only minutes after you entered, wealthy and free. Leave and live or stay and die.*

Dagger looked around at the rest of The Armory, and other than Vice whose head was bowed, they all nodded. Powder's face was drawn with pain as Pitch's chemicals began to fade. Dagger saw blood dripping down Vice's leathers.

"Dagger, please," Pitch said, his voice tense and urgent, "let's just go. Now."

Everything Dagger stood for seemed to urge her to stay, lay this demanding, fake god low. Twice she considered lifting her hammer, but finally she sighed and slung her weapon over her shoulder.

"Fine," Dagger said to the god that might be, "we'll leave."

*That is wise. Already, I can feel my control growing. Behold.*

The doors to the chamber swung open. Light flooded in like a fanfare.

Even then Dagger hesitated. Pitch gestured to the others to go on ahead, and with a reluctant glance at their leader, they stepped toward the light.

"Dagger," Pitch hissed under his breath, "Come on!"

Dagger relented. She turned and moved to the front of The Armory and led them out into the light.

The doors slammed shut behind them.

The stairs looked like they had when The Armory entered. The bodies of the guards they'd slain lay where they'd fallen. The Vigil had spoken true. It was as if they'd been gone for only minutes and not the years, decades or centuries it seemed like it had taken to climb the Citadel.

"Like it never happened," Dagger whispered to herself, staring down the vast flights of stairs. She looked behind her at the looming tower, tall and pristine in the daylight. It blazed like an insult.

Pitch was shifting nervously from foot to foot. "Dagger, we need to move."

She rounded on him and growled, "What is your fucking problem, Pitch? Since when is your spine this soft?"

From overhead a gunshot cracked and something nicked her shoulder. "Are you fucking kidding?" She raged even as she ducked and turned back. Above the door, that lone sniper was still alive and reloading.

Dagger stared at the shooter's perch and gestured to the rest of The Armory. "All of you, get out of range. I'll be right back."

"Fuck him," Pitch said. "We need to get off these stairs."

"Fuck the whole thing," Powder said, as she fired back at the sniper with her pistol. "We need to leave the whole kingdom. I don't we want to be here when the queen finds out we bailed on the job."

"Don't worry about that," Pitch said, already speed-walking down the stairs.

"Why not?" Dagger said, following him despite herself. Saber, Vice and Powder kept pace.

Pitch looked at Powder. "What was it you said outside the mine while we were waiting for your bomb? Give it a minute?"

"I guess?" Powder said.

"So, give it a minute," Pitch said.

"Pitch," Dagger said," what did you do?"

The ground lurched and buckled. The Armory stumbled and fell. Behind them the entire Citadel lurched, a rippled wave in stone worked its way up from the tower's foundations, all the way to its peak. A single brick broke loose from the battlements that punctured the clouds and hurtled down to shatter to dust where they'd been standing only moments ago.

Pitch looked at Dagger. "Can we fucking run now?"

"Move your asses!" she shouted.

More bricks fell. The tower sprouted cracks that spidered out with a ripping noise that tore at the mercenaries' ears. The sniper's death scream was smothered by a pile of falling rubble and the stairs under their feet aged, cracked and turned to dust as they fled. New, time-aged holes opened in the ground and threatened to catch and hold their feet, to swallow them. Saber ducked under Powder's good arm to help her run, and Dagger aided Vice in their mad sprint from the rain of stone.

They staggered and slid, falling and scraping themselves. They bled from dozens of new cuts and dents, and finally hurtled down the last shattering steps and rolled to a gasping stop in the dusty thoroughfare that led to the village.

The Citadel pitched and yawned. The Armory watched in shock as its shadow swayed. They waited tensely for it to pick a direction.

It fell. Away from them. Toward half of the village.

It crushed several buildings under its bulk. Dust blew out from the impact in a tempestuous exhale that filled their throats and blinded them, sticking to the blood and sweat on their faces. A collective wail went up from the town as some of the citizens ran toward and away from the destruction, their screams wordless, dumb and awed as this perennial fixture of their lives collapsed.

"What the fuck?" Dagger coughed and hacked, spitting blood and dust between her knees as she sat with her hammer by her side.

Pitch was on his hands and knees, wiping his eyes and vomiting. Saber sat in the dirt, his eyes two shiny pools in a face painted matte white. Vice was on his knees praying and defiantly watching the fallen tower with streaming eyes. Powder holstered her pistol in disgust and groaned as her broken arm shifted.

Pitch puked and spat dust. Then he chuckled and wiped his mouth. It built into back-wracking laughter. He clutched his sides.

"Pitch?" Dagger said.

But the alchemist was laughing too hard to answer her.

"The fuck is so funny?" Dagger croaked around the dust caking her throat. She spat to clear it.

Pitch collected himself with effort and wiped his face, dragging clean streaks through the dust. He took a deep breath. He looked extremely pleased with himself.

"Remember the test devices left over from the Dahlsvaart job?" Pitch said, beaming.

"You've had that in your pocket this whole time?" Powder asked with horror, recalling how volatile they were.

"Just a little one, but I kept the pieces separated. Wouldn't do much, but I hid it at the base of the clock. Just enough to erase two of the key glyphs. I wasn't sure if it would work but..." He gestured at the crumbled tower.

"How'd you hide that from a god?" Powder asked.

"That was not the Vigil," Vice said.

"*I see. I watch*," Pitch said, mimicking the god's sepulchral voice. "My entire ass. Vice is right. Whatever that thing was, it wasn't a god. It had power, sure, but it was full of shit and trying to con us. Us! It understood a lot, and sure, it knew the nature of the tower, but that was the old magic. Mine is the new."

"Just a little one..." Saber repeated and chuckled his way into helpless laughter.

"What is so funny?" Vice asked.

Saber gasped. "It just reminds me of that time we were in that town with the vineyard. They had that possessed vole problem. Remember how tiny everybody was? With the hairy little feet? Well, there was this one little guy and—"

"I do not want to know, Saber," Vice said, cutting him off.

"Vice, you're allergic to fun."

Powder shook her head. "Didn't we get chased out of there with torches and pitchforks?"

"Yes!" Saber said, still giggling, "very, very small torches and teeny tiny pitchforks. I still have a scar on my ass. Looks like I sat on a dinner fork."

Dagger nodded at the destruction with a satisfied sigh. "Job's done."

# — CHAPTER 14 —

## No loot for you.

When the Queen and her soldiers eventually showed up, The Armory were still sitting in the dust and the rubble, watching the royal procession march toward them. One of the people who lived nearby had been kind enough to bring the mercenaries water and beer. It was up for debate which had the stronger flavor. The queen's guards stopped a few feet from The Armory, the carriage door banged open, and a very angry queen emerged.

"I. This. This was not..." the queen started and then stopped to gather herself and take a deep breath. "What the fuck did you do?!"

"You said you wanted the tower gone. It's gone," Dagger said and after a pause added, "your majesty."

366

"I didn't say knock it down and crush the seawall! You flooded half the fucking village!"

"Trust us, it had to go," Saber said, "there was no cleansing the shit in there. Not if the whole world was made of soap."

"That was very poetic," Powder said.

"Powder, was that a compliment?"

"Don't get excited."

The queen's face turned, if possible, an even angrier shade of red.

"Arrest them," the queen hissed to her guards.

As the guards started forward, The Armory got to their feet, weapons ready. One man grabbed at Vice, perhaps assuming some advantage based on wound and lack of weapons. Vice snapped out a fist with his good arm and the soldier fell wheezing for air, his chest plate sporting a brand-new dent.

"No, your majesty," Dagger said. "You're going to pay us. And then we're going to leave."

"Somebody has to answer for this," the queen raged," and it won't be me!"

"There she is," Dagger said, "I finally see the queen in you, your majesty."

"If you think I'm paying for wanton destruction like this," the queen said, "much less allowing you to leave, well, I'll let my Minister of Pain explain it to you."

"Minister of pain?" Saber asked.

"Really all in the name, isn't it?" Powder muttered.

"It's just a bit dramatic," Saber said. "It'll just be some bent fuck in a hood. It's always just some bent fuck in a hood. Right, your majesty? Bent fuck? Hood?"

The queen glared at the duelist.

"See?" Saber said to Powder.

Dagger looked at each of the queen's guards, addressing them as much as their ruler. "Your majesty, what else do you want to lose today?"

"I beg your pardon?"

Dagger shrugged. "If you attack, we'll kill at least a dozen of your guards. One of us will reach you in the chaos. Hell, Powder here could run away and still kill you from the other side of town."

The queen looked at the sharpshooter, who winked.

"Just pay us," Dagger said. "We'll leave. Your lands are free."

"Somebody has to—" the queen said.

Dagger cut her off. "Put us on a ship, your majesty, or in a carriage. You don't want us around. Believe me." She paused to gesture at the carnage around them. "Pitch here did this with a little box he had in his pocket. Imagine what havoc we'd wreak if you kept us here. I once saw him make a bomb out of dust, piss and rat shit."

The queen stared hard at the rubble.

"Captain," she finally grated between her teeth, "take them to the harbor. I believe there is a rare merchant in port."

"And our gold?" Dagger asked.

"Consider it a donation," the queen said. "Disaster relief. Get out of my sight before I change my mind."

Dagger decided not to argue. They had the Vigil's gold after all.

A contingent of guards formed up around The Armory and escorted them through the rubble-choked town. Dozens of homes had been crushed beneath the hurricane of stones. People searched desperately, wailing and calling for their loved ones as The Armory passed. None of them so much as turned to watch their saviors pass.

At the harbor the leader of the guard had a brief word with the merchant vessel's captain and The Armory was put aboard. They gathered at the aft deck wordlessly and looked out over the destruction they were leaving behind. The sailors bustled around them, their bare feet slapping on the deck, and glanced at the new passengers' weapons and expressions nervously. An hour later the ship set sail, and The Armory watched the jutting bit of coast until it was just a single point in their back trail.

They moved toward the prow of the ship to watch the horizon. Pitch opened the bag of gold, glanced inside and swore.

"Boss," he said, "you'd better look at this."

"What now?"

He handed her the heavy bag. She jerked open the strings, already half knowing what she'd find. The gold they'd seen was now just a collection of brass counterweights a merchant might use to measure grain. Dagger groaned in disgust and heaved the bag over the side of the ship.

Saber chuckled. "A fake god with fake gold. All that, and we're still broke."

Dagger looked around the ship, then walked to the rail and leaned over the side. The ship's hull had been scraped clean of barnacles while in port, and her name had been freshly painted along her side: The Malevolent Scamp

"It's not a bad ship," she mused to the rest of The Armory. "Stupid name, though."

She looked around at the bustling sailors. The captain was standing by the wheel, deep in conversation with the first mate. They both looked back at Dagger, and the captain nodded at her cautiously.

"So," she said to her crew in a low voice, "have any of you ever considered piracy?"

**THE END**

# AFTERWORD

The Armory came to life, and repeated death, in a series of microfiction pieces. They weren't ever going to be more than that, but these knuckleheads just kept kicking around my brain, not dying.

I guess it all left a mark: The Conan movies, Frazetta paintings, D&D novels, Aeon Flux episodes on Liquid Television, and playing Golden Axe in sweaty arcades quarter after quarter.

I'm a big From Software fan too, even though I suck at their games, because in every one of them you have this sense of a weight of time and history pressing down upon you. This crumbling world has existed long before you arrived to witness it, and will continue to do so long after you've put down the controller. You couldn't hope to fathom the full story of even one crumbling edifice, you're just a visiting speck. I find that mystery fascinating and comforting. I don't want answers, I want wonder. I hope I've managed to create something like that feeling here for readers, that the world The Armory calls home is infinite in its possible strangeness.

I have some people to thank directly involved with this project in one way or another. In no particular order:

Dan, you created a cover so good it overshadows the work it introduces. Your enthusiasm for these assholes outshone mine by far, and it's the only reason anybody is reading this. Love you, brother. Chuck it in the fuck it bucket. Roll it up.

Vinh, you read this in one of its rawer forms and enjoyed it, and encouraged me to give the self-publishing idea a shot. You took it a step further with line edits of the final product. Love you, brother.

Becca, an invaluable test reader with a love for all things nerdy. You fell in love with these dickheads in a way that probably isn't healthy, but I share it. I'll have Saber and Pitch plan your thank you party. Better get some rest.

Maya. You don't give a shit about any of this nonsense, except that I care about it. Somehow you manage to keep your eyes from glazing over while I try to explain why I balled up logic and hucked it into a burning dumpster. I love you.

Jack, your influence and friendship changed the way I write forever, and that's just the tip of the iceberg. Here's to more years, continents and trouble. Love you.

Todd, you were the first person to publish my fiction. I have no idea what you saw in that first piece, but thank you for taking a chance and for all the years and stories, real and fictional, that came after. Oh, I've since come around: Cheesedick doesn't have a hyphen.

And finally, Sam. You suggested I take a writing class and had the leverage to actually get me to do it. To this day it's the only higher education I have. You started this. Thank you.

Made in the USA
Middletown, DE
17 May 2024